A BODY UNDER THE BRIDGE

A gripping Welsh crime mystery full of twists

P.F. FORD

The West Wales Murder Mysteries Book 6

Joffe Books, London
www.joffebooks.com

First published in Great Britain in 2024

Cover art by Dee Dee Book Covers

ISBN: 978-1-83526-562-8

To my amazing wife, Mary — sometimes we need someone else to believe in us before we really believe in ourselves. None of this would have happened without your unfailing belief and support.

PROLOGUE

52 St David's Place, Llangwelli
Friday 6 April, 11.15

Gareth Jenkins made his way slowly around to the back of his house, pausing at the door to survey the garden with a mixture of guilt and sorrow. How lovely it had looked when Alma was alive. The garden in those days had been their pride and joy — flowers everywhere, vegetable beds bursting with life, the greenhouse crowded with plants.

He stopped tending to it five years ago. Everything changed when Alma passed away. It all seemed too much, somehow, not worth the effort. He tried for a while, but his heart just wasn't in it. The greenhouse was empty of all but a few half-empty flowerpots; the vegetable beds were neglected and overgrown, and the only things that bloomed were the weeds. Even his once pristine lawn had succumbed.

He shook his head sadly, and one or two tears trickled down his cheeks. Five long years since she had passed, and still it was no easier. He missed her so much. Thank goodness he had the dog — she was the single piece of joy in his life.

'Bella. Come on, girl,' he called. 'I have to leave in a minute.'

1

As soon as he opened the back door a small black cock-apoo emerged from the wilderness and scampered past him into the kitchen.

Gareth washed and dried his hands, slipped on a jacket and bent down to fuss the dog.

'Now, we talked about this, didn't we?' he said. 'I don't like to leave you, but I have to go out for a few hours. Hopefully, once I've done this, the unpleasantness will end and we can go back to our peaceful lives.'

He patted her head one last time, straightened his back and made for the door. She looked up at him inquisitively.

'You be good now,' he said. 'I'll be back as soon as I can.'

Pulling the door closed behind him, he locked it and slipped the key into his pocket. Then he made his way slowly around the side of the house, through the rickety, rusty iron gate that only opened easily if you knew how, and set off for town.

CHAPTER ONE

Detective Sergeant Norman Norman dropped the receiver into its cradle, pushed back his chair and stood up. Short, stocky with a shock of unruly grey curls, Norman was fast approaching sixty and had become a sort of father figure to the small team of detective constables based at Llangwelli station.

'I'm needed upstairs,' he told Detective Constable Judy Lane, currently the only other occupant of the room.

She looked up from her desk. 'Anything important?'

'He didn't say. I don't know whether to take that as a good or a bad sign.'

'You'll be fine,' said Lane. 'I'm pretty sure we haven't done anything wrong, so perhaps he's going to give you a pat on the back.'

'He didn't ask for Sarah,' said Norman. 'Don't you think that's odd?'

DI Sarah Southall was the leader of their small team.

'Perhaps he knows she's not here yet.'

'She should have been here by now,' said Norman. 'When she gets in, tell her I need her help upstairs.'

3

'With Superintendent Bain?' said Lane. 'I thought you two went back years.'

'Yeah, we do, but he was a detective inspector back then and we were on the same team. Now he's a pen-pusher I sometimes wonder if we even have the same objectives, which is why I could do with some backup.'

Lane laughed. 'Okay, I'll tell her as soon as she arrives.'

Norman grumbled his way through the double doors and up the stairs to Superintendent Nathan Bain's office.

The door to the office was open, Bain standing at the window, hands behind his back, gazing out. Well over six feet tall and slightly stooped, he resembled a thoughtful heron contemplating the fish swimming in the water below.

Norman tapped on the door, and Bain turned towards him, breaking into a broad smile.

'Ah, Norm. Sorry to drag you all the way up here.' He pointed to a couple of comfy chairs. 'Come on in and take a seat.'

'Sarah's not here yet, so you'll have to make do with me for now,' said Norman.

'Yes, I know she's not here,' said Bain. 'That's why I asked you to come up.'

'You know?' said Norman, alarmed. 'I thought something was wrong. I've been calling her, but she isn't answering. You aren't going to tell me she's left, are you? Is that why you called me up here?'

'Of course she hasn't left,' said Bain. 'And there's nothing wrong with her. It's her father's funeral, so she's gone back to England for a few days.'

'His funeral! Jeez, I didn't even know he had died. She never mentioned it. Why didn't she tell me?'

'She didn't tell anyone, Norm. I only found out yesterday evening. Apparently, they fell out years ago. I'm not privy to the finer details, but I do know that whatever it was nearly cost her her career. She wasn't even going to attend the funeral, but her partner persuaded her to change her mind.'

'Her partner's name is Bill, and he's the pathologist, as you well know,' said Norman.

4

'Yes, well, anyway, I told her he was right, she ought to go.'

'Yeah, she'd have regretted it if she didn't,' said Norman. 'Maybe not now, but in time—'

'The thing is, she's probably going to be off all week, so I need you to steer the ship while she's away. Can you do that?'

'Yeah, sure,' said Norman. 'We haven't got much on at the moment, just the usual paperwork and a few general enquiries.'

'Good,' said Bain. 'I knew I could rely on you.'

'Is that it?' asked Norman.

'Were you expecting something else?'

'I thought maybe I've stepped out of line or something.'

Bain inclined his head quizzically. 'Remind me, when was the last time I felt the need to haul you over the coals?'

'Er, well, now you come to mention it—'

'Exactly,' Bain said. 'I know we have our differences, Norm, but don't go looking for problems that don't exist. The job's hard enough as it is.'

'Yeah, sorry. I'm a bit on edge this morning. Dentist.'

Bain smiled. 'Look at it the way I do. Twenty minutes torture every six months is better than toothache and an extraction.'

'I've tried looking at it like that,' said Norman, 'but it doesn't help.'

* * *

Norman reached the office door just as DC Catren Morgan was on her way out.

'I'm just going over to Terry's,' she said. 'I think we all deserve a cup of decent coffee for a change. I'm sick of the crap we get here.'

Terry's was a small mobile coffee bar which was often to be found parked across the road from the police station.

'That sounds like a plan I can wholeheartedly endorse,' said Norman.

'Good,' said Morgan. 'And don't forget it's Tuesday.'

Norman turned to her. 'Yeah. And?'

'The boss always buys everyone sandwiches on Tuesday. And as I understand you're the boss this week—'

'Yeah, but. Hang on a minute. How come you knew Sarah was away? I only just found out.'

'Come on, Norm, you know nothing escapes me,' said Morgan, touching the side of her nose. 'I have ways of finding these things out. Anyway, lunch. I've already placed the order. It'll be ready at midday. All you have to do is pick it up — and pay for it, of course.'

'You've placed the order? But you haven't even asked me what I want!'

'You always have the same thing,' said Morgan. 'BLT, right?'

Norman sighed. He'd been outmanoeuvred once again.

'I suppose I don't have much choice, do I?'

'None whatsoever,' said Morgan. 'But think of the goodwill it creates within the team. Anyway, to soften the blow, I'll buy the coffees at lunchtime, too.'

'Big of you,' said Norman. 'But it doesn't soften the dent the sandwiches'll make in my wallet.'

* * *

In the course of a long and varied career, Norman had seen — and dealt with — things most people hope never to have to face, from violent death to hideous abuse. He had grown as immune to their effects as anyone could be. Nevertheless, there was one thing he never had got used to, and if at all possible, would never put himself through it again. However, terrible as it was, a visit to the dentist could not be avoided.

His only consolation was that after it was over, he wouldn't have to endure another visit for six months. Just as he parked his car outside the station, his mobile phone began to ring. He glanced at the number but didn't recognise it.

'DS Norman,' he said.

'Hi, Norm.'

'Sarah?'

'You sound surprised,' she said.

'I didn't recognise the number.'

'The signal here's rubbish, so I'm using the house phone.'

'How come you're calling me? Aren't you supposed to be at your dad's funeral?' he said.

'I'll be leaving shortly. I just needed to speak to someone normal for a few minutes.'

'You're seeking normality, and you want to speak to me at work? Really?'

'I'm not checking up on you, I just need to hear a friendly voice.'

'You could have told me, you know.'

'Told you what?'

'About your father,' said Norman. 'You never even mentioned he'd passed away. I had no idea until Nathan told me this morning.'

'He'd been ill for a while, so it wasn't a surprise.'

'Yeah, but even so—'

'You haven't been arguing with him again, have you?' asked Southall.

'Who? Nathan? No, not on this occasion. I was preoccupied with going to the dentist, so I managed to resist the temptation. I don't know why, but there's something about Nathan that brings out the devil in me, especially when he starts spouting crap about budgets.'

'Budgets aren't crap, Norm, they're a fact of life. Bain doesn't get to choose how much he has to spend, and you know that. It wouldn't matter who was occupying the super's seat, controlling the budget is a big part of the job.'

'Yeah, I know. I just get frustrated when we can't do our job because there's not enough money. I mean, what's going to happen in the future if they keep reducing our funding?'

'Regardless of the reason, provoking a senior officer seems an odd way to secure your future,' said Southall.

'Yeah, well, as I said, Bain brings it out in me,' said Norman. 'That's why I had to get transferred away from him all those years ago.'

'Yet when he asked you to come to Llangwelli, you jumped at the chance.'

'Ah, yes, but that was because I needed to make a fresh start. Besides, I knew I would be working with you, so I wouldn't be coming into direct contact with Nathan very often.'

'That's not true,' said Southall. 'I was a last-minute replacement. I had no idea I was coming here when Superintendent Bain first spoke to you.'

'That may well be the case,' said Norman. 'But I knew Nathan well enough to know he wouldn't settle for anything less than the best when it came to selecting a DI.'

'But he didn't select me. As I understand it, he got saddled with me, he had no choice in the matter.'

'And you know that for a fact?' asked Norman.

'Well, that's what I've always understood,' said Southall.

'There's one thing you should understand about Nathan Bain,' said Norman. 'When it comes to staff, he nearly always gets what he wants, and he doesn't settle for second best.'

'Is that a compliment?' asked Southall.

'It's a fact,' said Norman. 'But, yes, it's also a compliment.'

Two hundred miles away, Southall allowed herself a little smile of satisfaction.

'How long are you going to be there?' asked Norman.

'I'm supposed to spend the rest of the week helping my sister clear his house so we can sell it.'

'Well, you take as long as you need. You're not missing anything here.'

'That's a pity. I'd love an excuse to come back.' In the background, Norman heard a faint voice calling her name. 'Damn,' she said. 'The car's here. I'm sorry, Norm, but I'm going to have to go.'

'There's no need to apologise,' said Norman. 'I hope it all goes well. You take care now.'

Norman slipped the phone into his pocket and grabbed the bag of sandwiches he'd collected on the way back. He got out, locked the car and made his way across the small car park and in through the back door.

CHAPTER TWO

It was just before midday when the man who had been pacing up and down opposite the police station finally made up his mind. Alun Edwards was a sprightly, bright-eyed, seventy-two-year-old. Proud of his full head of silver-grey hair, his only concession to the advancing years was the walking stick he carried to support an occasionally troublesome knee.

He stepped in line behind the young woman placing her order, and fighting back one final second thought, cleared his throat.

'Excuse me, are you a police officer?'

The young woman he had addressed turned from the counter and eyed him quizzically.

'I saw you leaving the police station across the road,' explained Edwards. 'So, I assumed—'

'And you assumed correctly,' said the woman. 'I'm Detective Constable Catren Morgan. How can I help?'

'I don't want to interrupt your break.'

'It's not a problem,' said Morgan. 'Just give me a second to pay for these coffees, and I'll be with you.'

Morgan collected four coffees on a small tray, handed over her cash, and turned to Edwards.

'They'll get cold,' said Edwards, pointing at the tray. 'Your colleagues won't be pleased if you return with cold coffees.'

'Why don't you walk over the road with me,' said Morgan. 'If you don't mind waiting in reception I'll run upstairs with the coffees and when I come back down, we can have a chat. Is that okay?'

'I can come back later. As I said, I don't want to interrupt your break.'

'Nonsense,' said Morgan. 'You're here now, and as long as you don't mind me drinking my coffee, you can tell me what's on your mind.'

'Well, if you're sure,' said Edwards. 'That's very kind of you.'

Less than five minutes later Morgan, armed with a notebook and pencil, rejoined Edwards in reception.

'Now then,' she said. 'What's your name?'

'Edwards, Alun Edwards.'

'Okay, Mr Edwards, how can I help?'

'Please, call me Alun. It's about my friend, Gareth. I usually go to his house to play chess on a Monday evening, but he wasn't there last night. I tried to telephone, but I couldn't get through. I've been round to his house this morning, rang the bell and knocked several times, but he didn't answer the door. The thing is, he's not been well, and he doesn't seem to have any family to worry about him.'

'Perhaps he's gone away and forgotten to let you know,' said Morgan.

Edwards gave a sad little smile.

'I think that's highly unlikely. Gareth isn't the travelling sort. You need to like to meet people to do that and, to be honest, he's probably one of the most unsociable people I know. As far as I'm aware, he only ever goes out to walk his dog, and I'm the only person who ever visits him.'

'Perhaps he had to be somewhere at short notice,' said Morgan.

'If that was the case, he would have rung me. And why isn't he back this morning? Anyway, he'd never leave his dog

10

on her own, and she's in the house. I could hear her barking, last night and this morning,' said Edwards. 'He dotes on that dog. I'm sure he wouldn't go off and leave her for more than a couple of hours and even then, it would have to be for a very good reason.'

'Do you want to make a missing person report?' asked Morgan.

Edwards considered for a moment. 'Do you think I should?'

'It will make it official, and at least then you'll know you've done all you can.'

Edwards looked alarmed. 'Official, you say. Goodness, I'm not sure Gareth would be happy about that. I wouldn't want to fall out with him. It's not easy to find a chess partner these days, you know.'

'Why do you think he'd be upset?'

'Last time I saw him he told me he thought he had a cold coming on. I offered to help if he wasn't feeling well, but he told me that wouldn't be necessary and that he would be fine. He'll probably hate me for causing a fuss and involving the police.'

'Tell me, Alun, when was the last time you actually saw him?' asked Morgan.

Edwards looked into the distance. 'Well, it's Tuesday today, and I didn't see him last night, so it must have been last Monday, in the evening.'

'So that would have been Monday the second of April, is that right?'

'That's right,' said Edwards.

Morgan made a note and drew a large circle around it. 'And what's your friend's full name?'

'Gareth Jenkins.'

'How old is Mr Jenkins?'

'I don't know exactly. He's around my age, or maybe a bit older. So that would make him mid to late seventies, possibly even early eighties.'

'Address?'

'Fifty-two St David's Place.'

'Oh, yes, I think I know it,' said Morgan. 'It's only about five minutes from here, isn't it?'

'Yes, that's right.'

Morgan regarded him for a moment. 'I can see how worried you are. Tell you what. Leave it with me, and I'll pop round there this afternoon and see if I can find out what's happened to Mr Jenkins.'

'Are you sure? I wouldn't want to waste your time,' said Edwards.

'It's fine,' said Morgan. 'In the circumstances I think you're right to be concerned.'

'Oh dear, I hope he won't be annoyed with me.'

'I'm sure Mr Jenkins will be fine if I go unofficially and explain that you were concerned about him,' said Morgan. 'If it was me, I'd be glad to think someone cared enough to look out for me.'

'When you say you'll go "unofficially", what exactly do you mean?'

Morgan gave him a conspiratorial smile. 'I'll go in plain clothes. If he's worried about what the neighbours will think, he'll be a lot happier than if a couple of uniformed officers turn up at his front door. I'll tell him I'm doing it as a favour to you.'

'Can you do that without making it official?'

'Of course I can.'

'Will you let me know he's okay?'

'Of course. Just give me your address and telephone number,' said Morgan.

* * *

Morgan saw Mr Edwards to the door and made her way back upstairs. Finding her sandwich on her desk, she tore the bag open and took a huge bite.

'I thought perhaps I'd said something to upset you,' said Norman.

'Sorry?' said Morgan when she finished chewing.

'When you went back downstairs. I thought—'

'Oh. No, I met this sweet little old man outside who wanted to speak to someone. He's worried about his friend.'

'Worried in what way?' asked Norman.

'He says he went round to his friend's house last night and he wasn't there. He's still not there this morning, he's not answering his phone, and his dog's barking. Apparently, he's one of those people who would never go away and leave his dog.'

'Did your sweet little old man file a missing person report?'

'I think he'd like to, but his friend doesn't like a fuss, and he doesn't want to fall out with him. I get the impression they're both a bit short of company.'

'How old is this missing guy?' asked Norman.

'Late seventies, possibly early eighties.'

'Okay,' said Norman. 'So, based on the information you have, what do you think we should do?'

'Well, he's not been officially reported missing, but because of his age and what I've been told I think it wouldn't hurt for someone to go and see if he's okay.'

'Correct,' said Norman. 'But—'

'But Mr Edwards is worried his friend will be upset if we make a big fuss, so I said I'd go in plain clothes rather than send a couple of uniforms. And, as we don't have any uniforms to hand anyway . . .'

Norman smiled. 'You took the words right out of my mouth.'

'As you're acting boss, does that mean I have your blessing to carry on?'

'Sure,' said Norman. He looked at his watch and nodded towards his desk phone. 'I'm expecting a call from Forensics. If you want to wait, I'll come with you.'

'How long will that take?' asked Morgan.

Norman shrugged. 'How long is a piece of string? Unfortunately, I forgot to tell them it was urgent, so your guess is as good as mine.'

'And is it urgent?'

'No, it's not, but if you say it's urgent it makes them move a bit faster. At least it used to. These days it doesn't seem to make much difference.'

'That's because you told everyone here to say it's urgent when they call the lab, and we all took your advice,' said Morgan. 'As a result, Forensics no longer know what is and what isn't urgent, so they treat all enquiries the same.'

'Oh, is that right?' said Norman gloomily. 'I'll have to stop sharing my trade secrets if they're going to be counterproductive.'

'This guy's house is only about five minutes away,' said Morgan. 'Why don't I head there when I've finished eating my lunch? I can call you if I need any help.'

Five minutes later, Morgan was pushing her way through the doors. DC Judy Lane watched her go.

'Haven't you ever considered moving up the ladder, Norm?'

Norman smiled. 'I don't mind making decisions while Sarah's away for a few days, but permanently? No way. My face doesn't fit. And anyway, I've never been any good at all the political crap that goes with moving up. I get enough job satisfaction doing what I do.'

'She's had more than her fair share of family tragedy, hasn't she?' said Lane.

'Who, Sarah? Yeah, she's had a rough deal one way or another. But at least this time, it seems it wasn't unexpected,' said Norman.

'She's never mentioned her father before,' said Lane. 'I didn't even realise he was still alive.'

'I believe they had a major falling out a few years ago,' said Norman. 'And before you ask, no, I don't know what it was about because she's never told me. Just like you, I don't think I can recall her ever mentioning her father. It was only when Superintendent Bain told me earlier that I even knew he had died.'

'It's bad luck she's away while it's so quiet,' said Lane.

14

'She'd prefer it this way,' said Norman. 'She wouldn't want to miss anything. I just hope it stays this way until she gets back.'

* * *

Morgan made her way down to the car park wondering whether to walk to St David's Place. Thinking about it, she decided to take her car on the grounds that she would look a bit silly if she needed to rush off somewhere in a hurry and first had to run all the way back to the station for her car.

It took her less than five minutes to reach the quiet, tree-lined street, it being a short walk away from Llangwelli town centre — not that Llangwelli really had a proper town centre. Most people wouldn't even call it a town. In reality, it was more of a large village with a small harbour; perhaps that was what attracted the tourists.

St David's Place was a cul-de-sac consisting of a mixture of detached and semi-detached houses. Morgan came to a halt outside number fifty-two, about three quarters of the way down on the right-hand side.

From her car, she studied the small semi-detached cottage, comparing it with its neighbours. Number fifty-two was distinctly shabby, as if the owner had stopped caring for his property. The weeds smothering the small front garden and the unruly hedge separating the garden from its neighbour only added to the overall impression.

Morgan got out of her car, went up to the front door and rang the bell. Almost immediately, a dog began to bark. From the sound she guessed it to be small, maybe a spaniel or something similar. After a few minutes, she gave up. No one was about to answer the door, or stop the dog from barking.

She peered through a window into a room bare of all furniture apart from two ancient threadbare chairs on either side of a small table. A chessboard and pieces were set up in the centre of the table, waiting for a game to commence.

Morgan stepped back from the window and made her way around the side of the house. An untidy path led to a rusty wrought-iron gate that had evidently seen better days. It looked as though the gate was rarely used and she held her breath as she gingerly tried to push it open, afraid that it might collapse. Although it creaked and groaned alarmingly, the gate slowly swung open far enough for her to step through, before it dropped off the top hinge.

Cursing quietly, she tried to lift it back up, but it was stuck fast and, try as she might, she couldn't get it to budge. After one or two futile attempts, she gave it up as a bad job. After all, she hadn't come here to repair broken gates.

Morgan followed the path around to the back of the house. The back garden looked just as neglected as the front. Pressing her nose to the glass, she looked through the kitchen window. Like the room at the front, the kitchen appeared shabby, sparsely equipped, and badly in need of redecorating. Meanwhile, the dog had obviously worked out she was now at the back of the house and was barking frantically from the other side of the door.

Her mobile phone began to ring.

'It's Norm,' said the voice in her ear. 'Is everything okay over there?'

'It's a bit weird,' she said.

'Weird, how?'

'Well, the house looks almost derelict, and there's hardly any furniture.'

'What about the old guy? Is he there?'

'Well, his dog is going ballistic, but he's not answering the door. I'm tempted to break in, in case something's happened to him.'

'Yeah, that's what I'd do, but don't go in there on your own,' said Norman. 'We don't know what might have happened. I'm leaving now. Wait for me and we'll go in together.'

* * *

Ten minutes later, Norman joined Morgan outside number fifty-two. Morgan led him around to the back, insisting that he help her close the gate as they made their way through.

'Why is this so important?' he huffed, struggling to set the collapsed gate back on its hinge.

'The dog,' said Morgan. 'She's probably desperate to get out and I don't want her escaping.'

'How do you know it's a "she"?'

'Mr Edwards told me.'

'He's the guy who told you about this, right?'

'That's right.'

They carried on to the back door, Norman brushing rust from his hands.

'Talking of the dog, do you think it barks like that all the time?' he asked.

'There's no telling how long the poor thing's been in that house on her own. She's probably bursting for a pee by now. If that was me, I'd be yelling for someone to let me out.'

'Yelling,' repeated Norman. 'Is that what she's doing? D'you know, I hadn't thought of it like that. I guess if you're right about her being shut in for days, that means she'll be hungry, too. She won't attack us, will she?'

'You aren't going to suggest we wait for Animal Welfare before we go in, are you?'

'Heck, no, not when there might be someone inside who needs help. We'll just get inside and deal with whatever happens.'

'It sounds like a small dog, Norm, not the hound of the Baskervilles. I can't see it being too much trouble.'

'I suppose you've checked to see if there's a key hidden somewhere?' Norman asked as they reached the back door. 'You know, under the usual flowerpot.'

Morgan produced a key from her pocket and held it up.

'That's why I brought you round the back,' she said, pointing at some nearby upturned flowerpots. 'It was under the middle one.'

Norman sighed. 'Neither original, nor secure,' he said. 'The only good thing about it is that we don't have to break the door down.'

Morgan inserted the key and turned it. There was a satisfying click as it unlocked.

'Don't forget to watch out for the dog as I open the door,' she said.

'I hardly need reminding that she's there, do I, with all that noise?'

No sooner had she pushed the door open than a small curly-haired dog made a mad dash between Norman's legs and into the garden, where she squatted.

'There we are then,' said Morgan. 'Just a small dog dying for a pee.'

'Let's hope that's the only sort of dying we're going to come across,' said Norman, following Morgan into the kitchen. 'What's this guy's name again?'

'Gareth Jenkins.'

'Okay, you take the downstairs, and I'll go up,' said Norman. He started up the stairs, calling out, 'Mr Jenkins? Mr Jenkins, it's the police. I hope you don't mind us coming in like this, but we were worried something might have happened to you.'

It took barely two minutes for Norman to satisfy himself that there was no one upstairs. By the time he got back to the kitchen, Morgan was on her knees making a fuss of the dog, who, as soon as she saw him, rushed over and sat at his feet, looking up at him.

'Well, look at that,' said Morgan. 'I think she likes you.'

'Me and Faye have been talking about getting a dog,' he said, bending to fuss the dog. 'What sort of dog is it — a poodle?'

'My guess is a cockapoo,' said Morgan. 'It's a cross between a poodle and a cocker spaniel.'

'D'you think she's hungry?'

'Her water bowl is empty, and there's a bit of a mess under the table,' said Morgan, 'so I'm guessing she's been on her own for a while. That means she's almost certainly not been fed.'

The light wasn't good in the gloomy kitchen but after a brief search, Norman found some dried dog food, filled a bowl with it and placed it on the floor. At once, the dog began to noisily devour it.

'Jeez, what is that smell?' asked Norman.

Morgan pointed to the mess under the table. 'A mixture of pee and poo.'

'Eew,' said Norman. 'Really?'

'Well, what else was she supposed to do if she couldn't get outside?' said Morgan. 'It's not as if she could use the loo, is it?'

'The bathroom door was closed,' said Norman, 'so she couldn't have, even if she knew how.'

'There we are then,' said Morgan.

The dog had finished her snack and was now making eyes at Norman, who found himself succumbing to her charm.

'She's kind of cute, isn't she?' he said.

'Shouldn't we call Animal Welfare?' asked Morgan.

Norman bent down and gathered the dog in his arms. 'I suppose we should,' he said reluctantly. 'And we'd better make a start on finding out what's happened to her owner.'

'Alun Edwards said Gareth adored the dog and wouldn't dream of leaving her for more than a couple of hours.'

'Well, he either got that wrong,' said Norman, 'or he got it right and Gareth went somewhere, and something happened to him. What do we know about him?'

'Nothing, really,' said Morgan. 'Only that he lives here, he has a friend called Alun Edwards, and they play chess here every Monday evening.'

'They play chess here?' said Norman. 'It's not exactly the cosiest of venues, is it?'

'The place is a bit lacking in furnishings, isn't it?' said Morgan. 'I mean, this kitchen could best be described as spartan, and there are just two ancient, incredibly uncomfortable-looking armchairs and a small table in the living room.'

'The only bed upstairs is a camp bed,' said Norman. 'That's not the sort of thing an older person should be sleeping on. In fact, it's not the sort of thing anyone should sleep on for more than a night or two.'

'So, what do you think?' asked Morgan. 'Is this just another poor old pensioner without a penny to his name?'

'I guess it must be, looking at the state of the place,' said Norman. 'The only comfortable thing in the house seems to be the dog's bed. Let's take a closer look around. Maybe we can find some paperwork that will tell us something about him.'

'But where are we going to look?' said Morgan. 'There's no sideboard or chest of drawers to search. The only cupboards and drawers are in this kitchen.'

'Well, you'd better get searching then,' said Norman, holding the dog to his chest. 'I'd love to help, but I've got my hands full right now. There's only a couple of drawers anyway. As you said, I'm the boss. That means I get to supervise.'

Morgan rolled her eyes.

'There's not much in here,' she said, opening a drawer and rummaging through the contents. 'Just a couple of old tea towels and an ancient telephone directory. I didn't think anyone used these anymore.'

'How old is ancient?' asked Norman.

'Oh, hang on, it's not a telephone directory,' said Morgan, lifting the tatty book from the drawer. 'It's a *Yellow Pages*, from 1998. Why would anyone keep one of these?'

She flipped quickly through the pages. 'None of the pages seem to be marked, and there's nothing hidden in between them.'

She put the book back and moved onto the second drawer, which rattled when she opened it.

'A collection of old buttons, screws, nails . . . Three pairs of spectacles in cases. They look pretty old. But no correspondence.'

'Try the cupboards,' said Norman.

'Didn't you just do that?'

'I was only looking for dog food, and I found it almost straight away,' said Norman. 'I didn't check the rest.'

Morgan worked her way through the cupboards but, apart from the dog food and a few pots and pans, there was hardly anything to find, apart from a large square cake tin. She lifted it out.

'What's that?' asked Norman.

Morgan shook the tin. 'Don't get excited, I think it's empty.' She set it down on the worktop and prised off the lid. 'Nothing but a few crumbs,' she said.

'He baked cakes?' asked Norman. 'With no ingredients?'

Morgan turned her attention to the solitary cupboard attached to the wall above the worktop.

'Wow. Look at all this stuff! It's like a pharmacy. There must be remedies for everything in here.'

Norman stepped forward to look over her shoulder.

'It looks mostly like cold remedies from here,' he said.

'There are a few different herbal remedies as well,' said Morgan. 'He told Mr Edwards he thought he had a cold coming on.'

'It seems odd he should have all these medicines,' said Norman. 'That suggests he worried about his health, yet there's no food, and the general state of this place says he wasn't really looking after himself.'

'Yeah, it's a bit of a contradiction, but it doesn't help much, does it?' said Morgan heading back into the hall. 'I'm going to have another look around the house. Maybe he's got a hiding place for his personal stuff.'

'There's a telephone in the hall,' Norman called after her. 'Maybe we can do a reverse search or get a call history. At least then we might be able to identify a family member.'

'Now you mention it, I'm sure Alun Edwards told me he had tried calling Gareth but got no answer,' said Morgan. 'He even wondered why Gareth hadn't called him to say he wouldn't be here on Monday evening.'

'Maybe he didn't pay the bill and got cut off,' said Norman.

Less than a minute later Morgan called to him from the hall.

'It's no wonder Alun Edwards couldn't get through. The phone isn't working.'

'That seems just about right for this place,' said Norman.

* * *

'I don't get it,' said Morgan fifteen minutes later. 'I've been over the entire house and there's nothing here!'

'Did you check that bedside cabinet?'

'Completely empty,' said Morgan. 'How many houses have you ever searched where there's not even a single piece of correspondence?

'I can think of the odd derelict place I've been to, but this place is lived in,' said Norman. 'At least, we think it is.'

Morgan raised an eyebrow.

'There are clothes in the wardrobe upstairs,' she said.

'Yeah? Like a whole collection?' asked Norman.

Morgan shook her head. 'Just a few bits, and nothing remotely new.'

'No coat?'

'Only the blue anorak that's hanging in the hall.'

'What if our man isn't missing but has moved out?' suggested Norman. 'He could have taken papers and stuff with him but decided the clothes and furniture had seen better days so left them here. It would explain why the phone doesn't work. Maybe it's been disconnected.'

'I suppose it's possible,' said Morgan. 'I'll check that when we get back. But what about the dog?'

'Maybe he's coming back for her,' Norman said. 'Or he just can't look after her anymore. Perhaps he was relying on Alun Edwards to alert us because he wanted someone to find her.'

'Why not take her to a dog rescue centre if he can't cope?' Morgan said.

'Perhaps it would be too painful to leave her like that,' said Norman. 'Or maybe he's just too ashamed to admit he can't look after her.'

'I don't see it,' said Morgan. 'She doesn't look neglected, and even though she was hungry, she's not starving. Apart from a few tins of soup, the only decent food in the house is dog food, so he obviously cared about her, and he must have been feeding her properly. There's also a relatively new dog lead and harness hanging on the back of the door, which suggests she gets taken for walks. To me that implies he was a dog lover, and a dog lover wouldn't move out and leave their dog like that. I think he must live here, however unlikely it seems.'

'Yeah, but doesn't that suggest he's putting the dog's needs before his own?' said Norman. 'Maybe he just can't do it anymore.' Then he had a thought. 'You don't think this guy eats dog food, do you?'

Morgan shrugged. 'I suppose someone could live on tinned dog food if they were desperate enough, but that dry stuff? Surely not.'

Still holding the dog, Norman looked around the dingy kitchen. 'You know, if this is really how pensioners live, I'm having second thoughts about wanting to grow much older.'

'It's not just me thinking this whole situation is weird, is it?' asked Morgan.

Norman scratched his head. 'Yeah, it's weird all right. If it wasn't for that guy approaching you, no one would know anyone lives here, and the place would fall into rack and ruin.'

'Should we call Forensics in?' Morgan asked.

'We have no reason to,' said Norman. 'Strange as it seems, there's nothing here to suggest it's a crime scene. Are you sure about your guy?'

'Who, Alun Edwards? I haven't checked him out, if that's what you mean,' said Morgan. 'I haven't had time and, besides, I had no reason to doubt him.'

'Fair enough, I guess,' said Norman. 'I mean, why would you? I wouldn't have either, but given what we've found, I reckon it wouldn't hurt to make sure he's who he says he is. Did he warn you about the state of this place? He must have known it was like a hovel if he comes here every week.'

'He didn't say anything about it. He was just anxious about his friend.'

Norman pointed at a small pedal bin. 'Did you check that?'

Morgan stepped on the pedal and peered inside the bin. 'Nothing in here but an empty dog food bag.' She lifted it out. 'Oh, hang on. What's this?'

She picked up the bin, reached inside and brought out a number of torn pieces of paper, which she laid on the worktop. It took her a minute or two to put them together, but all the pieces were there.

'It's a photograph,' said Norman. 'Or at least it was until someone tore it up.'

Morgan rolled her eyes. 'I can see why you're the sergeant and I'm the gofer.'

Norman smiled benignly. 'When you have as many years of experience as me, you're allowed to state the glaringly obvious.'

'Technically, it's not actually a photograph, it's a print-out of one,' said Morgan.

'You split hairs if you want,' said Norman. 'Either way, it's a picture of a woman. I wonder who she is? Can you read what it says at the bottom? Is it a name?'

A few letters had been scrawled under the photo and then scratched through. Morgan squinted at them.

'The first letter is a "G", and I think the last two are "O" and "R". I can't make out the rest.'

'How many letters?' asked Norman.

'Six, I think.'

'So, what's a name with six letters that starts with "G" and ends with "OR"?'

'How do we know it's a name?'

'We don't,' said Norman.

'So, it could be anything.'

'Yeah, of course it could, but, just for a minute, try humouring the old guy who's been doing this since before you were born.'

Morgan thought for a moment. 'Wasn't there a Gaynor in one of our cases?'

'There we are,' said Norman. 'That wasn't so hard, was it? Gaynor. Yeah, that could be it.'

'How do you know she's relevant?' asked Morgan.

'Perhaps she isn't,' said Norman. 'After all, it's understandable that a lonely old man might have a photo of a glamorous, much younger woman to look at.'

'You mean you think she was some sort of fantasy woman?' asked Morgan. 'Yuck!'

'Not necessarily. She might be his daughter for all we know. But I can't help wondering why he would have scratched through her name like that and torn up the photo.'

'Alun Edwards says he didn't have any family,' Morgan said.

'Ah, but does he know that for a fact? Maybe they fell out and Gareth prefers not to talk about her. None of us knew about Sarah's father for exactly that reason.'

Morgan glanced at him. 'Had she fallen out with her father?'

'I believe so, but that's neither here nor there,' said Norman. 'My point is that, for whatever reason, she chose not to mention him. Maybe Gareth has a daughter but chose not to tell Alun Edwards about her.'

'But if she's his daughter, why hasn't he got any proper photos of her?' asked Morgan. 'You've looked around in here. There isn't a single photograph anywhere. It's as if he doesn't have a past.'

'I have to admit I can't answer that with any certainty,' said Norman. 'But if he has moved out, I would imagine he would have taken his photographs with him. There again, if the family fell out big time, he could have thrown them away.'

'Or Alun Edwards could be right, after all,' said Morgan.

'Yeah, that's also possible,' agreed Norman. 'But whatever the reality, standing here speculating isn't getting us anywhere. Whether Gareth Jenkins has a family or not, he's obviously not here. Why don't we try the neighbours? Maybe they can shed some light on this guy.'

'Are you going to put that dog down or is she part of the team now?' asked Morgan.

Norman looked down at the dog which had settled in his arms and appeared to be in no hurry to change the arrangement.

'We can't leave her here on her own,' he said.

'Isn't that where the Animal Welfare guys come in?' asked Morgan.

'Yeah, but there's no need to rush, is there?'

'Norm, you can't just keep her,' said Morgan. 'She already has an owner.'

'But Animal Welfare will just dump her in a dark, dingy kennel.'

'Well, she has to go somewhere. And anyway, it's just a temporary arrangement until we find the owner,' Morgan said.

'But what if we can't find him?'

'We certainly won't find him while you're standing here cuddling his dog,' said Morgan. 'Aren't you supposed to be the adult here, setting me an example?'

Norman sighed. 'I know you're right,' he said sadly, looking down at the dog. 'Normally I wouldn't think twice about it, but there's something about this little one . . .'

Morgan had a soft spot for dogs herself.

'How about I start knocking on the neighbouring doors while you call about the dog?' she suggested. 'Or do you want me to call them?'

'No, it's okay. I can handle it,' said Norman. 'You go on. I'll catch you up.'

* * *

Morgan made her way back out to the street and knocked on the front door of number fifty-four, the adjoining house. It

26

was soon apparent that no one was at home, so she made her way back to number fifty, the detached house on the other side of number fifty-two.

The front garden of the house had been turned into a parking space for a small cherry red hatchback. Morgan skirted around the car, stepped up to the front door and rang the bell. After a short wait, a harassed looking young woman opened the door, carrying a grizzling toddler on her hip.

'Sorry about the noise. He's teething,' she said.

'I'm DS Morgan from Llangwelli station,' said Morgan, showing her warrant card. 'Could you spare a couple of minutes to answer a few questions?'

'Sure, if you can put up with the whingeing,' said the woman, glancing down at the child. 'What's it about?'

'We've had a report that your next-door neighbour may be missing. I wondered if you've seen him recently, or if you can tell me anything about him.'

'You mean old grumpy?'

'I believe his name is Gareth Jenkins,' said Morgan.

'That's right. Miserable old bugger.'

'I was hoping you might be able to tell us something that might help us find him,' said Morgan.

The woman sniffed. 'How long have you got? Why don't you come in for a minute while I sort Billy out. You can probably smell that he needs changing.'

The idea of being within half a mile of a dirty nappy was about as appealing to Morgan as shingles, but her duty as a policewoman called on her to face terrible hazards such as this. Reluctantly, she followed the woman inside.

* * *

Fifteen minutes later, Morgan stepped back into the cool fresh air and took several deep breaths. Norman was leaning back against his car, watching her.

'Are you okay?' he asked. 'You look a bit green around the gills.'

'I grew up on a farm, so I've learned to handle any number of unpleasant smells. I can even deal with a rotting corpse without getting queasy, so why can't I cope with a dirty nappy?'

Norman chuckled. 'Bad, was it?'

'There are no words to accurately describe it,' said Morgan. 'And according to his mum, Billy, the poor little devil, is teething, which makes it ten times worse than normal. How's that for my luck?'

'To be honest, I've never had to deal with dirty nappies so I'm relying entirely on hearsay, but I was once told it's one of the worst smells known to man,' said Norman.

'Trust me, if that kid's anything to go by it's a fact,' said Morgan. 'And it's a damned good reason for not having any of my own.'

'But was it worth the pain?' asked Norman. 'Did the lucky mum know anything about our man?'

'Her name is Rose Mackie, and according to her, Gareth Jenkins wasn't exactly the greatest of neighbours. She says her and her husband used to get on well with Gareth and his wife, even doing odd jobs for him. But after his wife died, Gareth refused any more offers of help and became standoffish and rude for no reason. He was both aggressive and abusive when she approached him about his fence falling down, allowing his dog to get into her garden, which she took particular exception to as she hates dogs. He even told her to eff off when she asked him to do something about the state of his front garden.'

'Not your typical all-round good guy, then,' said Norman.

'Apparently he's alienated all his neighbours over the last five years,' said Morgan.

'Why? What happened five years ago?'

'That's when Alma, his wife, died. According to Rose, everybody loved Alma, and they liked Gareth, too, but he changed after she died. She says she tried to look out for him, but it was as if he had withdrawn from the world and wanted nothing more to do with it.'

'That could explain the state of the house and garden,' said Norman. 'Losing someone you've spent your life with can be seriously traumatic. Some people manage to adjust and find a way to carry on, but not everyone does. I think it's all down to how much you depended on each other. If you don't have a life beyond that person, it must make it really hard. You need to have things to keep you occupied, things to do . . .'

'Rose says she doesn't know what he does all day because she hardly ever sees him, and he won't speak to her unless he's telling her to mind her own business. She's heard he only goes out once a week to do his shopping, and he walks the dog in the early hours so he can avoid seeing people.'

'Jeez, if that's true he really has withdrawn from the world,' said Norman.

'And Rose wasn't surprised to hear there's hardly any furniture in there. She says she once saw people come in a van and take furniture and other stuff away. She says he used to play the piano, but that went about a year ago.'

'Does she know why?'

Morgan shook her head. 'She says she thinks they were people who do house clearances. At least that's what she thinks it said on the side of their van.'

'Did she remember the name of the company?' Norman asked.

'I'm afraid not. She says it was months ago and, as far as she knows, they've never been back. But then there's nothing left worth taking now, is there? I've left her a card in case she thinks of the name, but I wouldn't hold your breath.'

Norman nodded towards number fifty-four, the house on the other side of Gareth Jenkins's house.

'Did you try the other side?'

'There's no one in,' said Morgan. 'I'll come back and try again later.'

'Right. I think we can now officially class this as a missing person case,' said Norman. 'Although we know next to nothing about Gareth Jenkins, in view of what we've heard so far, I would suggest it's more than likely his mental state makes him extremely vulnerable. I'll head back to the station and get the wheels in motion. You find your friend Alun Edwards and see what else he can tell us about our missing person.'

'How did you get on with Animal Welfare?' asked Morgan.

'Er, yeah, okay,' he said.

'I didn't see them come and collect her,' said Morgan.

'Er, no, they haven't yet.'

'So, where is she? You haven't left her in the house, have you?'

'Of course not.'

'So where is sh—' said Morgan, just then spotting a small doggy face at the front passenger window of Norman's car.

'Jesus, Norm. Is this a good idea? You have spoken to Animal Welfare, haven't you?'

'Yes, I have. They said they couldn't get here for hours, and we can't afford to be hanging around here dog-sitting while we've got a missing owner to find, so I offered to look after her until they can get here.'

'You want to keep her, don't you?'

'Of course not. It's just a temporary thing.'

'You'll regret it.'

'It'll be fine.'

'It won't though, Norm. You'll get attached to her, and then it'll be hard to give her back to her owner.'

'I won't get attached—'

'I think you'll find you already are,' said Morgan. 'She's in the passenger seat of your car, for goodness' sake.'

'You needn't worry about me getting distracted by her or getting too attached to her. I've arranged for Faye to look after her for the time being.'

'That's your solution? Faye's going to look after her?' said Morgan. 'That's your partner Faye, who just happens to live with you at your house, right?'

'I'm going to drop her off at home on the way back to the office.'

'And you really think that's a good idea? Hasn't it occurred to you that Faye will get attached to her too?'

'I think you're making a mountain out of a molehill, Catren. I bet you the guys will come and collect her before the day's out.'

'I just hope you know what you're doing,' said Morgan.

'Didn't you say earlier that I was the adult here?' asked Norman.

'Yeah, I did, and usually you are, but right now, I'm not so sure.'

'Well, whatever you think, I've made my decision and, right or wrong, I'm not going to change my mind.'

Morgan sighed.

'Okay, whatever,' she said, getting into her car. 'But don't say I didn't warn you.'

* * *

It was four thirty by the time Morgan returned to the office.

'I checked with the phone company,' Norman told her. 'Apparently, his phone was cut off over a year ago for non-payment. And because it's been over twelve months they've deleted his call history because of their data protection rules.'

'That's a dead end, then,' said Morgan.

'Yeah, it looks that way,' said Norman. 'What about you? Was Alun Edwards any help?'

Morgan went over to her desk and slumped into her chair.

'Not really. Despite their weekly chess games, it turns out they weren't exactly bosom buddies.'

'He must know something,' said Norman. 'I mean, what about the state the house was in? Does he know where all the furniture went?'

'Apparently, he's always been ushered straight into the lounge where the chess board is, and he says that in the year or so he's been going there, that room hasn't changed.'

'Okay, but they must have talked about stuff. What about Gareth's dead wife?' Norman asked.

'The only thing he ever said about his wife was how much he missed her.'

'He didn't reminisce about the times they had together?' Norman asked.

Morgan shook her head. 'It seems that Gareth only invited Alun Edwards to his house to play chess, nothing more. Edwards might have thought they were friends, but in reality, that was all Gareth wanted, and he only ever spoke about chess.'

'Jeez, that must have been one boring conversation. They never engaged in idle chat?'

'I know. It's hard to believe, isn't it?' said Morgan.

'What about the dog? Didn't he talk about her?'

'He says the dog was always there with Gareth, and he obviously loved her to bits, but he didn't say much about her, or anything else.'

'Are you sure he's telling you the truth and not keeping some sort of secret?' Norman asked.

'I don't think he even realised how little he knew Gareth until I put him on the spot. He says, apart from chess, the only thing they ever discussed was the weather, and that was just the odd comment.'

'And he didn't think it was strange?' asked Norman.

'He says chess partners are really hard to find, but I get the impression Alun Edwards is someone who offers himself as a friend to the lonely. It seems he's out most evenings visiting different people.'

'You mean he's a sort of free "rent a friend"?' Norman said.

'Yeah,' said Morgan. 'I'm sure he means well, but I think it's actually him that's most in need of friends, and he wouldn't want to risk falling out with those he has. So, if his chess partner didn't want to talk, he wasn't going to press him.'

'What about this woman, Gaynor?' Norman asked.

'He'd never heard of her.'

'I suppose he's got no idea where we should start looking for Gareth? A special place, perhaps?' Norman said.

'He says Gareth has never mentioned anything like that.'

'Did you at least manage to get a description?'

'Yes, but he doesn't remember any distinguishing features, so it's anyone's guess as to how accurate it might be.'

'Jeez, this is going to be a challenge,' said Norman. 'We've got nothing to go on but a vague description, we've no idea what clothes the guy might be wearing, and we're not even sure how long he's been missing.'

'I don't think he would have left the dog on her own for long,' said Morgan.

'Yeah, I agree,' said Norman. 'What if he only intended to be gone for an hour or two, but something happened while he was out?'

'Happened like what?' Morgan asked.

'I dunno. He could have passed out, had a heart attack or anything. He could be in hospital, and with no one to miss him, he could have been there for days.'

'I disagree,' said Morgan. 'Unless that's the world's cleanest dog, I'm sure she hadn't been on her own for more than a day — two days at most.'

Judy Lane came over to join them. 'I've checked every hospital within twenty miles,' she said. 'None of them have admitted anyone who sounds like our missing man.'

'Okay,' said Norman. 'I hate to say it, but with what we have so far, there's not really anything we can do but circulate a description and hope someone spots him somewhere.'

'I'll do it now,' said Lane.

'We need to speak to the neighbours again,' Norman said to Morgan.

'Already in hand,' said Morgan. 'I'm going back this evening, and I'll make sure I speak to all of them and ask when they last saw him.'

'You shouldn't do that on your own at night,' said Norman. 'Let me call Faye and tell her I'll be late home.'

'It's okay, Norm. I've asked Frosty to come with me.'

'Hasn't he got his own work to do?'

'Yeah, but he's only twiddling his thumbs waiting on search results. He's gone to have something to eat and then we're meeting over there at seven.'

'I don't suppose it occurred to you he might have had plans for tonight?' said Norman.

'Who, Frosty?' said Morgan. 'I think you'll find he's often at a loose end in the evenings. I bet he's glad of an excuse to get out of that tiny bedsit he lives in.'

CHAPTER THREE

Wednesday 11 April

Next morning, Norman was just getting out of his car when Morgan pulled up next to him. Noticing Detective Constable 'Frosty' Winter in the passenger seat of her car, Norman raised a quizzical eyebrow.

'What?' she said innocently.

'What's happened to Frosty's car?'

'It wouldn't start when we finished last night,' she said. 'We had to leave it at St David's Place.'

Winter got out and joined them. 'I'll need to call a mechanic. I haven't a clue about cars.'

Both returned Norman's suspicious glance with bland expressions. Anyway, was it really his business what they got up to in their own time?

'Okay, go and get that done first, Frosty. You need to be mobile in case anything comes up. I expect Judy knows a mechanic, she seems to know everything else.'

Winter headed for the office. Norman waited while Morgan locked her car.

'How did you two get on last night?' he asked as they made their way across the car park.

'Is that supposed to be a leading question?' asked Morgan. Norman frowned. 'I'm sorry?'

'We didn't sleep together if that's what you're thinking,' said Morgan. 'I have a spare room.'

'Actually, that wasn't what I meant,' said Norman. 'As far as I'm concerned, what you do in your own time is none of my business as long as it's legal. I was referring to your visit to St David's Place to speak with the neighbours.'

'Oh, right, I see. Well, we managed to speak to most of the residents in the street apart from number fifty-four.'

'Are they avoiding us?' asked Norman.

'The lady at number fifty-six says they've gone away and won't be back until next weekend.'

'Fair enough,' said Norman. 'What did the others have to say?'

'Nearly all of them knew there was an old man living at number fifty-two, but none could recall when they last saw him. And, apart from his wife being a lovely woman and isn't it a shame she passed away, hardly anyone knows anything about Gareth, except that he's become a miserable so and so.'

'Maybe Alma was the sociable one, and Gareth was an introvert who let her speak for both of them,' said Norman.

'Yeah, that's what I thought. It wasn't all bad news though. I had another chat with Rose Mackie. She said he loves the dog so much he would never willingly leave her on her own. She believes he's suffering from depression, and that's why he's the way he is.'

'Dog or no dog, if he was lonely and depressed, we have to consider suicide as a possibility,' said Norman.

'Yeah, I know,' said Morgan. 'I hate to think he might have done that. Anyway, wouldn't he have done it at home? You know, taken a few pills with the dog at his side?'

'Well, yeah, that sounds like the easier option, but we're not lonely and depressed, are we?' Norman pondered for a moment. 'Anyway, we shouldn't write him off just yet. We only put out a description late yesterday.'

'There's something else,' said Morgan. 'They couldn't be specific, but two or three of the neighbours thought Gareth had been at home over the weekend.'

Norman stopped and turned to face her. 'So, he's only been gone a day or two?'

Morgan nodded. 'Two people said they heard the dog barking out in the garden one night over the weekend. And a guy in one of the houses opposite said he hasn't seen Gareth himself, but there's definitely been lights on in the house at night.'

'Did he say which nights?' asked Norman.

'He can't be sure, but he thinks it's probably been every night, and he's sure there was a light on in the front room on Sunday night. He noticed it at about eleven when he was checking that his front door was locked.'

'That suggests someone was in the house, but has anyone actually seen Gareth?'

'A man called David Williams lives at the end of the road in number two. He works weird shift hours, and he says he often sees Gareth walking his dog when he's on his way home. This is between two and three a.m.'

'Yeah, but didn't Rose Mackie tell you she thought he walked in the early hours to avoid everyone?'

'Yes,' said Morgan. 'But that was more of a vague impression. This is a specific sighting, because David Williams says he arrived home at two thirty a.m. on Monday, and he saw Gareth walking the dog.'

'He definitely saw Gareth? Is he sure it was him?'

'He described the dog to a "T" and he said it was an older man wearing a blue anorak.'

'There was a blue anorak hanging up in the hall, wasn't there?' said Norman.

'That's right.'

'So, the neighbour opposite says he saw a light on in the house over the weekend and another neighbour thinks he saw Gareth walking his dog in the early hours of Monday morning,' said Norman. 'But did he see Gareth's face?'

'No,' said Morgan as they pushed through the doors into their office. 'He says it was raining quite heavily, so the old man had his hood up. He also said who else would be mad enough to be walking their dog in the pouring rain at that time of night?'

'Yeah, I suppose he has a point there,' said Norman.

Seeing them arrive, Judy Lane put down her receiver and called out, 'Ah. Good morning, you two — perfect timing.'

'Good news, or bad?' asked Norman.

'I think we might have found Gareth Jenkins,' said Lane.

'Well, that's a relief,' said Norman. 'I was beginning to think we'd never find him—' He stopped, seeing Lane's expression. 'Oh. Is he—'

'Someone has found a body in a village called Pont Daffyd,' said Lane.

'Oh, bugger!' said Morgan. 'Please don't let it be him.'

'Pont who? Where's that?' said Norman.

'It's a small village about ten miles from here,' said Lane.

'And they're sure it's him?' Norman asked.

'They can't say for sure, but it does match our description,' Lane said.

'It wasn't exactly a great description, was it?' said Norman hopefully.

'True enough,' said Lane, 'but there again he is the only man who has been reported missing within fifty miles.'

'When you put it like that, it probably is him,' said Norman. 'But what the heck was he doing out there? I thought he never went anywhere.'

'Here. I've written it all down for you,' said Lane, handing Norman a sheet of paper.

Norman glanced at it and passed it to Morgan.

'Come on, Catren. Let's go and see if it's our man.'

* * *

'Am I correct in thinking a "pont" is a bridge?' asked Norman as Morgan pulled out of the car park.

She smiled. 'I see someone's still doing their homework.'

'This village we're heading for is called Pont Daffyd. Would that translate as "David's Bridge"?'

'Correct,' she said.

'You're impressed, right?'

'Let's not get carried away,' said Morgan. 'Knowing one simple word doesn't make you fluent in Welsh, and anyway, there are only so many circumstances when you could use that word in a sentence.'

Norman sighed. 'It's frustrating, you know? I can see some words and know what they mean, but recognising them and pronouncing them so someone else can understand is a whole different ball game. There seem to be a lot of place names that start with "pont". Why so many?'

'I'm guessing there's a river runs through them all,' said Morgan. 'And I know there's a disused railway in Pont Daffyd that used to run down the valley, through the villages and on to the coast.'

'Ah, yeah,' said Norman. 'But would the railway be old enough to figure in the naming of the villages? I'm guessing the railway was originally built to transport coal from the mines to the sea, but wouldn't the villages have been there before the railways were built?'

'Good point,' said Morgan. 'I suppose in that case there must be a bridge over a river somewhere in the village.'

'You suppose?' teased Norman. 'Don't you know? You are supposed to be my indispensable source of expert local knowledge. Isn't that what you told me?'

'Be fair,' said Morgan. 'I can't be expected to know everything about every single place in the country.'

'All I'm saying is that anyone claiming to be an expert ought to know all the answers.'

She smiled. 'I do know the reason why there are so many rivers — it's because of all that rain you're always complaining about.'

'Even I managed to work that one out, Catren, which, by definition, means it doesn't count as expert knowledge. Therefore, you earn zero brownie points.'

'Now you're making the rules up as you go along,' protested Morgan.

'Which I am entitled to do through the privileges of both rank and age.' Norman looked out at the sky. 'Anyway, today we don't need to worry about the rain. We have a perfect blue sky and warm sunshine, so I have nothing to complain about, weather-wise. How much further is this place?'

'That signpost might give you a clue,' said Morgan, slowing the car and turning left by a sign that said, *Croeso i Pont Daffyd*. 'It says—'

'Welcome to Pont Daffyd,' finished Norman. 'Yeah, I know that one.'

Morgan laughed. 'We'll make a Welsh speaker out of you yet.'

'I appreciate your optimism, but somehow I doubt that will ever happen,' said Norman.

The road they had turned into wound steeply around to the left, then straightened, passing a chapel with a small cemetery followed by a cluster of houses. A hundred yards further on, the road narrowed as it approached a humpback bridge. A uniformed policeman stood to one side of it.

'The old railway runs under this bridge,' said Morgan. She pulled up beside the PC and wound down the window.

'DC Morgan and DS Norman. Is the body down there?'

'Aye,' called the PC, 'but you need to park around the corner on your right, opposite the pub.'

Morgan gave him a thumbs up and drove on.

'It looks like we have to park further on and walk back,' she said.

'I can see why,' said Norman. 'If we parked where he's standing, we'd block the road.'

Morgan crossed the bridge and turned into an even narrower road that led to a small trading estate. Police vehicles and a forensic van were parked on the grass verges on either side. Morgan added their car to the collection.

'So, this is it,' she said.

'Didn't Judy say the body was under the bridge?' asked Norman, getting out.

'I'm not sure,' said Morgan.

They went back over the bridge and presented themselves to the uniformed officer. He made a note of their details, and their time of arrival, and raised the tape. 'Go down the steps, and then follow the path,' he said.

Norman looked dubiously at the steps, which had been hacked from the bank some time in the past, and reinforced with timber.

'They're quite safe,' said the PC.

'Is the body under the bridge?' asked Norman. 'Only we were told it was in a tunnel.'

'It's not an actual tunnel,' said the PC. 'It's what the locals call the path that runs alongside the old railway. You'll see why when you get down there.'

'Is it far?' asked Norman.

The PC looked Norman up and down as if to assess his age and condition. 'There are about twenty steps down to the path, then you have to walk for about half a mile or so. It's just a gentle slope downwards for the first part but when it levels out it's uneven for a hundred yards or so. After that it's not too bad, and it's mostly flat, so you should be okay.'

Norman was about to offer a retort, but Morgan beat him to it.

'It's okay, I'll look after him,' she assured the PC. She turned to Norman and took his arm. 'Come on, Granddad, let me help you down these steps.'

Norman shook off her hand, wondering why Morgan always managed to catch him on the wrong foot by veering off into the unexpected.

Morgan turned and winked at the PC. 'He's always a bit cranky when he hasn't had his afternoon nap.'

'It's a good job I'm not the sort to take offence,' he said as she caught up with him at the bottom of the steps. 'That PC probably thinks I'm a right idiot for putting up with it.'

'I think it's more likely he's pleased to see we can do our jobs without having to be po-faced all the time,' said Morgan. 'Anyway, I wouldn't do it if I didn't think you could take a joke.'

'Yeah, that's all very well, but you need to bear in mind that in the course of your career, you're going to come across plenty of senior officers who don't have a sense of humour.'

'I do realise that,' said Morgan. 'I'm just making the most of this situation while I can.'

Norman had stopped to survey the path ahead of them. From the bottom of the steps it sloped gently downhill. Over to his left, he could see the old railway track. The line was relatively clear under the bridge, but further ahead nature had done its best to reclaim the land.

'Oh, wow,' he said. 'Look at that. It's like it was closed a hundred years ago.'

'It was originally built to carry coal to the coast,' said Morgan. 'They added a few passenger services over the years, but it was transporting the coal that made it pay. Once the mines started closing, the railway was always going to be doomed.'

'I suppose it closed for good in the eighties then,' Norman said, 'When all the mines shut down.'

'I don't know exactly when it closed,' said Morgan. 'I'm guessing it must have been around then, but it could have been before that. A lot closed in the sixties.'

They continued down the gentle slope until they were walking alongside the railway lines, which were just visible though the undergrowth.

'It's amazing that you can still see the actual lines, and the sleepers,' said Norman. 'It almost looks as if it could be restored as a tourist attraction. I mean, who doesn't like an old steam railway?'

'Good idea, except it would cost the earth,' said Morgan.

'Yeah, I can imagine,' said Norman. 'I bet as soon as you started moving these trees, the whole thing would fall apart. Can you hear running water?'

Morgan found a relatively clear path across the railway line and stepped across to the far side, where she peered through the trees. 'There's an embankment on the other side. It sounds like there's a stream down there.'

'I'm beginning to like this place,' said Norman. 'It's so quiet, with just the sound of the water — and look at that.' He pointed up at the trees ahead. 'I see now why they call it the tunnel. You can barely see the sky through the treetops. It's a living, green tunnel.'

He surveyed the path ahead.

'Jeez, I can see why he warned us about this part of the path. What the heck are all these rocks doing here?'

'They're not exactly rocks,' said Morgan. 'It's the granite chips from under the sleepers. Maybe some of the locals have been digging them out.'

'What for?'

'I don't know. Maybe they use it for hardcore when they're doing DIY stuff.'

'You could easily break an ankle out here.'

'All the more reason to be careful,' said Morgan. 'Sure I can't take your arm?'

Norman marched ahead, leaving Morgan staring at his back.

'I don't think that will be necessary, thank you, Catren. Just remember I'm approaching sixty, not ninety, and I'd prefer not to be reminded of it all the time.'

'Okay, point taken,' said Morgan.

They trudged on in silence for a few seconds.

'I suppose I could take being called "Dad" as a sort of backhanded compliment,' Norman continued, 'but "Grandad" is taking it a step too far.'

'Right,' said Morgan. 'That's fair enough. But you're too cool to be my dad.'

'Why? What's wrong with your dad?'

'Nothing, he's great, but he's not cool like you.'

Norman laughed. 'Me? Cool? How does that work?'

'Well, think about it,' she said. 'My dad's part of the farming community, and he's anxious to fit in, cares what people think of him.'

'And what's wrong with that?' asked Norman. 'Don't we all want to belong in some way?'

'Yes, of course we do, but I always thought that as you get older you care less about what others think of you, and are happy to just be yourself.'

'I've never gone in for that "mine's bigger than yours" bullshit, if that's what you mean,' said Norman.

'Oh no. My dad doesn't try to impress, he just wants to be like everybody else. Sometimes I think he tries a little too hard, and when he does, he hides his real self. That's not cool. You'd never do that.'

'From what I've heard you say about your dad, he sounds like a great guy,' said Norman.

'Yes, he is, but the difference between him and you is you don't give a damn what anyone thinks.'

'And you think that makes me cool? Some people would say that makes me arrogant, or ignorant.'

'Yeah, but that's probably because they're jealous,' said Morgan. 'Unhappy people often have nothing better to do than find someone with a bit of confidence to criticise.'

'I'm not cool, Catren, I'm just me.'

'But that's exactly what I'm saying,' said Morgan. 'As far as I'm concerned, you can't get any cooler than being yourself whatever anyone thinks, can you? I mean, isn't that what being cool really is?'

'It may surprise you to hear this, Catren, but I've never given much thought to what makes someone cool.'

'Trust me, I'm right,' she said. 'And you, Norm, are one cool dude.'

'Dude? Isn't that what cowboys call each other in old Westerns?'

Morgan smiled. 'There, you see. Some people would say knowing something like that makes you old-fashioned, but I think it just proves how cool you are.'

'You know, working with you is often the weirdest experience,' said Norman.

'Why?'

'I've worked dozens of murder cases in my time, but I don't ever recall having a partner tell me I'm a cool dude just as we're about to view a dead body. I mean, how did we even get onto the subject?'

'It's because I called you Grandad, don't you remember? Anyway, it's good to pass the time in abstract discussion. Don't you always tell me I shouldn't let the job take over my life?'

Norman couldn't think of an answer for that. Fortunately, just then another uniformed PC stepped out of a clump of trees and waved to them, so he didn't have to.

'This must be it,' he said.

The PC stepped forward and produced a clipboard, took their details, and raised yet another length of blue and white tape.

'Across the rails?' Norman asked the PC.

'The body's down by the stream,' said the PC pointing across the track. 'Once you get to the other side and look through the trees you'll see the pathologist and the SOCOs down the embankment.'

Norman ducked under the tape, and followed by Morgan, made his way through the trees and almost stepped out into the air. Below them, at the bottom of a steep slope, a suited and booted forensic team were beavering away around where the body must be lying.

'Jeez, we could do with a toboggan to get down there,' Norman said.

'It's not that bad,' said Morgan. 'I'll go first if you like.'

Norman grinned. 'Good call. Then if I slip, you can break my fall.'

CHAPTER FOUR

In the event, the slope wasn't as bad as it looked. Someone had considerately put up a makeshift rope handrail to hang onto, and they reached the bottom still on their feet.

A short way along the bank, a figure in a white forensic suit was busy taking photographs. As they watched, he stepped back and gesticulated to his team, who began to manoeuvre a pop-up tent over the body. He glanced up at Norman and Morgan and waved a casual hand in their direction.

'It's Dr Bridger,' said Morgan. 'How come he always manages to get here before us?'

'He probably doesn't get distracted by weird conversations about how cool he is,' said Norman, heading towards him.

'Well, of course he doesn't,' said Morgan. 'He's not cool.'

'Cool, or not, can we just try to focus on the job in hand?' asked Norman.

'I am always completely focused once we get to the job,' said Morgan.

'Good,' said Norman. 'Let's keep it that way.'

'What kept you?' asked Bridger as they approached.

'A question of national importance,' said Norman. 'And before you ask what it was, I should warn you I'd have to kill you if I told you what it was.'

'As you have DC Morgan with you, I assume you mean gossip,' said Bridger. 'I'd expect nothing less really.'

Morgan opened her mouth, but Norman raised a hand in warning.

'So, what can you tell us?' he asked.

'It's a dead body,' said Bridger, his face deadpan.

'No kidding,' said Norman. 'And here we were hoping you'd found ET. We were told it's a man. Is that right?'

'Correct,' said Bridger.

'Is this the crime scene?' asked Norman.

'I'm not sure it is a crime yet, but either way, I don't think anything happened here. I'm told people often walk their dogs down here because the stream is shallow enough to cross. I'm sure he would have been found before now if he'd died here. My bet is that he went in further upstream and was washed down here. I've got people searching the river to see what they can find, but there's miles of it to get through.'

'Does that mean he was actually in the water, and you fished him out?' asked Norman.

'He's sodden, Norm. Of course we dragged him out. How else are we going to get him back to the lab?'

'Jeez, Bill, did you miss breakfast this morning?' asked Norman. 'I'm just trying to do my job and establish a few facts, much the same as you are. Believe it or not, we're on the same side here.'

Bridger sighed. 'Sorry,' he said. 'I've had a shit start to my day, but you're right, I shouldn't be taking it out on you guys.'

'Okay,' said Norman. 'How about you give us a few details about the body to be going on with?'

'Sure,' said Bridger. 'As you correctly guessed, this is the body of a male, around seventy to eighty years old.'

'That sounds like our man,' said Norman.

'Don't you recognise him?' asked Bridger, pointing at the dead man's face.

Norman squinted. 'I suppose it could be him. There's just one problem with us trying to identify him. You see, we're not actually sure what he looks like.'

'Really?'

'We have a description but no photograph, and the description is a bit vague. That's why I say it could be him, but I can't be sure,' said Norman. 'Can you tell us the cause of death?'

Bridger frowned. 'I can't say right now.'

'What about time of death?'

'He's been in this cold water which is acting like a refrigerator and slowing decomposition down, making it difficult to work out. My best guess right now is that he could have been here for three or four days. But that really is only a guess.'

'Three or four days?' echoed Norman. 'Then it can't be our guy. He's only been missing for two.'

'Well, I'm sorry to disappoint you, but that's my initial impression,' said Bridger.

'And there are no injuries?' asked Norman.

Bridger pointed to the man's head.

'All I can see at this stage is a wound to the back of his head,' he said.

'He was attacked?'

'Maybe, but he could also have fallen and hit his head on a rock.'

'Okay. So, it could be an accident,' said Norman. 'Either way, even if it's not the guy we're looking for, we still need to know who he is.'

Carefully, Bridger searched the man's soggy jacket pockets. 'Hello, what's this?' he said, pulling something from an inside pocket. He studied it for a second. 'I think I've found his bus travel card.'

'Travel card?' said Norman.

'Anyone over the age of sixty in Wales can apply for a card which permits them to travel free on a bus,' said Morgan.

'Really? Is there a bus that comes out this way?' asked Norman.

'That's not actually my area of expertise,' said Morgan, 'but I would imagine there's probably some sort of service to the village.'

'What's the name on the bus pass?' asked Norman.

'Gareth Jenkins,' Bridger announced.

Norman was momentarily stunned into silence.

'Are you sure?' asked Morgan.

'Here, see for yourself,' said Bridger, slipping the card into a clear evidence bag and handing it to her. Morgan stared at the card and then handed it on to Norman, who stared at it, his brow furrowed.

'But this makes no sense,' he said. 'Our understanding is that he's only been missing for a day or two. How could he have been in the water for four?'

'Maybe it's a different person who has the same name,' said Bridger. 'Gareth and Jenkins aren't uncommon names in Wales.'

'Yeah, but how many of them would fit the correct age profile and be reported missing?' said Norman. 'It's too much of a coincidence.'

'Just because he has a bus pass with that name on it doesn't mean it's him,' said Morgan. 'Perhaps he found it, or he could even have stolen it from Gareth Jenkins.'

'I think you might be clutching at straws here,' said Bridger. 'I'd say his face matches the photograph on the card.'

Morgan squinted at the card and then at the body. 'I don't know. This photograph is tiny, and you said this man has been dead for days.'

'Ignoring the face,' said Norman. 'If it was a credit card or a wallet, I might be persuaded that it could have been stolen, but a bus pass? Really?'

'It might not mean much to you, but for an older person who doesn't drive, a bus pass is worth a fortune,' argued Morgan.

'All right, I'll accept it's a possibility, but at this point I'm not convinced.' Norman turned to Bridger. 'Are you sure he's been in there that long?'

'You know I can't be certain of anything until I get him to the lab, Norm,' said Bridger testily, 'but I've been doing this long enough to know I'm not a million miles off with my estimate.'

'I'm sorry, Bill,' said Norman. 'I don't mean to question your findings; I just can't understand how it's possible.'

'Maybe you need to question what you think you know,' said Bridger. 'If this really is your man, it seems to me he must have been missing for longer than you were told. Anyway, that's your problem. Right now, I want to move this body, if that's okay with you. We'll let you know if we find where he went in.'

'Yeah, go ahead,' said Norman. 'There's not really much we can do here anyway.'

'Are you available for a post-mortem this afternoon?' asked Bridger. 'I know Sarah's away, but I think she'd expect it to be done sooner rather than later.'

'Er, yeah, I suppose so,' said Norman reluctantly.

'Shall we say two thirty?'

'Does that work for you?' Norman asked Morgan.

'Me?'

'Yeah. I thought you might like the opportunity for a change, but I can manage on my own if you have something better to do.'

'No. It's fine, I'd love to be there. Thank you,' said Morgan.

'That's it then, Bill. We'll see you at two thirty,' said Norman. 'Now we'll get out of your way.'

* * *

'Is it me, or is he in a crabby mood?' asked Morgan as they set off for their car.

'Who, Bill? I think you'll find that's my fault. He always gets a bit tetchy if someone questions his findings, and if he's having a bad day anyway that would only make it worse.'

'But isn't that just plain arrogant?' asked Morgan.

'Oh, he can be arrogant, for sure,' said Norman. 'The thing is he rarely gets anything wrong, so he's got something to be arrogant about.'

'And what did he mean about me and gossip?'

'Take no notice,' said Norman. 'I'd probably be a bit crabby if I was having a bad day and then I had to drag a body out of a cold stream.'

A smile spread slowly across Morgan's face. 'Perhaps it's got nothing to do with work, and he's just missing the boss.'

'She's only been away a couple of days,' said Norman.

'Yes, but look how cosy they are together now,' said Morgan. 'I bet he's finding it hard sleeping on his ow—'

'Think for a minute about what Bill said back there, and what you're doing right now,' said Norman. 'Do you think there might be a link?'

Morgan was momentarily silenced.

'But I don't mean any harm by it,' she said finally. 'It's just a bit of fun.'

'Yeah, I know that Catren, but not everyone sees it that way, and anyway, there's a time and a place. Maybe there's times when you need to rein it in a bit.'

'Have I pissed him off somewhere along the line? Tell me what I did, and I'll apologise to him.'

'He's not said anything to me,' said Norman. 'As far as I know you haven't upset him, but that doesn't mean you won't. I suggest you just focus on the fact that we now have a potential murder case on our hands and forget the idle gossip.'

'Yes, right. Sorry,' said Morgan.

Their silence lasted until they were back in the car.

'What if it really is a coincidence and it's a different Gareth Jenkins?' asked Morgan.

'You know how I feel about coincidences,' said Norman. He reached for his mobile phone. 'But just to be sure, I'll call Judy and ask her to search the missing persons database again.'

* * *

'Any luck, Judy?' asked Norman, as soon as they got back to the office.

'Sorry, the only Gareth Jenkins on the database is ours.'

'But we're not totally sure it's him, are we?' said Morgan. 'And I still think that bus pass could have been stolen.'

'Right,' said Norman. 'Let's try to take some of the guess-work out of this. Whether this is our missing man, or not, the only thing we know for sure is that he was carrying a bus pass. So, Catren, I want you to find out who's responsible for those bus passes and check if our man was ever issued with one. And I want to know how many bus passes have been issued to anyone called Gareth Jenkins in the last twenty years.'

'Twenty years?' echoed Morgan.

'You said anyone over sixty can apply, and we've been told the guy may have been eighty years old. According to my old-fashioned arithmetic, that means he could have applied any time during the last twenty years, but make it twenty-five years just in case he's a little older than we thought.'

With a groan, Morgan headed for her desk.

'You do realise we have to attend the post-mortem this afternoon,' she called back.

'Yeah, of course I do,' said Norman. 'But it won't hurt to start the wheels turning now, will it?'

'Frosty,' called Norman. 'Did you get your car fixed?'

'They looked at it this morning but they couldn't fix it, so they towed it back to their garage. It's some sort of electrical problem. They've ordered the part, but it might take a couple of days to arrive. Judy's offered me a lift home.'

'I can pick him up in the morning,' said Lane. 'Or if we get called out tonight.'

'Are you sure?' asked Norman.

'Of course,' said Lane. 'It's fine.'

* * *

Dr Bill Bridger was in a much better mood when they arrived for the post-mortem. They followed him into his lab where the body, covered in a sheet, lay on a stainless-steel table.

'You'll be pleased to know you don't have to watch me wield a scalpel,' said Bridger. 'I've already done that part.'

52

'You know, I'm not sorry to hear it,' said Norman. 'I've always thought that watching you slice and dice a body is extremely overrated. The way I see it, we only need to know what you found. Seeing how you found it makes no difference, so why put us through it?'

'I wouldn't have minded watching,' said Morgan. 'I always find it interesting.'

Bridger smiled. 'It's funny how the older detective, who has probably attended dozens of post-mortems over the years, is the more squeamish.'

'Yeah, maybe,' said Norman. 'But I'm only like this when it's a dead body. Besides, being squeamish has never stopped me doing my job, and that's what matters. After all, that's what I get paid for.'

'That's a fair point,' said Bridger. Carefully, he pulled the sheet back to reveal the man's face. 'This is what his face looks like now he's been cleaned up.'

'That looks more like the face on the bus pass,' said Morgan.

'I thought so too,' said Bridger. 'Of course, that doesn't give us a definitive identity but if I were a betting man, I'd say it's him. Norm?'

'Yeah. I think I'd agree it's the bus pass face, but can we confirm he's the guy who lived in St David's Place?'

'I have requested dental records but that might take a couple of days.'

'That should be enough to confirm who he is, shouldn't it?' asked Morgan.

'Normally I'd say yes, but looking at his teeth, I'd say he hasn't been near a dentist in years. But you never know, we might get lucky.'

'Okay, so we think it probably is our man,' said Norman. 'What about time of death?'

Bridger consulted his notes.

'I originally said he could have been in the water for a few days, but I've managed to narrow that down. I now believe he died on Friday evening or possibly in the early hours of Saturday morning.'

Morgan thought this couldn't be right. She looked questioningly at Norman, who shook his head.

'Had he been in the water all that time?' asked Norman.

'As far as I can tell, yes, he had been completely submerged in that cold stream. That's why I can't be more precise about the time of death.'

'Did he drown?' asked Morgan.

'There's no water in the lungs,' said Bridger.

'So, he was already dead when he went in?' asked Morgan.

'Correct,' said Bridger.

'And you said he didn't go into the water where he was found,' said Norman.

'It's not deep enough there. We're still looking upstream.'

'What about a cause of death?' asked Norman.

Bridger pulled the sheet down to reveal the torso. It was covered in bruises.

'Jezuz!' said Norman. 'Look at those bruises. Are you sure he wasn't beaten to death?'

'It looks that way, doesn't it?' said Bridger. 'But these aren't impact bruises.'

'Is it some sort of illness?' asked Morgan.

'I'm not sure what caused the bruises yet,' said Bridger. 'When I get the lab results, I should be able to narrow it down, but I can tell you Mr Jenkins wasn't a well man. His liver appears to be diseased, and his gums aren't good. I would imagine they would have bled quite a lot, and he seems to have been anaemic.'

'Sounds like he wouldn't have been around for much longer anyway,' said Morgan. 'Was he being treated by a doctor?'

'I'll be checking that,' said Bridger. 'He certainly should have been. As I said, I've got no toxicology results yet. I did find the remnants of a couple of cold remedy tablets in his stomach, but not enough to kill anyone.'

'That figures,' said Morgan. 'We found a selection of medicines and herbal remedies at the house. There was enough there to treat an army, so maybe he ate them like smarties.'

'Yes, we bagged them up and brought them here,' said Bridger. 'I haven't had time to analyse them all yet, but I'd say it won't matter anyway. As I said, he wasn't a well man. The cause of death was most probably heart failure.'

'Are you saying he died of natural causes?' asked Norman.

Bridger shrugged. 'I'm saying he suffered a heart attack.'

'So, it was natural,' said Morgan.

'I'm not saying that for sure at this stage,' said Bridger.

'What about the head wound you mentioned earlier?' asked Norman.

'I'd say the blunt force trauma to the head would have been enough to cause the heart attack that killed him.'

'You have doubts?' asked Norman.

Bridger pointed to the dead man's face. 'You see these little red spots?'

'Petechiae, right?' said Norman.

Bridger smiled. 'So you do listen to my post-mortems.'

'Sometimes,' said Norman. 'That means he might well have been strangled, right?'

'It's a good indicator that his jugular vein could have been compressed, which would interfere with the blood flow to his brain.'

'You mean he was strangled,' said Norman.

'Possibly, but not necessarily,' said Bridger.

'Doesn't a broken hyoid bone prove that?' asked Morgan.

'That's very good, and if it was broken, I'd be more or less certain he'd been strangled,' said Bridger. 'But in this case the hyoid bone is intact, and there is no obvious bruising around his neck, which you would expect if he had been strangled.'

'You've removed his brain,' said Norman. 'Can't you tell from that?'

'I haven't dissected his organs yet, but his body had been in the water for so long, I'm not sure what I'll find.'

'Okay, to summarise then,' said Norman. 'We're still not completely sure if he's our missing man, but the likelihood is that it is him.'

Bridger nodded.

'I think it's him,' said Morgan.

'And, as he was in poor health,' continued Norman, 'the chances are he died of a heart attack brought on by a blow to the head, but it's also possible something happened to interfere with the blood flow to his brain or, in layman's terms, he might have been strangled.'

'I can't say for sure yet,' said Bridger.

'But with that blow to the head, surely we have to treat this as a murder?' asked Norman.

'As I said, that could have been caused by a fall so I can't give you a definitive answer yet, Norm.'

'Okay, but you spoke of being a gambling man earlier. How about you gamble on an educated guess about the probability.'

'When we find the place where he went into the water, we'll know more about what happened to him. Until then, I'm not prepared to commit myself one way or the other.'

'Jeez, Bill, if you sit on that fence too long, you'll get splinters in your arse,' said Norman.

Bridger smiled. 'You're probably right about that, Norm, but as it's my arse that'll be on the line if I get it wrong, it's a risk I'm willing to take.'

Norman managed a rueful smile. 'Well, don't call me when you need help picking the splinters out.'

'I'll bear that in mind,' said Bridger, 'but, splinters or not, I'm still unwilling to commit one way or the other.'

'Are you sure?' asked Norman.

'Absolutely.'

'Crap,' said Norman. 'In that case, we might as well get going.'

'Can I have quiet word before you go?' asked Bridger.

Norman looked at Morgan, who recognised a hint when she saw one.

'I'll wait in the car,' she said.

* * *

A couple of minutes later, Norman walked slowly out to the car. He decided he wouldn't tell anyone what Bridger had just said. They would find out when they arrived for work the following morning.

'Why didn't you tell him he was wrong about the time of death?' asked Morgan, once he was in the car. 'We have a witness who says he was walking his dog early on Monday morning. He can't have been doing that if he was lying dead in a stream ten miles away, can he?'

'Sometimes you have to stop and think before you jump in with both feet,' said Norman. 'You're suggesting we question the judgement of a pathologist with an impeccable record. I've worked with Bill Bridger for years, and he's never been more than a couple of hours out when it comes to estimating time of death.'

'But we're not talking a couple of hours, Norm,' argued Morgan. 'We know he's a few days out.'

'Or perhaps our witness was mistaken,' said Norman. 'Did he say he actually saw Gareth's face?'

Morgan fished in her bag for her notebook, thumbed back a few pages and then handed it to Norman who quickly scanned what she'd written.

'So, what the witness actually said was that it was pouring with rain, and the man had his hood up,' he said.

'Well, yeah,' conceded Morgan.

'That means your witness didn't say, beyond all doubt, that it was Gareth he saw.'

'Are you saying it was someone else walking their dog at two thirty in the morning?'

'I'm saying it's possible,' said Norman. 'And this is precisely why I think we always need to be one hundred per cent sure of our facts before we question the pathologist's findings.'

Morgan thought Norman was giving Bridger far more credit than he deserved, but it was clear he wasn't going to back down.

'You don't believe it's natural causes, do you?' she asked.

'If Gareth was as sick as Bill suggests, it would explain why he stayed at home all the time and only went out to walk his dog.'

'Yes, I suppose it does,' said Morgan.

'Which then begs the question, why did he go all the way out to Pont Daffyd?' said Norman. 'That's what bothers me about all this.'

'I see what you mean,' said Morgan. 'What do you want to do?'

'I think we should treat this as a murder until we know different. And now we have reason to think it's murder, you'd better call Forensics and get a team around to St David's Place.'

'So much for me getting home early,' said Morgan.

Norman smiled. 'Being a detective constable is a shit job sometimes, but someone has to do it. If it's any consolation, we've all been there too.'

CHAPTER FIVE

Thursday 12 April

Norman guessed that Southall would arrive before seven, as it was her first day back from leave, so he made the effort to get in early himself. When she walked in at six forty-five, he had a mug of coffee waiting for her.

'How was it?' he asked.

'It wasn't a holiday, Norm. I went for my father's funeral.'

'Yes, I realise that, but I thought you were going to stay for a few days to help sort out the house. We would have been fine here.'

'I haven't come back because I thought you couldn't cope without me, Norm. Being up there listening to my sister droning on about how great my dad was only reminded me why I left and came down here in the first place. I honestly couldn't wait to get away, and when Bill told me about the body, it was the perfect excuse for me to make my escape.'

'We were all sorry to hear about your father's death.'

'You needn't be sorry, Norm. I'm not.'

'Oh, really? I didn't realise,' said Norman. 'Although I suppose, thinking about it, I should have guessed you didn't get on with him.'

'What do you mean, you should have guessed? How?' asked Southall.

'It doesn't matter,' said Norman. 'Maybe we should talk about something else.'

'You must have a reason for saying that,' insisted Southall.

'It's just that, in all the time we've worked together, I don't think you ever mentioned him once. You didn't even tell me he was ill.'

'Is that right?' said Southall. 'I've never mentioned him?'

'Maybe once or twice in passing, but never at length.'

'Then that probably tells you everything you need to know about our relationship,' she said.

'I'm sorry to hear that, Sarah. I wasn't trying to pry.'

'To be honest, Norm, it's quite a long story and I don't feel up to sharing it right now.'

'That's okay,' he said. 'It's really none of my business.'

'I'd much rather you told me what's been going on here,' said Southall.

Norman was surprised that Bridger hadn't brought her up to date with their case.

'You haven't seen Bill? I assumed—'

'That he would have told me all about it,' finished Southall. 'Well, didn't he?'

'All I know is what he told me yesterday lunchtime, which was that he was about to do a post-mortem on a body.'

'He didn't tell you anything else?' Norman asked.

'Although we spend a lot of time together, we don't actually live in each other's pockets,' said Southall. 'I didn't get back until late last night, so I haven't seen him. Besides, he knows you take the lead on any case in my absence, and he wouldn't want to tread on your toes.'

'Oh, right,' said Norman. 'In that case, let me fill you in. We started off on Tuesday morning with an old guy missing from home. Then, yesterday, someone found a body just outside a village ten miles from here.'

'And you think there's more to it than just an unfortunate accident?'

60

'There are enough peculiarities to make me very suspicious,' said Norman. 'And I think you'll feel the same when you hear the story.'

'Is this the case that's on the whiteboard?'

'Yeah, it's a bit sketchy so far, but that's one of the things that bothers me about it.'

Southall headed for the board. 'Come on, then. Bring me up to speed before the others get here.'

* * *

By the time the rest of the team arrived, Southall was inclined to agree with Norman that he was right to have his suspicions.

'Good morning, everyone,' she said. 'Norm has been helping me catch up with the Gareth Jenkins case. At the moment, Dr Bridger is unable to give us a definitive cause of death but, even so, I think it's fair to say there are enough anomalies to warrant further investigation.'

'There is one new thing we know,' said Norman. 'Yesterday afternoon the SOCOs found the site where they believe Gareth Jenkins went into the water. It's about a hundred yards further upstream from where the body was found. We'll be going to take a look a little later today. So, unless anyone has anything else to add . . .'

The three younger detectives shook their heads.

'Okay,' said Southall. 'Judy, I'd like you to do your normal excellent job here in the office. Catren, I'd like you to look into Gareth's background and family and, Frosty, see if you can find any sign of a bank account. I'd also like to know who took all the furniture away, and why. Norm's going to take me to Gareth's house, and the scene of the crime, and then we'll take a look at where the body went into the water.'

'That works for me,' said Norman. 'Let's start with the house.'

* * *

Norman turned the car into St David's Place and parked outside number fifty-two. Blue and white police tape had been stretched across the front door with a warning sign attached: *Crime scene. Keep out.*

Norman, followed by Southall, went up to the front door, removed the tape and sign, produced a key and led the way inside. Reluctant to have to endure the smell from under the kitchen table, he waited in the hall while she had a quick look around.

'I see what you meant when you said it was sparsely furnished,' she said.

'It makes you wonder how it got this bad, doesn't it?' said Norman.

Southall took a step into the kitchen, stopped and waved a hand in front of her nose. 'Good grief!'

'Sorry,' said Norman. 'I should have warned you.'

'Didn't you say there was a dog in the house?'

'Er, yes, that's right,' said Norman. 'We think the poor thing had been shut in for a day or two before we got here.'

'That explains the smell then,' said Southall. 'Where is it now?'

'Animal Welfare couldn't get here on Tuesday, so she's with me and Faye at the moment.'

Southall raised an eyebrow. 'But it's Thursday today. Surely they should have got to you by now.'

'They said they didn't have any spare kennels, so I offered to let her stay at my house for the time being.'

'You know you may not be able to keep her, Norm. If we find any family members and they want her, you'll have to give her back.'

'Yeah, well, we'll cross that bridge when we come to it,' said Norman, hoping he wasn't going to get another lecture about becoming attached to the dog and then regretting it. But he needn't have worried.

'Have you thought about how our dead man managed to be seen walking the dog?'

'I don't believe in ghosts,' said Norman. 'So that leaves two possibilities. Either we're completely wrong about the body being that of our missing man, or someone else has been walking the dog.'

'If Gareth Jenkins isn't the dead man in the morgue, where is he?' asked Southall.

Norman shrugged. 'There's no doubt in my mind that it's his body in the morgue.'

'But if the man at number two saw him walking the dog in the early hours, how could that be his body on the slab?' asked Southall. 'He did identify him, didn't he?'

'Not exactly,' said Norman. 'What he said was that he saw an old man walking the dog, and that the man was wearing a blue anorak. But he also said it was pouring with rain and the man had his hood up.'

'So, it could have been anyone,' said Southall.

'That's what I'm thinking,' said Norman. 'He said the old guy was stooped, but what if it was just someone keeping their head down so they wouldn't be recognised, or because of the rain?'

'You said something about the lights being on.'

'Yeah. The next-door neighbour, and one across the road, claim they have seen lights on at night, just as normal. To me that suggests someone wanted people to think Gareth was still alive.'

'Any idea why?'

'Right now, your guess is as good as mine,' said Norman. 'Maybe they were looking for something.'

'For several nights? It's not a big house, is it? How long could it take to search a house this size?'

'It took us about half an hour,' he said. 'Even if you were taking the house apart, it shouldn't take more than a couple of hours.'

'Do you think they found what they were looking for?'

Norman shrugged. 'Let me put it this way. This is what it was like when we got here, and the SOCOs say they didn't take anything away.'

'Do you think it was all removed by whoever was here?'

Norman nodded. 'I reckon they took everything that might have told us something about him, or about what's been going on. That's why we know hardly anything about the guy. We couldn't even find a photograph to help us identify him.'

'But why keep feeding the dog, and why walk her in the early hours?' asked Southall. 'Why not just get rid of her?'

'To make it look more convincing?' suggested Norman. 'As the guy at number two said, who else but the grumpy old guy at number fifty-two would be walking their dog at that time of night?'

Suddenly, they heard a noise; a sort of rattle. Southall raised a finger to her lips and pointed towards the front of the house.

'It's coming from there,' she whispered.

Norman crept slowly towards the front door. As he drew nearer, he recognised the sound. Someone was trying to put a key into the lock. The door creaked open and an elderly woman stepped inside, dragging a wheeled suitcase behind her. Norman retreated into the shadows and watched her. He was always wary of guessing a woman's age, but this one was evidently in her seventies and presented no danger.

He stepped forward. 'Can I help you?'

The woman gasped. 'Who the hell are you?'

Norman had his warrant card ready. 'I'm DS Norman.' He pointed to Southall, standing in the kitchen doorway. 'And this is DI Southall. Can I ask who you are?'

'My name's Rhiannon Pugh.'

'What are you doing here, Rhiannon?'

'I might ask you the same question,' she said. 'Why are you in my brother's house?'

'Your brother? Gareth Jenkins is your brother?'

'Yes, of course. I wouldn't let myself into a stranger's house, would I?' She gazed past Norman into the living room. 'What's happened to this place? Where's all his furniture gone?'

'We were rather hoping you might be able to help us with that,' said Norman.

'You haven't told me why you're here,' she said. 'Has his furniture been stolen?'

'I think perhaps you'd better come and sit down, Rhiannon,' said Southall. 'We've got some rather bad news.'

'Is he dead?'

'What makes you ask that?' Southall said.

'Well, I know something's happened to him, and you just said you had bad news.'

'You sound as if you were expecting it,' Southall said.

'Well, he was no spring chicken, and we've all got to go sometime. Anyway, I'm here because Gareth's solicitor contacted me on Tuesday afternoon and suggested I should get down here. I've come all the way from Warwick, you know.'

'Why would the solicitor ask you to come all that way?' asked Southall. 'Didn't he say?'

Rhiannon shrugged. 'All he said was that I needed to get down here.'

'But why?' insisted Southall.

'I assume it's because he believes something has happened to Gareth, and as you're here it sort of proves he must be right, doesn't it?'

'So, let me get this straight,' said Norman. 'You're saying Gareth's solicitor told you there was a problem back on Tuesday. That was before we knew anything about it. Is that right?'

'Well, it was definitely Tuesday.'

'That's a bit strange,' Norman said with a glance at Southall.

'I don't see why,' said Rhiannon. 'Isn't it normal procedure for the solicitor to notify me since I'm his nearest relative? I mean, it's down to me to make the necessary arrangements.'

'What arrangements?' said Norman.

'The funeral, of course, and to sort out his affairs.'

'Ah. Now I'm beginning to understand,' said Southall. 'You're Gareth's executor.'

'That's right. That's why I'm here.'

Southall exchanged a puzzled look with Norman.

'How well do you know this solicitor?' asked Southall.

'Oh, I don't know him as such. Gareth must have appointed him and given him my contact details.'

'He'd have had to if you're executor,' said Norman.

'Well, there we are then,' said Rhiannon.

'Perhaps you could give us his name,' said Southall. 'We'll need to speak to him.'

Rhiannon opened her handbag and began rummaging around inside it.

'I've got his card in here somewhere. . . ah, here it is.'

She handed a business card to Southall.

'Were you and your brother close?' asked Norman.

'We kept in touch now and then, but no, I wouldn't say we were that close.'

'When was the last time you saw him?'

Rhiannon thought for a moment. 'It would have been a while ago. Warwick's a long way from here and I'm not a good traveller. It's probably been ten years, possibly even longer.'

'How does he contact you, Rhiannon?' asked Southall.

'Email.'

'Email?' said Norman. 'How does he do that? We couldn't find a mobile phone, or laptop.'

'He didn't have a mobile, he detested them, but I'm sure he had a laptop.'

'But how did he access the internet? Did he use an internet cafe?' Norman asked.

Rhiannon gave a half smile. 'I wouldn't have thought so. He wasn't the sociable sort. As I understand it, he didn't like to go out in public.'

'But there's no landline here.'

'Isn't there? Well, I'm sorry, I can't tell you how he did it, only that he did.'

'Look, Rhiannon, we'd like you to tell us all you can about Gareth, but I think there's something we need to do before that,' said Southall. 'There's no easy way of saying this — you see, we have a body that we think is Gareth's.'

'I guessed as much,' said Rhiannon.

'If you don't mind me saying, you're taking this very well,' said Norman.

'Yes, well, we all have to go some time, don't we? And as I said, we weren't close.'

'We need someone to confirm it's Gareth's body,' said Southall. 'If we take you to the mortuary, would you identify him?'

'I haven't seen him in ten years,' she said doubtfully.

'Nevertheless, he was your brother,' said Southall. 'He can't have changed that much. Would you be willing to help us?'

Rhiannon sighed. 'I suppose it won't hurt. As you say, he can't have changed that much.'

CHAPTER SIX

Southall and Norman knew from experience that there was no telling how relatives would react when called upon to formally identify the body of their nearest and dearest. In the case of Gareth Jenkins, Rhiannon had simply nodded, whispered, 'Yes', and bowed her head for a moment. Then she headed for the exit. It was all over in seconds.

Norman and Southall had to almost run to catch up with her. It was quite an effort to persuade her to accompany them to the family room and tell them about Gareth.

'Are you sure you're okay?' asked Southall.

Rhiannon took a sip from the cup of tea Norman had made for her.

'He looks much older than I expected,' she said, 'and so ill.'

'The dead are always pale,' said Norman.

'I expected that,' said Rhiannon. 'But he always looked young for his age. Last time I saw him he was sixty-eight but could have passed for a man twenty years younger. Now he looks twenty years older. How can he have changed so much?'

'Death can do strange things to a body,' said Southall, 'and he had been underwater for a few days before he was found.'

Rhiannon's eyes widened.

'Oh? You mean he drowned?' she asked. 'Was it an accident?'

'That's what we're trying to find out,' said Southall.

'You think he was murdered?'

'Now, why would you ask that?' said Southall.

Rhiannon's eyes narrowed. 'What are you suggesting?'

'I'm not suggesting anything,' said Southall.

'Would a detective inspector be investigating if there were no suspicious circumstances?' said Rhiannon. 'And, before you ask, I was at home in Warwick when he died. And, as I said, I haven't set eyes on him in ten years.'

'I didn't say *when* he died,' said Southall.

'It doesn't matter whether you said when he died or not,' said Rhiannon, testily. 'I didn't know anything about it until the solicitor called me, and I didn't leave my home in Warwick until early this morning.'

'He seemed to live a very quiet life, almost as if he was penniless,' said Norman, hoping to defuse the situation.

Rhiannon let out a little snort of derision. 'Penniless? I don't think so. He wasn't a millionaire or anything like that, but he was certainly comfortable enough.'

'You've seen inside the house,' said Norman. 'There's nothing there except a few sticks of furniture. It doesn't look like he was living well, does it?'

'I honestly don't know anything about that and, if you recall, I didn't get any further than the hall before you brought me down here to identify his corpse!'

'There's almost no furniture and no personal stuff in the house,' said Norman. 'No photographs, no bank statements, documents, or anything like that. And you said you thought he had a laptop. We didn't find one.'

'Well, I don't know what to tell you. Perhaps he found God and had chosen to live as a monk. Whatever, I can assure you that, last time I saw him, he was doing just fine.'

'And when was that?' asked Norman.

'I already said it must have been ten years ago. He told me that if I didn't tell anyone where he was, he would be leaving it all to me when he died.'

'You actually stood to gain from his death?' asked Southall.

'He had no kids and I'm his sister. What's so unusual about that?'

'You said he asked you to keep his location a secret?' asked Southall. 'Why did he want you to do that? What was he hiding from?'

'I didn't ask, but if I had to guess I'd say it was because of his past. And if you think his death is suspicious, maybe you should consider that. Maybe his past had caught up with him.'

'His past? What does that mean?' asked Norman. 'Was he some sort of criminal?'

'You really don't know anything, do you?' said Rhiannon.

'As I said, there was nothing in the house to tell us anything about him,' said Norman.

'So, anything you can tell us would be an enormous help,' added Southall.

'Was he really murdered?' Rhiannon asked.

'We can't say for sure at this stage,' said Southall.

'But you think he might have been, don't you?' said Rhiannon. 'Of course you do. As I said, why else would a detective inspector be sitting here asking me questions?'

'All I can tell you is that we have one or two questions about the cause of your brother's death,' said Southall.

'Well, if you think it's murder, you should be asking his wives where they were when he died, not me.'

'If you mean Alma, she died about five years ago,' said Norman.

Rhiannon sniffed. 'Alma wasn't his wife. She was just a girlfriend. At least, that's what Gareth told me. If you ask me, I think she was just a gold digger. If all his money's gone, she probably spent it for him. And if she hadn't died before he did, I'd have her down as a prime suspect.'

'And he'd been married twice before?' asked Southall.

'Still is, as far as I know,' said Rhiannon.

Norman sat back in his seat. 'Both of them? You mean he was a—'

'A bigamist?' She smiled at Norman. 'Oh yes. One wife in Birmingham and another in Swansea. Remember those men on the TV who used to set plates spinning on sticks? Well, my brother was like that with his women. He even had a girlfriend on the go as well.' Rhiannon seemed to be warming to the subject. 'He got away with it for years, but it turned out he couldn't keep more than three plates spinning at once. He was doing fine until Alma came along. Once she got her hooks into him and figured out what he was worth, she decided it was time the other three found out about each other.'

'I imagine that didn't end well,' said Norman.

'I don't know what happened to his girlfriend, but I know the two wives became the best of friends. And here's the bit you need to know — they told me they were looking for him.'

'What did they intend to do when they found him?' asked Southall.

'They never said, but I got the impression they weren't planning a joyful reunion.'

'Do you know them well?' asked Norman.

'No, but they did turn up at my door a few years ago, looking for him.'

'Did you tell them where to find him?' Norman said.

'If they've killed him, that would make me an accessory to murder, wouldn't it?'

'Did you tell them where he was?' asked Southall.

'What, give up my own brother? Of course I didn't. What sort of sister would do a thing like that?'

'One who stood to gain a lot of money,' suggested Southall.

'If I was going to bump him off for his money, I would have done it ten years ago while I still had the energy to enjoy spending it.'

'You're saying this is the reason he never went anywhere and had no friends?' asked Norman. 'He was hiding from his two wives?'

'I wouldn't be surprised,' said Rhiannon. 'He was definitely scared of what they might do if they found him.'

'Do you know their names?'

'One's called Bethan, and I think the other one is Melanie. I presume they took his surname.'

Norman made a note of the names.

'Your brother's body was found in a village called Pont Daffyd,' said Southall. 'Is there any reason he might have gone there?'

The beginnings of a smile appeared on Rhiannon's lips. 'Pont Daffyd. Now that name brings back some memories. We had an uncle and aunt living there when we were kids, and we used to go there during the summer holidays. We'd spend hours down by the railway track with our cousin, and watch the steam trains hauling coal wagons from the mines to the coast, and we'd try to catch fish in the stream.'

'Does your cousin still live there?' Southall asked.

'How would I know? I'm talking about more than sixty years ago. I lost touch with most of my family after I married and moved to Warwick, but I suppose he could still be living there.'

'And you don't think Gareth would have been in touch with him?' Southall asked.

'Not to my knowledge, but what do I know?' said Rhiannon. 'Although it would be a bit of a risky thing to do if he wanted to keep a low profile, wouldn't it?'

'Would this cousin be from the Jenkins side of the family?' asked Southall.

'That's right. The uncle was my father's brother.'

Norman found a photograph on his mobile phone and showed it to her.

'Have you ever seen this woman before?'

Rhiannon squinted at the screen. 'Are those scars across her face?'

'No,' said Norman. 'It's taken from a photo that had been torn to pieces. The marks that look like scars are where we pieced it back together.'

'You found it in his house?'

Norman nodded. 'Torn up and thrown in the bin.'

'Who is she?' Rhiannon asked.

'That's what we'd like to know,' said Norman.

'He's not been at it again, has he?' asked Rhiannon. 'Good grief, she must be half his age. You'd think after Alma he would have learned his lesson.'

'We're not even sure she knew Gareth,' Norman said.

'But you're thinking that if he had her picture, she must be important,' said Rhiannon.

'We can't ignore the possibility,' said Southall. 'We think her name might be Gaynor.'

Rhiannon sniffed again. 'Well, whatever her name is, I've never seen her before. I'd remember a face like that.'

'Okay, no problem,' said Norman. 'Apart from the two wives, can you think of anyone else who might want to harm Gareth?'

'If you mean do I know anyone who would want to murder him, I'm afraid I can't help you. He always took risks with women, so there could be any number of husbands and boyfriends who would have liked him dead, but I wouldn't know who they were, and anyway, all that was years ago. Why wait until now?'

'We'd better get you back to the house,' said Southall. 'Will you be staying here long?'

'That depends. When can I have his body so I can arrange a cremation?'

'I'm afraid I can't say at the moment,' said Southall.

'That's a nuisance. I wasn't intending to stay any longer than I have to,' said Rhiannon. 'Still, I'm sure I must be able to arrange some way of dealing with the body so I don't have to hang around. Assuming I can do that, and unless you intend to keep me here, I'll be off in a couple of days.'

'It would help us if you could stay for a few days, but if you really have to get back home, we can always let you know when Gareth's body is ready to be released.'

'I don't have to stay in that dump of a house, do I?' asked Rhiannon. 'Is there a decent hotel anywhere nearby?'

'There are three small ones in Llangwelli,' said Southall. 'I can get someone to arrange that for you.'

Rhiannon looked unimpressed. 'I don't think that will be necessary. I think you'd be better off getting someone to find out who murdered my brother, don't you? I'm quite capable of finding myself a hotel.'

'As you wish,' said Southall. 'But can you let us know where to find you?'

Norman handed her one of his cards.

'I'll probably be at Gareth's house in the daytime,' said Rhiannon.

'Yeah, but even so,' said Norman. 'And I'd be grateful if you could let us know when you're heading back home. Just so we know in case we have any more questions.'

'I suppose that will be okay,' she said, 'but I really don't see what else I can tell you.'

After they had taken Rhiannon back to the house, Southall decided they should have lunch and then go back to the office before they visited the crime scene.

* * *

Norman had barely settled back at his desk after lunch when his mobile phone began to ring.

'DS Norman.'

'It's Rhiannon Pugh.'

'Oh, hi, Rhiannon. I wasn't expecting to hear from you so soon. What can I do for you?'

'Do you think you could come to the house?'

'What? Now? Are you okay? Is there something wrong?'

'I'm not in any danger, if that's what you mean, but there's definitely something odd going on. I think I need to report a crime.'

'What sort of crime?'

'All my brother's money is gone.'

'I can't say I'm surprised, looking at the state of his house. But how do you know he didn't just spend it all?'

74

'He wouldn't do that,' she said.

'And how do you know it's all gone? We searched the house and couldn't find anything to do with his finances.'

'I've just come back from his solicitor. I went to ask about the will, and he told me I'm not going to inherit a brass farthing as there's nothing left. It's all gone, every single penny!'

'How much are we talking about, Rhiannon?'

'The best part of half a million.'

Norman couldn't help letting out a long, low whistle. 'Jeez, really? Gareth had that much money in the bank and he was living like a pauper? And you have no idea where it's gone?'

'The solicitor says Gareth told him he was broke about a year ago, but he wouldn't say where the money had gone or how it happened.'

Norman thought for a second. 'Okay, Rhiannon. Don't worry. I'll be there in about twenty minutes.'

He ended the call, and headed for Southall's office.

'Have you got that phone number for Gareth Jenkins's solicitor?'

'Yes, I took a photo of the card on my phone,' she said.

'And didn't you say it was the old guy down by the harbour who should have retired years ago?' Norman asked.

'That's right. Elwyn Thomas. Why?'

'How long is it since we left Rhiannon at the house?' he said.

'A couple of hours.'

'Right,' said Norman. 'Well, she's just called to say she's been to see the solicitor and he's told her Gareth was broke, and she's going to inherit nothing. She claims he wouldn't have spent it and that the money's been stolen. She wants to report a crime.'

'Right,' said Southall. 'And your point is?'

'Am I right in thinking that old-school solicitors like Elwyn Thomas prefer to enjoy extended lunch breaks — say, of around two hours rather than one?'

'Yes. I'm still not with you,' said Southall.

'It's just after two p.m. now,' said Norman, 'and we dropped Rhiannon at St David's Place at around midday. I might be wrong, but I'm guessing that old guys like Elwyn Thomas don't take appointments at short notice, and especially not between twelve and two, because they might interfere with his lunch.'

'You think she's lying?' Southall said.

'It sounded like she hadn't expected me to ask how she knew the money was gone,' Norman said. 'I also think it's unlikely she would have been able make an appointment with the solicitor during his lunch break.'

'She could have made the appointment when he called to tell her about Gareth,' said Southall.

'Yeah, I'll admit that's possible, but it wouldn't hurt to call his office and check, would it?' Norman said.

'Of course not. We need to arrange an interview with him anyway,' said Southall. 'Are you heading out to see Rhiannon now?'

'I thought it might be the chivalrous thing to do,' said Norman.

'And you hope you might be able to catch her out,' said Southall.

'Do you think I'm out of line?' he asked.

'Not at all,' said Southall. 'There's something distinctly iffy about her story, and I'm not sure I buy this idea that the solicitor called her down here because he knew Gareth was dead. Is she suggesting he's clairvoyant, or that he murdered his client?'

'She's a slippery one for sure,' said Norman.

'But at least now she'll have to give us his bank account number,' said Southall. 'I've got Frosty trying to find it, but it would save a lot of time if we had the details.'

'I'll see if she's uncovered any hiding places we might have missed, too.'

'Take Catren with you,' said Southall. 'I'll get Judy to call the solicitor's office. She can let you know what they say.'

'What about visiting the site where the body was found?' Norman asked.

'That'll have to wait until later,' said Southall.

* * *

Fifteen minutes later, Norman was knocking on the door of number fifty-two St David's Place.

'This is Detective Constable Catren Morgan,' he told Rhiannon when she opened the door. 'It was Catren who realised something was wrong when she first came here.'

Rhiannon ushered them into the kitchen.

'I'd offer you somewhere to sit,' she said, 'but, as you know, all the decent furniture seems to have gone.' Rhiannon turned to Morgan. 'Can I ask you a question?'

'Of course,' said Morgan.

'What made you come here in the first place?'

'A man called Alun Edwards told me he was worried because he hadn't seen Gareth for some time and couldn't get an answer when he knocked at the door. I offered to come and check, to put his mind at rest.'

'Who is Alun Edwards?' Rhiannon asked.

'You don't know him?' Morgan said.

'Never heard of him,' said Rhiannon.

'He is — was — Gareth's chess partner.'

'Ah. That explains the chess board then,' said Rhiannon. 'That shows you how little I knew about my brother. I had no idea he even knew how to play chess.'

'Maybe it was a recent thing,' said Norman. 'Why don't you tell us about the missing money?'

Norman's phone beeped. He pulled it out of his jacket pocket.

'Excuse me a moment. I just have to see what this is.' He read the text, slipped the phone back in his pocket and smiled at Rhiannon.

'Now, when you phoned, you said you found out about the missing money after we dropped you off here at midday.'

'That's right. The solicitor told me.'

'And how is Elwyn? You're lucky he was willing to fit you in at such short notice. Did you have lunch with him?'

'Yes. He's a very nice man.'

Norman's smile broadened. 'Now that's funny. According to his secretary, he's out of the office today playing golf with two of his clients.'

Rhiannon swallowed, hard.

'I think it's your turn to speak now,' said Morgan quietly.

Rhiannon stood looking down at her hands while they waited.

'All right,' she said at last. 'I haven't spoken to any solicitor. I know how to access Gareth's bank account.'

'You told us you had almost no contact with Gareth, yet you have access to his bank account? Is there any particular reason for that?' asked Norman.

'My having access doesn't change the fact that nearly all his money has gone.'

'But how do we know you didn't take the money yourself?' asked Morgan.

'If I had, do you really think I'd be telling you it's gone?' said Rhiannon.

'Okay, so perhaps he moved it to some other account,' suggested Morgan. 'Did he have any others?'

'He had a savings account with the same bank but it's empty. Apart from that, he had no other accounts that I'm aware of,' Rhiannon said.

'We'll be needing those account details,' said Norman.

Rhiannon said nothing.

'We can get authority easily enough, if you really want us to do it that way,' said Norman. 'It'll take a little longer, but we'll still get what we want. And in the meantime, we'll make sure you can't access this account or any others Gareth may have had. Your choice.'

'Okay,' Rhiannon said reluctantly. 'I'll give you the information, but you need to understand that I couldn't have taken any money from it. I knew the sort code, but I didn't know the account number or password until I arrived here.'

'We've only got your word for that,' said Morgan.

'Yes, that's right,' said Rhiannon. 'But once you start looking at the account, you'll find I haven't been near it.'

'Like I said, we didn't find anything remotely like bank account details when we searched,' said Norman. 'In fact, we didn't find a scrap of useful information anywhere. So where did you get them?'

Rhiannon pointed to the kitchen cupboard where they had found the dog food.

'That's because you didn't know where to look,' she said. 'Try inside the cupboard under the worktop. There's a piece of paper stuck up there with the details written on it. Look for yourself if you don't believe me.'

Norman got down on his knees and felt around the underside of the worktop. Just as she said, his fingers touched a piece of paper. He pulled it out and took a photo of the account number and password.

He hauled himself up on his feet. 'Why didn't you just tell us about this, Rhiannon? Why lie when you knew we'd be able to check anyway?'

'I don't know. Shock, I suppose. After all, I've just discovered that my brother's dead. I'm just not thinking straight.'

'And yet you told us this morning that you thought he was dead on Tuesday when the solicitor asked you to come down here,' said Norman. 'What is this now — delayed shock?'

'Yes, I did say that. I was hoping it was a false alarm. I didn't really believe it until you took me to the morgue.'

'Oh, right,' said Norman. 'But the shock didn't stop you remembering where he kept his bank details and checking his account.'

'It's not just the money,' Rhiannon said. 'It's worse than that. It looks as though he cancelled all his insurance policies.'

'Maybe he just forgot to keep up the payments,' suggested Norman. 'And anyway, how did you know about them?

'He made a point of setting them up when he first came to me about going into hiding. He said everything would be taken care of and was already paid for.'

'Just so we're clear, are you saying he actually cashed the policies in and got his money back, or he just hadn't been paying the premiums?'

'I don't know if he cashed them in, but he certainly hadn't paid any premiums in months. That's why I was checking the bank account. I need money to pay for a funeral, and there's not even enough left to buy a coffin!'

'I think you should arrange to speak to Gareth's solicitor before you jump to conclusions about things like that,' said Norman. 'As my colleague said, perhaps Gareth moved his money to another bank account that you don't know about.'

Rhiannon sighed. 'Yes, you're probably right. I think this has hit me harder than I thought.'

'You say Gareth used to contact you by email,' said Norman. 'Can you tell us his email address?'

'You won't find anything useful there. He never really said anything in his emails. He even used to copy and paste from previous messages.'

'Even so, we should check to see whether he was in contact with anyone other than you,' Norman said.

'I see what you mean,' said Rhiannon. She reached for her mobile phone. 'Hang on a minute. I'll find it for you.'

Morgan made a note of the email address, and reminded Rhiannon to tell them where she was staying.

'That's a nice little hotel,' she commented. 'You'll be well looked after there.'

Norman had been considering taking Rhiannon back to Llangwelli station, but, looking at her face, he decided to give her the benefit of the doubt; she really did look shocked and upset. They had the email address and bank details. It would do for now.

'Can we give you a lift back to the hotel?' he asked.

'Thank you, but no. I have a taxi booked.'

* * *

80

'For a minute there I thought you were going to take her in,' said Morgan when they were back in the car.

'I did consider it for about a millisecond,' said Norman. 'Then I decided she'd been through enough for one day. She doesn't present a flight risk, and I really don't see how she could have murdered her brother when she was a couple of hundred miles away in Warwick.'

'Why did she lie about the solicitor?' asked Morgan. 'If she's Gareth's executor, she has every right to know the state of his affairs.'

'At first I thought she might be intending to take the money and run,' said Norman.

'Wouldn't that be a bit obvious?'

'I reckon,' said Norman.

'Aha!' said Morgan. 'So you do think she's up to something.'

Norman smiled.

'I'm not certain, but the possibility has crossed my mind. And I think if we wait and see, we'll find out what it is soon enough. In the meantime, it won't hurt for her to think we're not really interested in what she's up to.'

'That's a relief to hear,' said Morgan. 'For a minute there I thought you had taken pity on her because she cleaned up the dog poo from under the table.'

'I can't deny I was a bit reluctant to follow when she led us into the kitchen,' said Norman. 'I'm not sure I could have coped with that awful smell again. So, yeah, I admit I was genuinely pleased to find she'd cleaned it up.'

'What with you taking the dog home, and now this, I wondered if perhaps you're beginning to go soft,' she said.

'I think you'll find it's called compassionate policing,' said Norman.

Morgan smiled. 'Yeah, right, if you say so. Hey. Didn't you think it was funny she didn't ask about the dog? I mean, if you had to clean up that mess you'd want to know how it got there in the first place, wouldn't you?'

'Maybe she doesn't like dogs and she's just glad it's not there and she doesn't have to deal with it,' said Norman. 'In fact, if she really hasn't seen or spoken to Gareth in ten years she might not even know he had a dog.'

'I would imagine finding all that poo on the floor might have given her a clue, don't you?' Morgan said. 'And if that wasn't enough, what about the dog food in the cupboard?'

'Yeah, I suppose you're right,' said Norman. 'It's funny, that little dog hasn't done anything like that in my house. She's been as good as gold.'

'I expect that's because you and Faye let her out to relieve herself,' said Morgan. 'I'm sure she only messed in the house because she was desperate. Even the best trained dogs can't hold it in forever.'

CHAPTER SEVEN

Friday 13 April

First thing on Friday morning, Southall briefed the team on the progress of the case — such as it was. 'You'll be disappointed to know that Forensics didn't get any useful evidence from the house. It seems someone went to a lot of trouble to wipe the place down so there were very few fingerprints. Most of the prints they did find seem to have belonged to the victim, but there are a couple that aren't his. They don't match those of anyone on the database, but they'll help if we find a suspect.'

'If they were in the lounge, or on the chess pieces, they could belong to Alun Edwards,' said Morgan.

'Good thinking, Catren,' said Southall. 'We'd better take a sample of his prints.'

'I'll ask him,' said Morgan.

'Forensics didn't find any useful evidence from where the body went into the water either,' said Southall.

'What? Nothing at all?' asked Morgan.

'Oh, there's plenty there, but it's a popular spot for dog walkers and hikers, so it's impossible to say whether any of it relates to our case. It's disappointing, I know, but it is what it is,' said Southall. 'It means we'll just have to carry on with the boring stuff. However, it does raise a question we need to address. We're told Gareth never went anywhere, yet we found his body ten miles from his home. It appears he had no car, so how did he get there?'

'He got the bus!' said Winter excitedly. 'That's why he had a bus pass on him.'

'Exactly,' said Southall. 'And, as you were so quick off the mark, Frosty, you can have the job of finding which bus service runs between Llangwelli and Pont Daffyd.'

'Okay, boss, no problem,' said Winter.

'Where are we with the bank account?' asked Southall.

'I'm only just getting started,' said Winter, 'but I can tell you there's nothing in it now and, despite what Rhiannon says, there's never been more than fifty thousand there.'

'What about his current account?'

'Up until a year ago there was two or three thousand in the current account, but now it looks as though he lives month to month on his pension, and the actual balance at the end of each month is less than a hundred.'

'What happened a year ago?' Southall asked.

'He seems to have withdrawn all his money.'

'Do you know where it went?'

'Not yet. I'm working my way back through the statements. So far I've looked at nine months and haven't found anything yet.'

'Okay,' said Southall. 'According to Rhiannon, Gareth told his solicitor he was broke a year ago, so keep digging, Frosty, you've only three months to go.'

'What about the email address Rhiannon gave us?' Southall asked Lane.

'Pretty much useless,' said Lane. 'From what I can make out, he only ever used it to send messages to Rhiannon, and none of them say anything meaningful. Even so, he must have had access to the internet and some means of—'

'Rhiannon said she thought he had a laptop,' said Norman.

'That's right, she did,' said Southall. 'So where is it?'

84

'Someone must have taken it,' said Norman.

'In that case,' said Southall, 'find that person and we've probably found our killer. By the way, did you have time yesterday to check out the two wives?'

'I'm sorry,' he said. 'I didn't even get started. I dropped everything after Rhiannon called.'

'Right then. Catren. Rhiannon claims the two wives, Bethan and Melanie, were looking to get even with Gareth. We can't ignore the possibility that they did, so see what you can find out about them.'

Morgan nodded and turned to her computer.

Southall was about to continue when Norman's phone beeped.

'It's a message from Bill,' he said, looking at the phone. 'He wants us to go and see him. He says it's important.'

'Okay, everyone,' said Southall. 'I'm taking Norm to visit his favourite mortuary, then we're going on to interview Elwyn Thomas. Keep on digging, and we'll catch up when we get back.'

* * *

'Are you two not speaking?' Norman asked Southall, as he started the car.

'Pardon?'

'You and Bill. Are you not speaking?'

'Of course we are.'

'I just wondered why he texted me and not you.'

'Oh, I asked him to,' said Southall. 'He said the lab results might come through this morning, and I thought I might be called upstairs to talk about this possible reorganisation, so it made sense for him to call you.'

'Oh, right. I see. Their plan to change everything is still alive, is it? I was rather hoping it might have got kicked into touch and forgotten about.'

'If it comes to fruition, Norm, the way we work may well change. You will become even more of a "go-to" man than you are now, and you'll be Bill's first point of contact.'

'That's not what worries me,' said Norman.

Right now, Southall really didn't feel like embarking on a discussion about what Norman would do if Llangwelli station was to close.

'I understand your concerns, Norm, really I do, but nothing has been decided yet, I promise.'

'Even if it had, you wouldn't be allowed to tell me, would you?' said Norman glumly.

'Strictly speaking, that's true,' said Southall. 'But if I was to tell you, who's to know?'

'Huh?'

'Well, how would they know? I'm certainly not going to tell them, and I'm sure you won't, will you?'

'Well, yeah, of course,' said Norman. 'I wouldn't stab you in the back.'

'And I won't keep you in the dark,' said Southall. 'It'll be months before anything happens, but as soon as I hear anything definite, I promise I will tell you. In the meantime, I need you to focus your mind on our murder case and not worry about what might, or might not, happen to the station.'

'You're right, and I'm sorry,' said Norman. 'I know worrying about it won't help. It's just that I've never been happier, and I don't want that to change.'

'You know the way you're always telling people they shouldn't apologise for being human,' said Southall. 'Well, it applies to you too. So I don't want to hear any more about it, okay?'

'Whatever you say, boss.'

* * *

Bridger was waiting for them at the lab.

'What was so urgent you had to drag us away from our office?' asked Southall. 'Found the killer, have you?'

'Much as I'd love to solve the case for you, I'm afraid that's not why you're here,' said Bridger. 'If anything, I'm about to make it even more complicated.'

86

'Oh, terrific,' said Norman. 'As if having nothing to go on wasn't making it complicated enough.'

Southall frowned at Bridger. 'Come on, then. What's the big deal?'

'When I did the post-mortem I noticed a bit of gum disease in his mouth. It wasn't a surprise as it was obvious the man hadn't been in the best of health. Indeed, when I examined the organs, I found signs of liver disease, and his heart wasn't in a very good state. Again, no great surprise.'

'He doesn't seem to have looked after himself very well,' said Norman.

'Exactly,' said Bridger. 'And when the blood results came back, they confirmed he was anaemic and his white blood cell count was low. Again, this wasn't a surprise, especially given his age. But when I read the full report, I realised it wasn't just age and lifestyle that contributed to his demise.'

'Come on then,' said Southall. 'Don't keep us in suspense.'

'Do either of you know what warfarin is?' asked Bridger.

'Isn't that rat poison?' asked Norman.

'It was,' said Bridger. 'But nowadays rats have become immune to it, so it's not used for that. Nowadays it's prescribed for people, as a blood thinner.'

'Ah, yeah. It's to stop blood clots, right?' said Norman.

'Normally, yes, but Gareth seemed to be overdosing. That's what caused the bruising I showed you,' said Bridger.

'Jeez, no wonder he looked so ill. Are you sure he wasn't trying to kill himself?' Norman said.

'Well, that's the thing,' said Bridger. 'I've been through all the medicines and remedies that were in his house and there's no warfarin tablets among them.'

'Maybe he ran out,' suggested Norman.

'I've spoken to his doctor,' said Bridger. 'Apparently, he hasn't seen Gareth in years, and he definitely wasn't prescribed warfarin.'

'I don't understand,' said Southall. 'Can you get the tablets without a prescription?'

'Of course, it's possible to get just about anything if you know where to find it, but I think it's unlikely,' said Bridger.

'What if he was taking actual rat poison?' asked Norman.

'Again, I think it's unlikely,' said Bridger. 'As I said, it's no longer used to kill rats.'

'What about if it's been kicking around for a few years?' asked Norman.

'Honestly? I doubt it,' said Bridger.

'So, what are you suggesting?' asked Southall. 'Are you saying he was taking someone else's medication?'

'Again, it's possible, but people are prescribed warfarin for a good reason. If you need it, you don't give it to someone else.'

Southall raised an eyebrow. 'I don't like the sound of that. How do you think he was getting hold of this stuff? Are you suggesting someone was giving it to him without his knowledge?'

'Well, he must have got hold of it somehow. And why haven't we found any at his house? He lived on his own, so who would he be hiding it from?'

'Is this medicine really dangerous then?' asked Norman.

Bridger nodded. 'Basically, it's a poison that's prescribed in strictly controlled doses, and like many drugs, if the amount is exceeded it can cause considerable damage.'

Norman grimaced. 'So, even if a healthy individual took it, they'd still come to harm, right?' he asked.

'Especially if they were overdosing,' said Bridger.

'What are the side effects?' asked Southall.

'They can include a high temperature, feeling cold and shivery, headaches, cough, sore throat, general aches and pains.'

'So, he could have mistakenly thought he had a cold,' suggested Southall.

'He could,' said Bridger. 'The problem is, some of the herbal remedies he was taking are known to react with warfarin and cause serious issues, such as the liver damage I found.'

'You think he was being poisoned?' said Southall.

'I'd suggest he was, yes.'

'Is it a quick, or a slow way to go?' asked Norman.

'It would depend on the dose,' said Bridger. 'But I'd say probably long and slow.'

'I think we can rule out suicide, then,' said Southall. 'There must be a hundred easier, and quicker, ways to do it than slowly poisoning yourself.'

'Yeah, I reckon so,' said Norman. 'My money says someone's been helping him along without him knowing.'

'The warfarin couldn't have been hidden inside one of those cold and flu remedies, could it?' asked Southall.

'We're going through them now, as a matter of urgency,' said Bridger.

'And if you did find it in one of them, there's no way it could have got there by accident, is there?' asked Southall.

'Impossible,' said Bridger.

'Right,' she said. 'Any other nasty surprises?'

Bridger smiled. 'If there are, I promise you'll be the first to know.'

* * *

'So, if he hadn't been knocked on the head and thrown into the river, Gareth Jenkins was slowly being poisoned, and would have ended up dead anyway,' said Norman when they were back in their car.

'Sounds like he was already well on the way,' said Southall.

'So why bump him off then?'

'Maybe he wasn't going fast enough,' said Southall.

'Jeez, that's one determined killer,' said Norman.

'Or perhaps it's two killers, each unaware of what the other was doing,' said Southall.

'Now who's complicating things?' asked Norman.

'We can't ignore the possibility,' said Southall.

Norman sighed. 'Yeah, I guess you're right about that. Where do you want to go now?'

'I think we'd better keep our appointment with Elwyn Thomas, and then go back to St David's Place and see if Rhiannon knows anything about blood thinners, don't you?'

'That works for me,' said Norman, and started the car.

* * *

Elwyn Thomas was a small man, wiry, despite a distinct paunch, his white hair the only evidence of his advancing years. He wore round, rimless spectacles, which made his clear brown eyes appear larger than they really were. He greeted them with a cheerful smile and a firm handshake, and invited them to sit in the armchairs grouped beneath his office window.

'Much more comfortable,' he assured them. 'I only use the desk when I want to put a barrier between myself and my adversary.'

'I'm sure that won't be necessary,' said Southall. 'We understand you are — or were — the solicitor for Mr Gareth Jenkins of fifty-two St David's Place.'

'That's correct,' said Thomas. 'I was shocked to hear of his death.'

'How did you hear about it?' asked Southall.

'His death? Mr Jenkins's sister, Rhiannon Pugh, told me. I believe you asked her to identify his body.'

'That's odd. We were given to understand that you knew about it before she did,' said Southall. 'In fact, Mrs Pugh says you called her and asked her to come and sort out Mr Jenkins's affairs.'

The cheery smile faded somewhat.

'It's true to say that I suspected Mr Jenkins had died, but I didn't know for sure until Mrs Pugh called to tell me.'

'When was that?' asked Norman.

'She called late yesterday afternoon. I was out playing golf, but my secretary took a message, and I called her back first thing this morning.'

'Can you tell us why you suspected he might be dead before Rhiannon called you?' asked Norman.

'To put it bluntly, Mr Jenkins was somewhat paranoid. He suspected someone, or perhaps more than one person, of being — well — out to get him.'

'Who were these people?' asked Norman.

'He never actually mentioned any names. In fact, I'm not even sure it wasn't just a figment of his imagination.'

'We have good reason to think it was a bit more than that,' said Southall.

'Yes, Mrs Pugh told me you thought he had been murdered.'

'Can we go back to why you called Mrs Pugh in Warwick, before we even knew who our victim was?' asked Southall.

'Mr Jenkins had set up a system whereby he sent me an email at the same time every Sunday evening, which would be waiting in my inbox first thing on the Monday morning. If the message wasn't there for just one Monday, I was to assume the worst and contact Mrs Pugh.'

'Why Mrs Pugh?'

'After Alma passed away, Rhiannon became the executor of his will,' Thomas said.

'You said you assumed Gareth was dead,' said Norman. 'You didn't think you should report it to the police?'

Thomas raised an eyebrow. 'Report what exactly? That I hadn't received an email?'

Norman conceded the point. It was unlikely anyone would have taken it too seriously.

'And you didn't think there might be some other reason why he failed to contact you?'

'He had been sending that message, regular as clock-work, for the last ten years. Why would I think otherwise?'

'You said he sent an email,' said Norman. 'How did he do that? When we searched his house, we couldn't find a mobile phone, or a laptop, or any other device he could have used.'

'I think he despised smart phones, so I just assumed he must have had a laptop or a PC.'

'Do you know how he got access to the internet?' asked Norman. 'There is no landline to his house.'

'I'm sorry, I can't tell you how he did it, only that he did.'

'What did actually he say in these emails?' Norman asked.

'It was the same three-word message every week: *Everything OK here.*'

'And what was your reply?'

'Oh, he told me not to bother sending a reply. To be honest I thought the whole thing was rather ridiculous, but he was a long-standing client, so I humoured him. I believe he set it up to work automatically, so that he wouldn't have to remember to send the email every week.'

'There must have been an email address on it,' said Norman. 'Can you tell us what it was?'

'Of course. My secretary will find it for you.'

'If you handled his will, I assume you were aware of the extent of his assets, and of his financial position,' said Southall.

'When we originally drew up the will, he had the house in St David's Place, and some savings in the bank.'

'Do you know how much he had in the bank?'

'I seem to recall him telling me he liked to try to keep it at around fifty thousand pounds, in case of emergency. When we updated the will after Alma died, he told me he still had fifty thousand in his savings account.'

'Mrs Pugh seems to think there should be half a million,' said Southall.

Thomas stared at her, the eyes behind the spectacles even larger. 'Good heavens, really? Where on earth did she get that figure?'

'She says Gareth told her,' Southall said.

'Well, I don't see why he would do that,' said Thomas. 'She seems to have added an extra zero to the real figure. Perhaps he put it in an email, and she misread it.'

'Rhiannon also said that a year ago, Gareth told you he was broke.'

Thomas shook his head. 'I think Rhiannon's got her wires crossed somewhere. I hadn't spoken to Gareth since we amended his will. I had a feeling Rhiannon didn't really understand what I was telling her.'

'Didn't understand what exactly?' asked Southall.

'When Alma was first diagnosed with cancer, she was told she only had months to live. She had always wanted to travel the world, and Gareth wanted to make sure she could do that before she died, but he didn't want to blow all his savings. So, instead of using the savings, he went to one of those equity release companies. They gave him a lifetime mortgage of fifty thousand.'

'For those of us in the dark about these things, how does that work?' asked Norman.

'Put simply, it's a loan taken out against the value of the house. It is to be repaid when the borrower dies, and in the meantime, interest is added to the loan every month.'

'So, in theory, the house could be worthless,' said Norman.

'Theoretically, if you lived long enough, I suppose it could, but to stop that happening there's a limit to how much they'll lend, and the interest is fixed rate, so you won't get any nasty surprises. At the time when Gareth took out his loan, I believe the interest rate was a round three per cent.'

'Do you know what the house is worth now?' asked Southall.

'I'm no estate agent, but as a ballpark figure, I would imagine a semi-detached house in St David's Place would be worth somewhere around two hundred and twenty thousand,' said Thomas. 'Repay the fifty thousand, plus seven years' interest and you'd still have in excess of a hundred and fifty thousand.'

'That's hardly worthless,' said Southall.

'Of course not,' said Thomas. 'I obviously need to sit Rhiannon down and explain how it works.' He looked at his watch. 'I'm awfully sorry, but I have an appointment in a few minutes.'

'That's okay,' said Southall. 'Thank you for your help. I take it we can call again if we have any more questions?'

'Of course,' said Thomas. 'Anything I can do to help.'

'One more thing,' said Southall. 'Did Gareth ever mention a woman called Gaynor?'

'Gaynor?' said Thomas thoughtfully. 'No, I don't think I recall him ever mentioning anyone of that name.'

'So she's not mentioned in his will?'

'The only beneficiary is Gareth's sister, Rhiannon. Where does this Gaynor come into it?'

'We're not sure,' said Southall. 'We're just trying to establish whether Gareth knew anyone by that name.'

'I'm not aware that he had any lady friends, though Gareth wasn't one for small talk.'

'You didn't know him well?'

'Not really. I only knew him professionally, you might say.'

* * *

Southall and Norman walked slowly back to their car. 'What do you think of that?' she said. 'Just because an email fails to arrive, you're to take it he's dead?'

'No, you're right,' said Norman. 'It sounds a bit James Bond, doesn't it?'

'What if a server goes down, or there's a power cut?'

'If it's a reputable service, I imagine there would be some sort of backup for that sort of thing,' said Norman.

'Okay, but what if the backup system fails?'

'You've got me there, Sarah,' said Norman. 'Anyway, aren't I the wrong person to be asking? I mean, you're always quick to point out that I'm a technological philistine. It seems to me you're clutching at straws here.'

Southall grinned. 'You're right. I am clutching at straws.'

'You don't have to agree with me,' protested Norman.

'Sorry, Norm, but in this case, I do.'

'What about Rhiannon? Do you think she genuinely believes the house is worth nothing?'

'I'm sure there was a scandal over these equity release things when they first came out,' said Southall. 'It was years ago, but as I recall, there was no proper regulation and people were effectively being conned out of their homes. The rules have been changed so that can't happen now, but maybe Rhiannon heard about the scandal and she's assuming Gareth was ripped off too.'

'Perhaps we should ask her,' said Norman.

'I'm not sure about her yet, so let's save our questions about Gareth's money for later,' said Southall.

They got into the car and set off for St David's Place. As Norman drove, Southall called Judy Lane.

'I'm going to text an email address to you,' she said. 'It's from an automated message that Gareth sent regularly to his solicitor. As soon as one of you has a few minutes, I'd like you to see what you can find out about it. I'd also like someone to do a background check on Rhiannon Pugh, and the solicitor, Elwyn Thomas.'

* * *

In his years on the force, Norman had grown used to not being welcomed with open arms, but Rhiannon regarded him as if he were a lump of dog poo she'd just trodden in.

'I hope you've come to tell me you've found my missing money,' she said.

'Not yet, but we're working on it,' said Norman.

'Well, you won't find it here, will you?'

'We'd like to ask you a few more questions about Gareth,' said Southall, before Norman could retort.

'I have enough to do without you people hassling me all the time. I've already told you everything I know about my brother.'

'I'm sorry you feel that way,' said Southall, 'but we're investigating a suspicious death. I would have thought that as the dead man's closest relative, you'd be interested in helping us.'

Rhiannon glared at Southall. 'All right. I suppose you'd better come inside.'

'Thank you,' said Southall.

'But make it quick,' said Rhiannon, turning her back on them. 'I'd like to get finished here and go back to my hotel. This place gives me the creeps.'

'Fine,' said Southall, following her to the kitchen.

Rhiannon stood leaning back against the sink, her arms folded. 'Well?'

'Okay, as you're in such a hurry, I won't beat about the bush,' said Southall. 'Did Gareth ever tell you he suffered from heart disease, or that he was at risk of having a stroke?'

Rhiannon's mouth dropped open. 'What? No, he never mentioned anything like that.'

'So, you're not aware that he was taking warfarin?' Southall asked.

'Warfarin? I don't understand. Why are you asking me this now? I thought you said his death was suspicious!'

'Trust me, Rhiannon, it's suspicious all right,' said Southall. 'The reason we're asking is because the pathologist has found evidence from his blood tests that he was taking warfarin. His GP never prescribed it, so we're trying to establish why he would be taking it.'

'He never discussed the state of his health with me. I've already told you that he never said anything to me about his life,' said Rhiannon. 'Why would he be taking these drugs if he wasn't ill?'

'Did he ever mention anyone he knew who was taking warfarin?' asked Norman. 'He took a lot of home remedies. Maybe they got mixed up somehow.'

'Didn't I just tell you he never spoke about his life? He certainly didn't chat about his friends. Anyway, as far as I'm aware, he didn't have any, healthy or otherwise. You've already been through this place, so you know there's nothing here, and I can't tell you anything further. I knew he kept himself to himself, but it's like he didn't have a past, or even a present.'

* * *

96

Back in the office, Southall asked Judy what she'd found out about the automatic email message Gareth had set up. 'Did that email address provide anything useful?'

'Not really,' said Judy Lane. 'It's just a no-reply mailbox address that goes with the automated system he was using. He couldn't have used it for his own personal mail.'

'Do we know anything about the system? Is it legit?' Southall asked.

'There don't seem to be any issues with the service. It's something anyone can use,' said Lane. 'You set up the message, then add the parameters which govern when it sends.'

'What parameters?' asked Southall.

'You could use a trigger, like a certain time. Or it could be the other way around, and the message is only sent if there isn't a trigger.'

'So, if the solicitor was telling us the truth, we can assume that the service didn't get the trigger signal. Judy, can you find out from the service provider if that's correct?'

'Sure.' Lane made a note.

'So, Gareth must have been communicating with the service in some way for the last ten years, in order to activate the trigger every week,' said Norman.

'Everyone seems to think he hated smart phones, and he never went anywhere near an internet cafe,' said Southall. 'As far as I'm concerned, this confirms he must have had a laptop, and someone was searching the house to find it.'

'That's a big risk to take,' said Norman. 'I mean, if the body had been found earlier, we might well have been knocking on the door while they were there.'

'Which suggests there has to be something on that laptop that this person doesn't want us to see,' said Southall.

'Yeah, and if they found it, it will have been destroyed by now,' said Norman.

'But what if they haven't?' said Southall.

'What? Found it?' said Norman. 'It took Catren less than twenty minutes to search the place.'

'Ah, but if it was so easy to find, why were they there for so long?' asked Southall. 'It was days between the time Gareth went missing and the time Catren first went to the house, and yet the neighbours say they heard the dog barking out in the garden, they saw lights on every night, and someone was even seen walking the dog in the early hours. And we know for sure that someone was feeding her.'

'Are you saying you want to search the house again?' asked Norman.

'Not necessarily,' said Southall. 'We need to get a SOCO team down there first thing on Monday, but this time ask them to search the garden, especially the shed. Tell them they're looking for warfarin in any shape or form, and they're also looking for a laptop. If they can't find it out in the garden, then they can take the house apart.'

'That garden's like a jungle,' said Norman.

'Then there are probably lots of great hiding places in it, aren't there?' said Southall.

'Good point,' said Norman, reaching for his phone.

'Catren,' said Southall. 'Please tell me you've found the two wives.'

'I have,' said Morgan with a smile.

'Both of them? Well done!'

'I got lucky,' Morgan said. 'I only had to find one, and bingo, the other was there too. It seems being the victims of a bigamist decided them against having anything more to do with men. They're now living as a couple in Brighton.'

'Did you manage to speak with them?' Southall asked.

'I couldn't contact either of them, but I eventually got hold of Melanie's mother. She tells me Melanie and Bethan tied the knot in a civil ceremony in Brighton, on Friday the sixth, and that they're now on their honeymoon in the Maldives. I'm running checks on their passports, but I'm pretty sure Mum was telling me the truth.'

'I thought they were already both married to Gareth,' said Southall.

'Rhiannon may think so, but Melanie's mum says they both had their marriages to Gareth annulled on the grounds that they'd had no contact with him for more than seven years. Is it really that easy?' Morgan said.

'I couldn't say,' said Southall. 'And frankly, I don't care. We've got much bigger fish to fry. So, Melanie's mother says they got married and went on their honeymoon the very weekend Gareth may have been held somewhere. Is that a convenient coincidence, do you think? Remember, Rhiannon said they came to her looking for Gareth's address.'

'Yeah,' said Morgan. 'But maybe she got it wrong about why they wanted to know where he was. What if they just wanted him to agree to annul the marriages so they could get on with their lives?'

'You could well be right about that,' said Southall. 'I get the impression Rhiannon tends to distort the facts to suit her.'

'If it was down to me, I'd give them the benefit of the doubt,' said Morgan. 'The fact they're now a couple suggests to me that they've put him down to experience, and moved on. Besides, would they plan a wedding and a murder at the same time? I mean, how many accomplices would that involve?'

'I agree,' said Southall. 'They're still possible suspects, but definitely not top of the list.' She turned to Judy Lane. 'Have you also been checking Rhiannon Pugh and Elwyn Thomas?'

'Yes, I have,' said Lane.

'Anything worth knowing?'

Lane smiled. 'There was nothing of note on either of them as adults, so I thought I'd go right back to when they were kids to see if that threw up anything. And I came across something you may find quite interesting. Did you know they both grew up in Carmarthen?'

'It doesn't really surprise me,' said Southall. 'I guessed from what Rhiannon said that she had been raised in the area, and I assumed Thomas was probably fairly local.'

'Ah yes, but they didn't just grow up in the same town,' said Lane. 'They all went to the same school. Rhiannon and Elwyn were even in the same class!'

'Oh, were they?' said Southall with a wry smile. 'That's more than quite interesting, Judy, that's very interesting, because Rhiannon told us she'd never met Elwyn Thomas.'

'And there's a brother,' said Winter.

'A brother! Who has a brother?' Southall said.

'Gareth and Rhiannon. They have a younger brother called Rhys.'

'That's something else Rhiannon didn't mention,' said Southall. 'Is he still alive?'

'Well, I haven't found a death certificate,' Winter said.

'How much younger is he?'

'He was born when Rhiannon was ten and Gareth was fourteen. So that would put him in his mid-sixties now.'

'That's quite a bit younger,' Southall said. 'Did you find where he lives? It's probably too much to hope for, but Rhiannon did say they had family who lived in Pont Daffyd when they were kids.'

'I'll get onto it,' said Lane.

'Not tonight, Judy,' said Southall. 'I want you all to call it a day, go home and get some rest. You can continue on Monday.'

She headed back to her office and slumped into her chair. Having finished his call to Forensics, Norman came in and joined her.

'Tough few days, huh?' he said.

'Does it show that much?'

'Actually, you hide it pretty well, but I have a nose for these things,' said Norman. 'Anyway, I get that you don't want to talk about it, so tell me what I missed while I was on the phone.'

'For a start, Rhiannon forgot to tell us she went to school with Elwyn Thomas,' Southall said.

'So there is a connection.'

'She also forgot to tell us she has a younger brother called Rhys.'

'What? A younger brother? That's not something you're likely to forget, is it? And Thomas didn't mention him either,' said Norman. 'You'd think he'd be included in the will.'

'We're obviously only getting half the story,' said Southall.

'It looks that way,' said Norman. 'Perhaps we need to give Rhiannon and Elwyn a wakeup call on Monday and find out why that is.'

'That's exactly what I'm thinking,' she said.

'Who do you want to start with then?' Norman said.

CHAPTER EIGHT

Monday 16 April

'I hope you all had a good rest over the weekend,' said Southall. 'The downside, of course, is that we're no further forward than we were on Friday afternoon.'

With a discreet cough, Winter raised his hand.

'We're not at school, Frosty,' said Norman.

'Er, yeah, sorry,' said Winter.

'Do you have something you'd like to share with us?' asked Southall.

'I didn't have a car this weekend so I thought I might as well make myself useful by looking at bus timetables. I found there is a bus service three times a day that runs through Llangwelli on its way to Carmarthen, passing through Pont Daffyd.'

'That's good work, Frosty. Well done,' Norman said.

'Hang on, there's more,' said Winter. 'Having found out which bus company operates that service, I went to their main garage and asked to see the CCTV footage from that particular bus. Unfortunately, their records are a bit haphazard and it took ages to find the relevant footage, but I think I've found something important.'

He held up a memory stick. 'This footage is from Friday the sixth.' He plugged the stick into his laptop, and the others gathered around to look. 'The bus arrives at the stop in Llangwelli town centre at eleven forty. Here, you can see two women get on, along with this old man.' He froze the image.

'That looks like our dead man for sure,' said Norman.

'He shows the driver his bus pass,' said Winter, restarting the footage. 'The bus isn't busy, so he finds a seat on his own, away from the other passengers.' He fast-forwarded through the footage.

'In the half hour it takes to reach Pont Daffyd, the man doesn't budge from his seat. A few passengers get on and off at various stops, but he doesn't speak to anyone.'

He slowed the video to normal speed. 'At this point, the bus has to turn around because it's too wide to go over the humpbacked bridge. The old man gets off just as the bus comes to a stop. The time is now twelve oh eight.'

'This is excellent work,' said Southall. 'You must have spent nearly all weekend going through that footage.'

Winter shrugged, embarrassed. 'I'd have been bored stuck at home without a car. Besides, I'm relying on Catren and Judy for lifts at the moment, so I wanted to make up for the extra work I'm giving them.'

'You don't have to make up for that,' said Lane. 'It's what friends are for.'

'Okay,' said Southall. 'We now know Gareth Jenkins arrived in Pont Daffyd just after midday on Friday the sixth. Dr Bridger puts time of death at late in the evening of that day, or the early hours of Saturday the seventh. The question is, where was he in between?'

'I haven't found any footage of him getting on a bus at the village,' said Winter.

'Someone could have driven him back home,' suggested Lane.

'Then he must have got another lift back to Pont Daffyd later that same day,' said Winter, 'because there's no footage of him on the bus apart from that one journey.'

'This confirms the time of death, but it raises another question,' said Norman. 'If Gareth left home on the sixth and didn't come back, who was in the house, feeding the dog, turning lights on at night and generally convincing his neighbours that he was at home as usual? They were even seen walking the dog in the early hours.'

'Which brings us back to the million dollar question: why did they go to so much trouble?' mused Southall. 'What was so important that they were prepared to take such a risk?'

A silence ensued. No one was prepared to offer even a suggestion of an answer.

'Right,' Southall said eventually. 'Carry on with your research. Norm and I are off to rattle a couple of cages.'

* * *

Turning into St David's Place, they saw the familiar white van of the SOCOs parked outside number fifty-two.

'Well, they didn't waste any time getting here, did they?' said Southall.

'I believe there's heavy rain forecast for later today,' said Norman, 'so they're probably hoping to get done before it starts.'

'I wonder what Rhiannon will have to say about it,' said Southall.

'She'll probably kick up a stink,' said Norman. 'I have an idea she could win the lottery and still find something to complain about.'

As Norman parked up outside the house, the front door was flung open revealing Rhiannon, her face scarlet, her hands on her hips.

'Uh-oh. It looks as if I should have put on my drag-on-slaying armour before coming here,' said Norman.

'Let me handle this,' said Southall. 'She may not take too kindly to your sarcasm.'

'Sarcasm? Me?' said Norman.

'You know very well what I mean,' said Southall. 'I just don't want her wound up any more than she is already.'

'Okay. You're the boss,' said Norman. 'My lips are sealed.'

'Would you mind telling me what's going on?' demanded Rhiannon as they approached.

'I've asked a forensic team to search the garden,' said Southall. 'It's normal procedure to search the premises when there's been a suspicious death.'

'But you said he died in Pont Daffyd. That's miles from here. And it doesn't take an expert to see that no one has set foot in that garden for years.'

'Which makes it a perfect hiding place,' said Southall.

'For what?' demanded Rhiannon.

'We don't know yet,' said Southall. 'Maybe nothing. We'll just have to wait and see. Look on the bright side. At least they'll clear the garden for you before you sell the house. I assume you are going to sell?'

Rhiannon snorted in disgust. 'What good will that do? The damned thing's mortgaged to the hilt, not that it's any of your business.'

'Actually, right now any and everything concerning your brother is my business,' said Southall. 'And that brings us to why we're here.'

'What's that supposed to mean?'

'It seems you've been a little economical with certain facts.'

'I don't know what you're talking about.'

'Let us in, and I'll explain,' said Southall.

Rhiannon made a move to close the door.

'We can do it here, informally, or we can take you down to Llangwelli police station and make it official,' said Norman. 'It's your choice.'

Rhiannon considered this for a few seconds, before turning and marching into the kitchen.

'Do I need a solicitor?' she asked.

'That's for you to decide,' said Southall. 'We're not here to arrest you, but we will if you don't give us some straight answers.'

'I suppose you have a solicitor lined up, just in case,' said Norman.

'I beg your pardon?' said Rhiannon.

'Elwyn Thomas?' said Norman.

'What about him?'

'You told us you didn't know him, but it turns out you were in the same class at school.'

Rhiannon crossed her arms and her chin jutted forward.

'Is that it?' she said. 'You think we're bosom buddies because we were at school together?'

'You were at school together, though,' said Norman.

'Yes, I was, along with about twenty-five other kids,' said Rhiannon. 'I left that school over fifty years ago and I haven't set eyes on Elwyn or any of the other children since. Do you keep in touch with all the kids you went to school with?'

'But you can see how it looks,' said Southall.

'I can see that all right,' said Rhiannon. 'It looks as though you're trying to accuse me of something I haven't done, that's how it looks. Do you know how many Elwyn Thomases there are in Wales? I live two hundred miles away so how was I supposed to know the Elwyn Thomas I went to school with sixty years ago was Gareth's solicitor?'

'We're going to be checking what you say,' said Norman. 'If we find you've been in contact with him—'

'You can check what you damned well like,' said Rhiannon. 'If you're that desperate to accuse me of something, then fine, I admit I'm guilty of forgetting a boy I went to school with over fifty years ago. As far as I know, that's not a crime.'

Southall allowed Rhiannon her moment of triumph before asking her next question. 'What about your brother, Rhys? You didn't mention him either.'

Rhiannon's smile turned into a wince. 'Ah. So you found out about him. The reason I didn't mention Rhys is because we don't talk about him. He's no longer part of our family, and hasn't been for years.'

'What do you mean, "no longer part of your family"?' asked Southall.

'I'd rather not say,' said Rhiannon.

'Well, I'm sorry,' said Southall, 'but this is a murder enquiry, and so you're obliged to talk about him whether you want to or not.'

'He was always difficult to deal with, right from his birth,' said Rhiannon. 'Our parents spoiled him something rotten.'

'He's a lot younger than you and Gareth, isn't he?' asked Southall.

'Gareth was fourteen and I was ten when he was born. We were doing fine until Rhys arrived, and then everything changed.'

'A younger child like that is bound to need more attention,' said Southall.

'Probably, but Gareth didn't see it that way,' said Rhiannon. 'He deeply resented Rhys, and bullied him terribly whenever our parents weren't around.'

'How long did that go on for?' asked Southall.

'Rhys was just four when Gareth joined the army. He made Rhys's life a misery until the day he left home. He never went back, and I missed him, though it was a relief, too, because the bullying stopped.'

'What about you? When did you leave home?'

'I met my husband when I was sixteen, married him and moved to Warwick at eighteen.'

'So that left young Rhys at home with your parents?'

'Yes, that's right. Our parents punished us for leaving by cutting us out of their wills. Everything went to Rhys. It didn't bother me personally, there wasn't much of an inheritance anyway, and I'd fallen on my feet in Warwick. Gareth wasn't happy about it though.'

'Is that what caused the rift in the family?' asked Southall.

'No. That happened years later, after we'd all gone our separate ways. I'd more or less lost contact with Rhys, and I thought Gareth had too. Then, out of the blue, Gareth turned up at my house in Warwick and told me that he and Rhys had had a major falling out. He said I must choose whose side I was on — him or Rhys. Well, I didn't know what to think, or what to do. However, I'd already lost touch with Rhys, and Gareth was right there in my home—'

'You mean you chose Gareth,' said Southall.

'It sounds awful, doesn't it? Thinking back on it, it was a lazy and selfish decision, and I took the easiest way out.'

'Where is Rhys now?' asked Norman.

'I have no idea,' said Rhiannon. 'Ashamed as I am to admit it, I haven't seen or spoken to him in over forty years.'

There was a moment of awkward silence.

Southall considered her next move. 'We'll leave you in peace, but if there's anything else we should know, please tell us, Rhiannon. We don't want to have to keep coming back like this.'

'I honestly can't think of anything else,' said Rhiannon. 'Can I ask how long those people are going to be in the garden?'

'They'll be there as long as they need to be, but it's not the biggest garden, so I can't imagine they'll be too long,' said Southall.

* * *

They went back to the car in silence.

'Did you believe that stuff about not knowing Elwyn Thomas?' asked Norman.

'I think we should ask him the same question and see what he says,' Southall said. 'We should also check that they really haven't been in contact, but, yes, I think I do believe it. As Rhiannon said, do you actually know all the kids you went to school with?'

'Yeah, she has a point there for sure,' Norman said. 'I doubt I could recall the names of most of the kids I went to school with, and I haven't spoken to any of them in years. What about this brother, Rhys, though? If he fell out with Gareth so badly, maybe he's been waiting for a chance to offload that grudge. And would she really not have any contact with her little brother for forty years?'

'He's got to be a person of interest, hasn't he?' said Southall. 'And if it weren't for Frosty, we might have missed him altogether.'

'Yeah, he's pretty hot when it comes to research,' said Norman.

He was just about to start the car when he saw a figure in a white forensic suit running towards them.

'Hey up, Sarah. That SOCO looks pretty excited about something.'

Southall got out and went to speak with the technician. A few seconds later, she was back and leaning into the window.

'They haven't found any warfarin, but their metal detector has registered something. C'mon, Norm, let's go and see. They're just uncovering it now.'

Norman trotted after Southall, around the side of the house and into the back garden. Three SOCOs were gathered around a fourth, who was on her knees by the side of a small shed, carefully feeling underneath it.

'I can't believe whoever was here didn't search the shed,' said Norman.

The SOCO looked up. 'Oh, someone's definitely been inside, but they didn't think to look underneath. We would probably have missed it too, if we hadn't brought the metal detector.'

'Do you know what it is?' asked Southall.

'It seems to be wrapped in a thick plastic bag, but it feels like something slim and flat.'

'A laptop?'

'It could well be. Hang on a sec, and I'll show you.'

The technician sat back and handed Southall a slim, flat package wrapped in a heavy-duty black plastic bag. 'Here you are then. I'd say that's most likely a laptop.'

'That's fantastic work. Well done, everyone,' beamed Southall. 'I'll make sure to let your boss know what a great job you've done. Come on, Norm, let's get this laptop fingerprinted. Hopefully, it will tell us why Gareth Jenkins died.'

'Since it's so important, why don't you let us dust it for prints now?' said the SOCO. 'We've got the necessary kit in the van. We can have it back to you in an hour or so, if you like.'

'We've got another call to make, which will take us about an hour. We could come back and collect it from you here. How's that?' Southall said.

The SOCO grinned. 'You've got a deal!'

* * *

As Norman pulled into the small car park at the solicitor's office, Southall caught sight of Elwyn Thomas strolling towards the parked cars.

'It looks like we got here just in time,' she said.

Norman drew up alongside Thomas just as he reached a pristine Lexus.

'Nice car,' said Norman.

Thomas jumped, startled. 'Oh. Sergeant Norman, isn't it?' He bent and peered into the car. 'And Inspector Southall. You were lucky to catch me. I was just about to take the rest of the day off.'

'Not much on then?' asked Norman.

Thomas smiled. 'One of the benefits of being semi-retired and only having a handful of long-standing clients is that I don't have to be in my office all the time. Sometimes I don't come in at all.'

Southall leaned across from the passenger seat. 'Could you spare a few minutes to answer a couple more questions?'

'Of course,' said Thomas. 'As I said, I'm not busy. Shall we go into my office?'

'We can probably manage here, if that's okay with you?'

Thomas looked around the empty car park. 'Why not? It's a nice day, we might as well make the most of the weather while it lasts. I believe there's rain on the way again.'

Southall got out of the car while Norman parked up.

'So, how can I help, Inspector?' asked Thomas.

'Did Gareth ever mention his health? An illness, perhaps?'

'Good heavens, no. Is that why he died?'

'No, we don't believe so,' said Southall.

Elwyn looked baffled. 'So, why are you asking?'

'The pathologist found traces of warfarin in Gareth's blood. We're trying to figure out how that could have happened.'

'Oh. That's very odd,' said Thomas.

'Yes, isn't it?' said Southall. 'How long have you known Rhiannon Pugh?'

'Now that's a question I didn't expect.' He thought for a moment. 'Let me see now. I suppose it depends on what you mean by "know". I went to school with her. I knew her quite well when we were in our early teens.'

'How well?'

Thomas smiled reminiscently. 'I seem to recall a kiss and fumble one night behind the scouts hut, but we were never an item, if that's what you mean.'

Norman came across to join them, and stood beside Southall, listening.

'Did you stay in touch with Rhiannon after you left school?' she asked.

'No, we went our separate ways. I chose to go into further education and eventually to university. By the time I came back here to live, a lot of the people I knew from school had moved away.'

'And you didn't look for Rhiannon?'

'As I said, we were never really close. I'd forgotten all about Rhiannon until Gareth asked my advice on his will.'

'Did you contact Rhiannon then?'

Thomas frowned. 'I can't quite see where you're going with this, Inspector. Perhaps you're not listening to what I say. So, I repeat: yes, I knew Rhiannon at school. No, I had no further contact with her until last Tuesday, when Gareth's email failed to arrive and I was duty-bound to alert her to his possible passing. Does that answer your questions?'

'Yes, of course,' conceded Southall. 'I'm sorry. I didn't mean to imply anyth—'

'That's all very well, Inspector, but that's precisely what you did mean. I'm happy to help, but if you wish me to continue doing so, I suggest you keep your innuendos to yourself. I've done nothing wrong, and I take exception to your suggesting that I have.'

Norman had never seen Southall embarrassed before, and felt compelled to calm the atmosphere of tension.

'Er, there is something else you could help us with, Mr Thomas, if you don't mind,' he said.

Still frowning in annoyance, he turned to Norman.

'Yes?'

'We understand that Gareth had been married before — twice, in fact — and we understand he still is married to both women. You didn't mention them when you were telling us about the will. Would you like to tell us about them now?'

'Ah, yes. You realise this was a long time ago?'

'Yeah, we know that,' said Norman. 'But, according to Rhiannon, both wives came to her looking for Gareth, and they weren't planning a happy reunion.'

'You have to understand that Rhiannon and Gareth weren't the closest of siblings. The truth is they despised each other, and almost never communicated.'

'What does that mean?'

'The reason the two women were looking for Gareth wasn't because they intended to murder him. They wanted him to agree to annul the marriages.'

'And did he?' Norman asked.

'It took some doing to avoid alerting the authorities, but, yes, I managed to get it done for him.'

'You didn't think you, a lawyer, should report a case of bigamy?' asked Norman.

'The two wives just wanted a quick solution that would allow them to move on with their lives, and Gareth certainly didn't want a fuss.'

'But is what you did legal?' asked Norman.

Thomas appeared to be studying his shoes.

'Hey, look, don't worry,' said Norman. 'It's not our department, so it doesn't really concern us, but I'll be more inclined to forget about it if you could help us with one more thing.'

'Do I have a choice?'

'Not really,' said Norman.

Thomas sighed. 'Okay, Sergeant. What else do you want to know?'

'We have discovered that Gareth had a younger brother, Rhys. We were wondering why you didn't contact him when Gareth died.'

'Rhys was specifically written out of Gareth's will. He instructed me to ensure that Rhys was excluded from his affairs, even after his death.'

'I see,' said Norman. 'Do you know why?'

'All I can tell you is that it goes back fifteen, possibly even twenty, years.'

'Would it have anything to do with his bigamous marriages?'

'I honestly don't know. Whatever it was happened long before Gareth approached me regarding his will. I have an idea it may have been related to a woman, but I can't tell you any more than that.'

'Do you know where we can find Rhys?' Norman asked.

'I'm afraid not. Gareth said he didn't know where he was living, and didn't want to. I searched for him myself, but I couldn't find him.'

'You've looked for him?'

'It's been ten years since I tried to find him, but maybe I should try again. I get the impression Rhiannon may know how to contact him, but whether she will or not, I have no idea.'

'She knows where he is?' asked Norman.

'Rhys is her brother, and whatever bad blood existed between the two boys, I don't think it involved Rhiannon. In my experience, brothers and sisters usually know where to find each other, even if they don't actually do so. I hope she does. I think it's only right that Rhys should be informed of his brother's death, don't you?'

'Yes, I suppose you're right,' said Norman.

'There again, if you're looking for Rhys, I'm sure that with your resources, you'll have a greater chance of finding him than me,' said Thomas.

'We'd certainly like to speak to him,' said Norman.

'Well, there we are then,' said Thomas. 'Even if Rhiannon really doesn't know where he is, perhaps, when you find him, you might break the sad news to him. Now, if there's nothing else, I have things to do.'

'Yes, of course,' said Southall. 'Thank you for your help. And I apologise for being—'

But Thomas was already slamming his car door shut.

'Shit!' muttered Southall, watching him drive away. 'I'm sorry, Norm. That was a classic example of how not to interview someone when you have nothing to accuse them of.'

'But we do have suspicions,' said Norman.

'You think so? I'm not sure we have, after what he said.'

'Don't you think the stories were too similar?' said Norman. 'I mean, they would have known we'd check, and could easily have prepared for this eventuality. Just because he played the righteous indignation card, it doesn't mean we're wrong.'

'It's not just that, Norm. I think we actually are wrong,' said Southall. 'Rhiannon says she has no idea where Rhys can be found, and now Thomas says he thinks she probably does. Would he say that if they were working together?'

'Maybe they're trying to muddy the waters to confuse us,' said Norman.

'No. I'm still not convinced about Rhiannon, but I think Thomas is on the level. The problem is, I've now made sure the one man who might know something useful won't be in a hurry to help us again.'

'You seem to be forgetting we have the laptop. We might not even need his help,' said Norman. 'C'mon, let's go and see if the SOCOs have finished with it.'

'If there's anything on it,' said Southall gloomily.

Norman stood facing Southall across the car. 'You know, you're beginning to worry me, Sarah. It's not like you to be so negative. I don't know what you went through last week, and I don't want to pry, but you know you can talk to me, right?'

Southall slumped into the passenger seat with a sigh.

'That's very sweet of you, Norm, but there's really nothing to say. Yes, as days go, they were pretty crappy, but I knew they would be. The thing is I needed to be there, and I'm glad I went. But do you know what? I couldn't wait to get back. Being back there reminded me how much I love it here.'

Norman smiled. He knew that feeling only too well.

'You feel it as soon as you come over the bridge, don't you?' he said. 'It happened to me the very first time I came here, and that was before I even knew what it was going to be like.'

'Yes,' said Southall, a smile beginning to form on her lips. 'It's as if there's some sort of emotional unloading as you cross the bridge, like all your baggage somehow got left on the other side.'

'It'll be different for you because you're still young and ambitious, but I can't see me ever going back to live in England,' he said.

'Really? Never?'

'Not a chance,' said Norman. 'I mean, think about it, how could going back make my life any better than it is right now? So why do it?'

CHAPTER NINE

'Right,' said Southall, pushing her way through the office doors. 'Our fabulous colleagues at Forensics might just have given us a way to solve this case.'

She held up the laptop, still wrapped in a clear evidence pouch.

'This, we believe, is Gareth Jenkins's laptop. The forensics guys found it hidden under his garden shed.'

'Under his shed!' said Morgan.

'Yes, Catren. Not somewhere you'd normally keep your laptop, is it?' said Southall. 'Logic suggests it must have been put there for a reason, so if we can only get into the thing, it might give us some answers. It's been dusted for fingerprints, but the SOCOs didn't waste time trying to access it because the battery is flat. Frosty, I'm entrusting you with this job, as it's your area of expertise.'

Winter eyed the laptop dubiously. 'I wouldn't say "expertise". I'm more of a dabbler really. I'm sure the tech department would make a much better job of it than me.'

'You're being far too modest, Frosty,' said Southall. 'Besides, if we give it to them it'll be put in a queue and we all know what happens then. It could be weeks before they even notice it's there.'

'Come on, Frosty, at least give it a go,' encouraged Norman. 'You've done it before, and no one will hold it against you if you don't manage to get into the thing.'

'Okay,' Winter said, taking the laptop from Southall. 'I'll do what I can, but I'm not making any promises.'

He set it carefully down on his desk and stared at it as if it might explode.

'It looks a bit ancient,' he said. 'This model must have been discontinued at least ten years ago.'

'But will it still work?' asked Southall.

'I expect it'll be seriously slow, but if I can hook it up to a power source, we might just get lucky,' said Winter.

'Have we got the right connection?' asked Southall.

'There's a cupboard full of old computer leads downstairs,' said Winter. 'I'll see if I can find one that'll fit.'

In less than five minutes he was back, brandishing a handful of leads.

'I'm hoping one of these will do it. . . Ah. Here we go. We have lift-off!'

He flexed his fingers a couple of times, like a virtuoso about to take his seat at the piano, and opened the lid. The others crowded around his desk as he switched it on, and waited. After a few long seconds, the laptop began to whirr noisily, and slowly, into life. After what seemed like a further age, a screen saver appeared.

'Wow! I wasn't expecting an old guy to use a screen saver like that,' he said.

'What is it?' asked Southall.

Winter was blushing. 'I suppose you could call it a woman in a, er, provocative pose.'

'Come on, Frosty, we're all adults here,' said Morgan. 'Just turn it around so we can see.'

Gingerly, Winter turned the laptop around.

Morgan was first to speak. 'Oh, right. I see what you mean. That is a provocative pose. You might even say it's verging on the pornographic. No wonder Gareth had a weak heart if he was into things like that. I mean, at his age . . .'

'Now you've all had a good look,' said Winter, turning the laptop back, 'I'd like to get on with trying to crack the password.'

'Can I have another look at that, Frosty?' asked Norman.

Winter rolled his eyes, but did as requested. Norman leaned forward for a closer look.

'Steady on, Norm,' said Morgan. 'Are you sure you can handle this?'

'Never mind the funnies, Catren,' said Norman. 'I hate to disappoint you, but what I'm interested in is her face.'

'What about it?' asked Southall.

'Take a closer look and tell me who you see,' Norman said.

Everyone leaned in.

'Wait a minute,' said Southall. 'Isn't that—'

'Yep. It looks to me like the woman in that photo we found in the bin,' said Norman. 'It's Gaynor!'

'I think we can safely assume she's not his secret daughter, then,' said Lane.

'I certainly hope not, if she's posing like that,' said Southall.

'How are you spelling Gaynor?' said Winter.

'As in Gloria, I will survive,' said Norman.

Winter frowned. 'Sorry, Norm, but that's a bit too cryptic for me.'

'The song,' said Norman. 'You know. "I will survive" by Gloria Gaynor.'

Winter looked up at him, perplexed. 'Still no idea.'

'Isn't that one of your old sixties songs?' asked Morgan.

'Late seventies, actually,' said Norman.

'Sixties, seventies, eighties, it's all the same,' said Morgan. 'You forget that the rest of us are less than half your age.'

'It's not an age thing,' said Norman. 'You people just have no appreciation of classic songs.'

'Well, you can't expect us to appreciate what we've never heard,' said Morgan. 'Anyway, it's a matter of opinion — knowing your taste in music.'

'What's that supposed to mean?' asked Norman, bristling.

'Well, let's face it,' said Morgan. 'Your idea of a classic song and my idea of crap often come to the same thing. Now, if you were to—'

Southall clapped her hands. 'You two can argue the merits of your musical tastes in your own time. Right now, I'd prefer you to get back to your desks and get on with your work.' She turned to Winter. 'It's G A Y N O R, Frosty. Why do you need to know? D'you think it could be the password?'

'I think having her image as a screen saver suggests he was a bit obsessive about her, so it's probably worth a try.'

'Of course, he could have just had a thing about pornography, and the woman's identity is irrelevant,' said Southall.

Winter considered this for a few seconds. 'Yes, that's possible, but I've got to start somewhere, haven't I?'

'Fair enough,' said Southall. 'Go for it.'

Winter carefully typed in the name, hit return and held his breath.

'Bugger,' he said. 'Sorry, boss.'

'Password incorrect,' muttered Southall reading over his shoulder. 'Doesn't there have to be a mix of capital letters, numbers and special characters?'

Winter grunted. 'I was just assuming that this laptop's operating system is old enough to use a simpler system. Also, we're dealing with an older person, which is why I'm convinced the password will be something easy to remember, like a name.'

Southall shrugged. Maybe he was right. She waited patiently as he leaned forward, frowning in concentration and still flexing his fingers. Finally, he took a breath and typed in a few more letters. The screen went black. Southall stepped back. 'Never mind, Fr—'

Suddenly, the screen lit up, and the home page was displayed. She patted Winter on the back.

'Well done, Frosty,' she said. 'Still think you're just a dabbler, do you?'

'I got lucky,' said Winter, blushing again, this time from modesty. 'He spelled it backwards.'

'And you got it right in just two attempts,' said Southall. 'That's amazing. It must be a record. One thing's for sure, it's certainly not the work of a dabbler.'

'I suppose I am a bit of a nerd when it comes to this stuff,' said Winter. 'But it comes in useful sometimes.'

'Well, since you've got into it now, I'll leave you to see what you can find.'

'What am I looking for?' Winter asked.

'Anything that might tell us where the money's gone, or why, and anything you can find about Gaynor.'

'Okay, I can do that,' said Winter. 'By the way, I didn't want to interrupt when you came in with the laptop, but I went another twelve months into the bank account and found one or two big transfers of money going out.'

'How big?'

'Ten grand each time.'

'Ouch! That's a lot of money,' said Southall.

Winter nodded. 'Yes, it all but emptied the account.'

'Do you know who he sent it to?'

'It was sent via a money transfer service, you know, like Western Union, meaning it could have gone anywhere.'

'Both payments went the same way?'

Winter nodded again. 'I haven't had time to check out the transfer company yet. I was waiting to see how many more payments I could find.'

'That's good work again,' said Southall. 'But put it on hold for now. I'd like you to focus on the laptop first. You might get lucky and find a reference to those payments in his emails.'

* * *

Half an hour later, Lane called Norman over to her desk. 'You might want to take a look at this, Norm.'

He peered over Lane's shoulder at her screen.

'What have you got?'

'Well, it seemed to me that Gaynor must be important,' said Lane, 'so I thought I'd see what I could learn about her.'

'Good luck with that,' said Norman. 'If you don't have a surname, it's worse than trying to find a needle in a haystack.'

'That's true, but Frosty found some more photos on the laptop,' said Lane. 'Granted most of them are pretty racy, but there was one fairly decent headshot. So, I did a search using that.'

'And you found her?'

'Sort of,' said Lane.

'What does that mean?' asked Norman.

Lane brought up a social media profile on her monitor.

'See for yourself,' she said. 'Our mystery woman isn't Gaynor at all.'

Norman stared at the screen.

'That's her face all right, but Mary-Ellen Crosby?' said Norman. 'What is she, some sort of con artist?'

'On the contrary,' said Lane. 'She's a housewife living in Lafayette, Louisiana, in the USA.'

'Okay,' said Norman, 'but that doesn't necessarily mean she's not a con artist.'

'I don't think so,' said Lane. 'I believe this woman is an innocent victim, but I don't think she's lost any money, or is even aware of what's been going on. I think some of her photographs have been stolen, manipulated, and used to create a fake persona.'

'But what about the pornographic poses?'

'All you need is a woman with a similar body shape, and then you just superimpose the victim's face onto that to create someone quite new.'

'You mean like those deep fake blackmail videos?'

'Yes, why not? If people do it to create convincing blackmail videos, it must be even easier to make up a few still photographs.'

'And you're sure this woman isn't some sort of porn star herself? She looks as if she'd have the body for it.'

Lane looked at Norman and frowned.

'What?' he said. 'You saw the screen saver on that laptop, and you just said someone with a similar body shape could have created the poses. I'm just suggesting maybe they didn't need someone else.'

Lane shrugged. 'I suppose when you put it like that . . .'

'C'mon, Judy, don't hit me with this stuff,' said Norman. 'I'm only making an observation. I'm trying to make sense of what you're showing me. I'm trying to solve a murder here; it's my job, it's what I do.'

'What's going on here?' asked Southall, who had been standing behind Norman, unnoticed, for a while now. 'Am I missing something?'

'Er, no,' said Lane. 'We were just discussing what I've found.'

'And what have you found?' asked Southall.

Lane sat back, allowing Southall to see the screen.

'Mary-Ellen Crosby? Who's she, and why is she of interest?' asked Southall.

'I believe she's proof that our mystery woman, Gaynor, isn't a real person at all,' said Lane. 'I think someone has used images from her social media profile to create a fake persona, and manipulated them to produce racy photos like the one Gareth used as a screen saver.'

'Ah. Now that makes sense,' said Southall. 'When a bank account gets emptied like Gareth's was, I can't help but think it's an online scam. Do you think this Mary-Ellen person is involved?'

'There's nothing in her profile to suggest she's anything other than what she says she is.'

'What does it say?'

'That she's a housewife with a wealthy husband and three small children. She even preaches at her local church.'

'That isn't necessarily proof of her innocence,' said Southall.

'Yes, that's what Norm said, but I've read some of her posts. They all show her as a God-fearing, law-abiding citizen, and she obviously doesn't need the money, so why would she take the risk?'

'I admit it sounds unlikely,' said Southall. 'But you know as well as I do that you can't always take people at face value. Some of the most evil killers have come across as saints before they're found out.'

'That's true,' said Lane. 'Will it be all right for me to contact the police in the States and ask them for their help?'

'Of course,' said Southall. 'But I wouldn't mention that she's a possible suspect. If you tell them we believe she's an innocent victim, I'm sure they'll be more willing to cooperate.'

'Boss! I think I've got something,' called Winter.

Southall hurried over to his desk. 'Go on.'

'I've found a whole bunch of emails between Gareth and Gaynor. It looks as though she contacted him out of the blue two or three years ago, and she's been slowly bleeding money out of him ever since.'

'Is that where all his money went, then?' asked Southall.

'It looks that way,' he said. 'The emails stopped coming about a year ago. He kept trying to contact her after that, but got no reply. It looks as if he gave up about six months ago.'

'Well, fancy that,' said Norman. 'As soon as all his money's gone, so is she.'

'That's how these people work,' said Southall. 'They're parasites. Find a vulnerable victim, bleed them dry, and then move on to the next one.'

'But what made her pick on him?' asked Norman.

'Maybe they met online,' suggested Lane.

'Is there any evidence of that?' Norman asked Winter.

'Not so far, but I haven't got through all his mail yet — there's tons of it; I've hardly touched the surface.'

'What about her email address?' asked Southall. 'Does that tell us anything?'

'I'll check it out, of course, but it looks pretty anonymous, so I wouldn't hold your breath,' said Winter.

'What about his browser history?' asked Norman.

'Going back five years?' asked Winter. 'You'll be lucky.'

'I thought you said it started two or three years ago,' said Norman.

'Yeah, the emails started then, but I'm guessing he would have started looking before he came across her,' said Winter.

'Yeah, I suppose that figures,' said Norman. 'Wait a minute. Didn't his partner die five years ago?'

'You mean Alma? Yes, that's right,' said Southall.

'That's what made me think of it,' said Winter. 'He would have been lonely after she died, right? And we all know how desperate people can get when they're lonely. My theory is that he was tempted to try and find someone to replace Alma, and since he didn't like meeting people face to face, he tried online.'

'Yeah,' said Norman. 'I get what you're saying, but if they met that way, you'd think Gaynor would have mentioned it in their correspondence, especially if she thought he was losing interest at any point.'

'I think those racy photos would have made sure that didn't happen,' said Southall.

'You're probably right on the money there,' said Norman. 'It would be interesting to know which of the online dating sites he used, though.'

'What are you getting at?' asked Southall.

'Well, if he was looking for a replacement for Alma, would he really be interested in someone living in the USA?'

'Maybe Frosty's right and he had no wish to actually meet them,' said Lane.

'Yeah, maybe,' said Norman. 'But there are plenty of dating sites in the UK that cater for lonely seniors, why not use one of those? It doesn't make sense to me.'

'Didn't Rhiannon say he was hiding from his two wives?' said Lane. 'Maybe he was afraid they'd check out the dating sites.'

'I'd take everything Rhiannon says with a huge pinch of salt,' said Norman. 'Elwyn Thomas says the issue was resolved years ago, and he should know — he was the solicitor who dealt with it.'

'I believe we can safely assume that Gareth was being scammed,' said Southall. 'And if this woman has the technical know-how to fake an ID, she's probably capable of faking her way onto a UK dating site.'

'Don't they check these things out?' asked Norman.

'Yes, Norm, but if she's that good she'll get past any checks,' said Lane.

'Hang on, everyone,' said Southall. 'Before we get carried away with this scam idea, let's think about this for a minute. Aren't we getting side-tracked? No matter how clever this scam may be, is it relevant to our murder?'

'Side-tracked?' Norman said. 'But it's a classic online scam and it needs investigating, surely.'

'I think we can all agree it's a classic scam,' said Southall. 'But we're not here to investigate those, are we? We've a murder case on our hands.'

'Are you saying we should drop it?' asked Norman.

'My question is, are we wasting our time with this?' asked Southall. 'Is this online scam connected to our murder, or is it just a red herring?'

'Are you saying it's not connected?' asked Norman.

'Not necessarily, but I am saying it appears to have ended a year ago, and, while I agree that preying on the old and vulnerable is a despicable thing to do, as of this moment we don't have a single shred of evidence to link this particular online scam to Gareth Jenkins being found dead in a village just a handful of miles from here.'

'I appreciate your concern,' said Norman. 'But I'm convinced they're connected. It's too much of a coincidence for them not to be.'

'In that case, have you any idea about how?' Southall said.

'The way I see it, Gareth was getting by just fine until five years ago when Alma died,' said Norman. 'Within a couple of years of that, he starts an online relationship with this Gaynor and loses everything. And don't forget, some of the neighbours also said he changed completely after her death, going from Mister Nice Guy to Mister Pain in the Arse.'

'Yes,' said Southall. 'But that could be explained by Gaynor having taken all his money. That would make anyone bitter, wouldn't it?'

'I reckon she's the prime suspect,' said Norman. 'At the very least, she's involved in some way.'

'But if you're right, and Gaynor wanted him dead, why wait all this time?' asked Southall.

Norman shrugged. 'Maybe she wanted to bleed him dry first.'

'But why wait another year before killing him?' asked Southall. 'She had already taken every penny he had and got away with it, so why risk coming here to kill him?'

'When you put it like that, I admit it's difficult to see how it makes sense,' said Norman. 'Unless he somehow found out who she really was, and was about to expose her.'

'How would she have known that?' asked Southall. 'Frosty says he stopped trying to contact her six months ago.'

'Are we saying this woman has been operating from outside the UK?' asked Lane.

'I would say probably, but we can't be absolutely sure,' said Southall. 'Why do you ask?'

'We believe Gareth was lured to the place where he died, don't we? If so, would a woman from outside the UK, or even outside this part of Wales, know of the existence of a small village like Pont Daffyd? Even if they had been in the area on vacation, it's not a known tourist spot, is it?'

'Good point,' said Southall. 'And it adds weight to my argument that the two crimes aren't linked.'

'Maybe she has an accomplice who was watching Gareth in the weeks before he was murdered,' suggested Norman.

'What? And followed him to Pont Daffyd? You're forgetting that the man was sick, and was living like a hermit,' said Lane. 'The only time he ever went out was to walk his dog.'

'Jeez, yeah, you're right, Judy,' said Norman.

'Er, boss,' said Winter. 'Sorry to interrupt, but I'm getting nowhere trying to trace where Gaynor's emails were coming from, so I've asked a mate of mine in the tech department to try. They've got the software and know-how and they'll do it much quicker than I ever could.'

'I'm not sure that's a good idea,' said Southall. 'They always seem to prioritise their friends in Region, and put us at the back of the queue. It could take weeks.'

'I'm calling in a favour,' said Winter. 'He's going to work late on it. With any luck, he'll have something for us in a day or two.'

'I admire your optimism, Frosty, but they don't usually rush to help us.'

'Ah, yeah, but I think that's about to change. According to my mate, they've got a new boss who doesn't think Region deserve to get top priority every time.'

'Let's hope he means it,' said Southall. She turned back to Norman. 'Sorry, where were we?'

'We were just wondering if we were wasting our time trying to find a link between the scam and the murder and was it just a coincidence that they both happened to Gareth,' said Norman. 'And then . . .' He stopped mid-sentence. 'Jeez!' he said. 'Sometimes I'm so stupid I miss the obvious even if I fall over it.'

'What?' asked Southall.

'It's what Judy was saying,' said Norman. 'She's right. The key to this isn't the online scam, and it isn't the two former wives. It's Pont Daffyd. It must be.'

'There again, it could be Rhys Jenkins,' said Morgan, who was staring at her screen.

'And there I was thinking you'd fallen asleep you've been so quiet,' said Norman.

'I've been quiet because I've been concentrating on this search,' said Morgan.

'What have you found, Catren?' asked Southall.

'What about this for a coincidence?' said Morgan. 'Rhys Jenkins is a software development engineer who spent fifteen years working in Silicon Valley in the US. He retired just over a year ago.'

127

'Holy shit!' said Norman.

'Do we know where he is now?' asked Southall.

'I'm working on it,' said Morgan.

'If he's a software engineer, he would surely know how to create the fake images,' said Norman.

'And how to set up a fake ID and run an email scam,' agreed Southall. 'We need to find him urgently.'

'I hate to change the subject,' said Lane, 'but does anyone want a cup of tea? I'm gasping.'

To a chorus of 'yes, please' she headed for their tiny kitchen.

'What about Rhiannon?' Norman asked Southall. 'She's been economical with the truth every time she's spoken to us. Maybe she knows a bit more about Rhys than she's been willing to divulge up to now.'

'D'you want to head out there and ask her?' asked Southall.

'Sure,' said Norman. 'Should I take someone with me?'

Southall nodded towards the kitchen. 'Ask Judy.'

Norman went to the kitchen and stood just inside the door, watching Lane pour boiling water into their mugs.

'The boss suggested you might like to drive me out to St David's Place,' he said. 'We just want to put a little pressure on Rhiannon Pugh. She might well know where Rhys is.'

'Okay,' said Lane. 'Have we got time to drink our tea first?'

'Yeah, of course,' said Norman. 'Look, about earlier—'

'It's okay, Norm, honestly,' said Lane, turning to face him. 'You're right, it is what you get paid for, and I had no right implying anything else. It's my fault. I'm a . . . What I mean is, it's still a bit raw, you know?'

'You mean giving evidence against Marston?' he asked.

Marston, an unsavoury character, had been the detective sergeant at Llangwelli station before Norman arrived. Norman had reported him to Professional Standards when issues came to light regarding Marston's conduct during a previous case. It also turned out that Marston had made sexual advances to Lane, going so far as to send several intimidating messages to her mobile phone.

Encouraged by Norman and Southall, Lane had plucked up the courage to report Marston to Professional Standards herself, and had recently been interviewed. As she'd confessed to Norman, reliving those events had been more difficult than she had expected, and had brought back memories she would rather forget.

Lane nodded.

'I'm sorry. I should have realised,' said Norman.

'No, it's okay. I've got to get over it,' said Lane. 'It was hard, but it was something I needed to do.'

'Do you need to talk to someone?' he asked.

'You mean counselling?'

'It doesn't have to be a counsellor,' said Norman. 'Sarah's a good listener, and you can always talk to me.'

'That's okay. I have someone, thanks.'

'Oh, right. What about some time off, then?' said Norman. 'Whatever you need, just let me or Sarah know, and we'll arrange it.'

Lane managed a sad little smile. 'Frosty said you were kind, and he's right, you really are,' she said. 'But, honestly, I think the best thing for me is to keep busy.'

'Okay, but if you change your mind—'

'You'll be the first to know. Now, can you carry two of these mugs?'

'Sure,' said Norman, picking up two. 'I've got mine and Sarah's.'

He held the door open for Lane, then took Southall's tea to her office.

'Is everything okay between you two?' she asked as Norman set the mug down on her desk.

'Me and Judy? Yeah, we're fine.'

'I got the feeling there was a bit of tension between the two of you earlier.'

'Oh, that. Yeah, you're right. I made a remark, and she took offence to it.'

Southall raised her eyebrows. 'You offended Judy? How on earth did you do that? I've always had the impression she adores you — you know, rather like a father figure.'

'Yeah, well, even an adored father figure can step out of line,' said Norman. 'We were talking about those saucy photos on the laptop. Judy says they probably used a model and superimposed Mary-Ellen's face. I said I didn't think Mary-Ellen looked as if she needed a model, her own body would have done.'

'And she took offence to that?' said Southall. 'But it's true.'

'She says she took offence because she's still a bit touchy after giving evidence about that creep Marston.'

'I thought she was all right about that.'

'Only on the surface. I offered her counselling or some time off, but she says she wants to work through it. I don't think it helps that it's been hanging over her all this time. It's been months since I gave my evidence, yet she's only just been asked to give hers. The whole process should have been wrapped up months ago.'

'Yes, I know what you mean. When it drags on so long, it does make you wonder just how keen they are to get rid of the bad apples,' said Southall.

'It's not as if there's any doubt about his behaviour, either,' said Norman. 'The evidence is there on Judy's mobile phone for all to see, and yet the guy's been suspended on full pay. I can't see how that's a punishment to fit the crime, can you?'

'If it's any consolation, Norm, I understand that the delay is because Marston's punishment isn't just going to be dismissal for gross misconduct. The Criminal Prosecution Service are also preparing a sexual harassment case against him.'

'Does Judy know? That will mean her giving evidence in front of a jury. It will be much worse than talking to a couple of detectives from Professional Standards.'

'I don't think we should say anything until we know for sure,' said Southall. 'I'm sure she'll cope if we all support her, but there's no need for her to be worrying in the meantime. The good thing is, Marston will end up behind bars, thanks to you and Judy.'

'It's the best place for creeps like him,' said Norman.

'Anyway, enough about Marston. Are you and Judy going to be okay?'

'Oh, yeah, we're fine. Is that why you volunteered her to drive me?' he said.

'I thought you might need a bit of time to talk through whatever it was.'

Norman smiled. 'You don't miss much, do you?'

'I try not to,' said Southall. 'I find it's a good way to keep everyone happy.'

'In that case, you could keep me happy if you were to ask Catren to apologise for dissing my taste in music.'

Southall grinned. 'Sorry, Norm, I can't possibly do that.'

'Why not?'

'Isn't it obvious? How could I possibly ask her to apologise for something I agree with.'

'Ha! Right, I get it. It's gang up on the old guy time,' said Norman. 'Well, you're all wrong, you know. Everybody on the planet knows people of my generation grew up listening to the best music that was ever made.'

'Right. Of course you were, Norm,' said Southall. 'I'll try to remember that next time you start playing Led Zeppelin at full volume while I'm in your car.'

'Ah, now you're talking. Led Zeppelin — the very best of the best,' said Norman.

'That's as may be, but I have a meeting with Superintendent Bain,' Southall said.

'Oh, right,' said Norman. 'Actually, I've just thought of something I've been meaning to do anyway. And it might be useful if I do it before I speak to Rhiannon.'

'What's that?' asked Southall.

'Just a little research,' said Norman. 'It might be a waste of time, but you never know.'

Southall looked at her watch. 'I must go,' she said. 'This meeting might go on for a bit, so I'll see you tomorrow morning.'

CHAPTER TEN

Rhiannon Pugh flung open the door. 'Not you lot again?'

'And good afternoon to you, Mrs Pugh,' said Norman. 'It's a pleasure to see you again.'

Rhiannon looked down at Lane as if she were some sort of unpleasant insect. 'Who is this?'

'This is my colleague, DC Judy Lane. We'd like to ask you a few more questions.'

'Have you found my money yet?'

Norman smiled. 'I'm afraid our priorities and yours aren't quite the same. If you want my honest opinion, the money has either been spent, or it's stashed away in an off-shore bank account. Either way, I doubt we'll be recovering it any time soon. While we can't deny there's a strong possibility of a link between the money and Gareth's death, our real interest lies not in chasing a lost cause, but in finding out who killed your brother.'

Rhiannon sniffed. 'I dislike your attitude,' she said.

Norman's smile widened. 'I always aim to please.'

'And I don't like you,' she added.

'I stopped worrying about my popularity rating a long time ago,' said Norman. 'I don't care whether you like me or not, Rhiannon, I only care about doing my job. And when people keep offering half-truths or even outright lies every time I ask them a question, their opinion of me matters less and less.'

'Are you threatening me?'

'With violence? No way. That's not my style,' said Norman. 'I'm just saying there is a better way of getting you to answer our questions, one that doesn't waste so much of our time.'

'Waste your time? I don't know what you mean. I've answered all your questions as best I can.'

'But that's not quite true, is it?' said Norman. 'Sure, you've volunteered a few crumbs of information, but the only reason we've managed to get anything at all out of you is because we've been prepared to keep coming back. Well, I'm getting fed up with doing that.'

'Now that does sound like a threat.'

'I'm offering you a choice. You can either answer our questions truthfully here, or we can take you down to Llangwelli station where you will be formally interviewed, and that could take hours. You might even be there all night.'

Rhiannon stared at Norman and then turned to Lane.

'Are you going to let him threaten me like that?'

'It sounded like a perfectly reasonable offer to me,' said Lane.

'You can't treat me like this,' said Rhiannon. 'I know my rights. I've a good mind to make a complaint about both of you. Threatening me like that.'

'You're free to make a complaint about me any time you want,' said Norman. 'Be my guest. But as for my colleague, she hasn't said anything that could remotely be construed as a threat.'

'The thing is this, Mrs Pugh,' said Lane. 'If we take you to the station we'll have to faff around with reams of paperwork before we can even start the interview, it's official procedure. Making a complaint will only add to the paperwork, because you'll also have to wait for someone from Professional Standards to come and speak to you before we can proceed with the interview.'

Rhiannon was silent for a few seconds, clearly weighing up the odds. 'How long is this going to take?'

'No more than half an hour,' said Norman. 'But the longer we stand out here arguing, the more likely I am to run out of patience, and if that happens, it could take half the night.'

'Well, I'm not standing out here for another half hour, let alone half the night,' said Rhiannon. 'It's bloody cold.'

'You could let us into the house,' suggested Lane.

'I can tell you've not been here before,' said Rhiannon. 'If you had, you'd know it's not much warmer inside. Still, I suppose it's better than standing on the step.'

Rhiannon reluctantly stepped aside, and, muttering darkly about police brutality, led them to the kitchen.

'Oh, my,' said Lane, taking in the state of the house.

'Not the most welcoming place, is it?' said Rhiannon. 'I won't be sorry to get back home to Warwick, I can tell you.' She leaned back against the kitchen sink and folded her arms. 'Right, what's this about?'

'Your brother, Rhys,' said Norman. 'We need to find him.'

'I distinctly remember telling you that I haven't spoken to him in years.'

'Then let me help you out,' said Norman. 'Rhys is a software development engineer who spent fifteen years working in Silicon Valley in the US. He retired just over a year ago.'

'Well, there you are. You know more than I do,' said Rhiannon.

'Somehow I doubt that,' said Norman. 'But we can come back to that in a minute. What caused the big bust up between him and Gareth?'

'I don't know.'

'Was Rhys ever married?'

'I don't know,' said Rhiannon. 'He may have been.'

'It looks like we're wasting our time again,' said Norman. 'Perhaps we'd better take you down to Llangwelli station after all.'

'All right!' snapped Rhiannon. 'Yes, Rhys was married. But what does that matter?'

'It matters because, according to Elwyn Thomas, the reason Gareth and Rhys fell out was, in his words, "woman related". What do you think he meant by that?'

Rhiannon's eyes darted between Norman and Lane. She licked her lips.

'I have no idea.'

'Oh, come on, Rhiannon,' said Norman. 'You can do better than that. Didn't you tell us Gareth was a bit of a ladies' man? You said he had two wives and a girlfriend on the go when he met Alma.'

'Did I?'

'You know you did,' said Norman. 'Now I'm going to hazard a guess here, and you tell me if I'm right. Would I be right in thinking they fell out because Gareth had a fling with Rhys's wife?'

Rhiannon's eyes widened very slightly, but it was enough.

'Ah, so I am right,' said Norman.

'I didn't say so,' said Rhiannon.

'You didn't need to,' said Norman. 'I can see it in your eyes.'

'How could I know? I wasn't there.'

'But you know what happened,' said Norman. 'You told us Gareth came to see you and told you about the fallout, but I'm beginning to think that maybe it was Rhys who told you, not Gareth.'

'I haven't spoken to Rhys—'

'In forty years. Yeah, you said. The trouble is, I don't believe you,' said Norman.

'How dare you! You have no right to keep accusing me of—'

'Lying?' said Norman. 'Is that what you were going to say? Well, I hate to tell you this, Rhiannon, but I have every right. You see, I spent a few minutes online before we came out here, and I found your Facebook profile.'

Rhiannon's eyes widened further.

'It lists Rhys as one of your "friends".'

'There's nothing wrong in listing your family as friends. Anyway, that doesn't prove I've been in contact with him.'

'Of course it doesn't,' said Norman. 'But I can't believe he would have approved your friend request having not seen you for forty years.'

Rhiannon stared at Norman.

'And what about the photos you posted after you visited him in the US five years ago?' said Norman. 'How did that happen if you've not been in contact for forty years?'

Rhiannon continued to stare at him, her mouth working.

Lane, who had been taking notes, said, 'I think now might be a good time to offer some answers.'

Rhiannon ran her hands through her hair. 'All right. What do you want to know?'

'Rhys and Gareth.'

'As I said, Gareth bullied Rhys when he was little. What I didn't say was after he left home, when Rhys was only four, he still took every opportunity to interfere with Rhys's life. So when Rhys got married, I suppose it was inevitable that Gareth would see it as another opportunity to do him harm. I blame myself, because I should have seen it coming.'

'He stole Rhys's wife?'

'Oh no, he didn't steal her. He had an affair with her, but he had no intention of taking her away. It was all about destroying the marriage and messing things up for Rhys. I can't be sure, but I suspect Gareth arranged for Rhys to catch them together, and really rub salt into the wound. It's the sort of thing he would have done.'

'What did Rhys do when he found out?'

'He broke Gareth's nose, and then he kicked his wife out.'

'How did he end up working in the US?'

'He wanted to get away and make a new start. When the position in the US came up, he jumped at it.'

'Did he meet anyone while he was out there?'

'Yes, he met a widow with two teenage daughters. I went out there for the wedding.'

'So you were in touch, even though you told us you weren't?' Norman said.

'Only through Facebook. After all, he's my brother. Why shouldn't I keep in touch with him?'

'But we all know Facebook hasn't been going for forty years,' said Norman. 'Which leads me to think you've been in contact with Rhys all along.'

'Oh, what does it matter?' snapped Rhiannon. 'And why are you asking all these questions about Rhys anyway?'

'The money that's missing from Gareth's account wasn't stolen. We think he gave it away to a woman called Gaynor.'

Rhiannon laughed.

'Ha! Well, that's ironic. Having spent all his life taking from them, he ends up losing everything to a woman.'

'Yeah, something like that,' said Norman. 'Except Gaynor isn't real, and I'm beginning to think she isn't even a woman.'

'You're not making any sense,' said Rhiannon. 'I thought you said her name was Gaynor, so how can she not be a woman?'

'Gareth was scammed by someone pretending to be a woman called Gaynor,' said Lane. 'We think she managed to trick Gareth into sending her all his money.'

'You remember that photograph I showed you?' said Norman. 'It's that of a woman who lives in the USA. She has no idea her photo was being used to scam a man here in Wales.'

'He always did think from down there under his trousers,' said Rhiannon. 'I still don't see where Rhys comes into it, though.'

'He's a software engineer,' said Norman. 'He would know how to set up, and carry out, a scam like that, and now we know he also has a powerful motive.'

'What motive?' demanded Rhiannon.

'The one you've just given us,' said Norman. 'Gareth ruined Rhys's happiness, so Rhys found a way to ruin Gareth in return. Maybe he murdered him, too, who knows?'

'That all sounds very neat,' said Rhiannon. 'But that's not how it is. Rhys wasn't really happy with his first wife; now he says he's never been happier. Gareth certainly didn't intend it that way, but he did Rhys a favour.'

'Excuse me if I have doubts about that,' said Norman, 'but I'd rather hear it from Rhys himself. The thing is, we don't know if he's back in the UK or not, and we'd like you to tell us where he is.'

'That's it,' said Rhiannon. 'I've had enough. I have answered your questions about my younger brother, but when you accuse him of murder . . . It's outrageous. I want you out of this house, now!'

'Okay,' said Norman. 'But not until you tell us where Rhys is.'

'I don't know where he is.'

'Aw, come on, Rhiannon,' said Norman. 'You can do better than that.'

'On my life, I don't know where he is.'

'I tell you what,' said Norman. 'You can have tonight to think about it, and then tomorrow when you come into Llangwelli station and make a full statement, maybe you'll have remembered his whereabouts.'

Rhiannon smiled. 'I'm sorry, but I won't have time to make a statement. I'm going home tomorrow. I've booked a ticket for the midday train.'

'That's okay, you can still go home,' said Norman. 'After all, if you're not leaving till midday, you'll have plenty of time to come in and make that statement before then.'

'How am I supposed to get there? I don't even know where it is.'

'It's about five minutes' walk from your hotel,' said Norman. 'But I'll arrange for someone to come and collect you at nine. We'll even drive you to the railway station afterwards.'

'And what if I refuse?'

'Someone will still come and collect you at nine, only they'll arrest you first. Of course, if that happens, everything will take longer and you might miss your train.'

Rhiannon glared at Norman. 'You'd enjoy that wouldn't you? Humiliating an old woman.'

'I'm just asking you to come in and help us with our investigation, which is what you previously said you wanted to do,' he said. 'But if you want to set yourself up for that sort of humiliation, well, it's your choice.'

'I hate you,' she hissed.

Norman smiled. 'That's one thing you've said that I do believe. However, I have a very thick skin, and I can assure you I won't lose any sleep worrying about what you think of me.'

* * *

'Are you sure we shouldn't have taken her in now?' asked Lane when they were back in the car.

'What would be the point?' said Norman. 'I mean, she is in her seventies. And she didn't kill anyone.'

'She could warn Rhys.'

'Well, yeah, that is a bit of gamble, but I think she was telling the truth when she said she doesn't know where he is. Even if I'm wrong, I think it's worth the risk, because if we take her in now, we'll get nothing out of her.'

'She really hates you, doesn't she?' Lane said.

'Is it me, or is it the fact that we're not as dumb as she thought? I reckon she's one of those people who think that just because the Welsh aren't as rich as people in England, it means they're all thick as shit. That's a big mistake.'

'But you're English, not Welsh. Do *you* think we're all thick, then?'

'I hope I have more respect for people than to generalise like that,' said Norman. 'Besides, the people I work with are mostly Welsh, and they're all very bright, so I know what I'm talking about.'

'Thank you for the compliment.'

'It's not a compliment. I'm just saying how things are,' said Norman.

'Does that mean you'll stay, then?'

Norman stared at her. 'Are you kidding? I have absolutely no plans to go anywhere. I like it here so much I'm thinking of applying for honorary membership.'

'Membership of what?' asked Lane.

'The Welsh.'

Lane burst out laughing. 'Wouldn't that be wonderful?'

'I know I struggle with the language, but still . . . D'you think they'd let me join?'

'Less than twenty percent of the population speak the language, Norm, so you wouldn't fail on that account. If it was down to me, you'd get my vote every time, but there's no getting away from the fact that you were born English. I'm afraid the selection committee would probably find that a massive stumbling block.'

'Yeah, I guess you're right about that. Maybe I'll get lucky and be born here if I come back in another life.'

'Do you believe in that?' asked Lane.

'What, reincarnation? To be honest I've never really decided what I do believe in,' said Norman. 'I often think it doesn't matter anyway. The only thing we know for sure is that we're all going to die, whatever our beliefs. I suppose that makes me a fatalist. What about you?'

'I'm with you in the "not sure what to believe" category,' said Lane. 'The thing is, there are so many different belief systems, and they can't all be right, which means that whatever you believe in, there's a good chance it's the wrong one.'

'That's a fact,' agreed Norman. 'Maybe it's just about love, peace and kindness while you're alive. Surely, if you live according to those principles, then if there is anything after death, you'll be sure to qualify for acceptance.'

'Wow! I didn't realise I was going to get a lesson in philosophy when I came out today,' said Lane.

'I'm sorry,' said Norman. 'I didn't mean to lecture. I hate it when people try to force their beliefs on me.'

'Oh, I'm not complaining,' said Lane. 'I don't think anyone could argue against those values. I'm certainly not going to.'

Lane slowed the car, ready to turn into the station car park.

'You can drop me here, unless you need to call into the office,' said Norman.

'Are you sure?'

'Of course,' said Norman. 'You get off home. I'll see you in the morning.'

CHAPTER ELEVEN

Tuesday 17 April

'So, how did you two get on with Rhiannon yesterday?' asked Southall.

'I checked out her Facebook profile so I knew the real story before we even got there,' said Norman. 'She's been in touch with Rhys all along. She even went over to the US a few years ago to see him. But she swears she doesn't know where he is right now.'

'Do you believe her?' asked Southall.

'I'm not absolutely certain, but I think so,' said Norman.

'Do we need to bring her in?'

'She's going back to Warwick today on the midday train, but I've arranged for someone to bring her in at nine so she can make a statement.'

'And she agreed?' Southall asked.

'I told her we'd arrest her if she didn't. That seemed to persuade her. I also told her to think about where Rhys is and, if she does, whether she ought to tell us.'

'So, you'll be interviewing her, then.'

Norman shook his head. 'She hates me. I think she'll be more co-operative if you speak to her. I also think it'll be worth leaning on her, so as to get a straight answer about Rhys.'

'D'you think she's involved in Gareth's death?'

'I doubt it,' said Norman. 'She says she didn't know about the scam, and despite all her other lies, I think she really didn't.'

'In that case, I'll speak to her, but I don't want us to get too hung up on Rhiannon. If Rhys is back in the UK, I reckon, of the two of them, he is the more likely murder suspect.'

'Okay, so what next?' asked Norman.

'Yesterday you said you thought Pont Daffyd was the key to this case, and I agree with you. Gareth must have had a very good reason for going there, and so far we've no idea what it was. I think that's where we should focus our attention.'

'Didn't Rhiannon say they often went there when they were kids, because they had relatives there?'

'Exactly,' said Southall. 'If I'm right about Rhys being the prime suspect, and he isn't in the area, it might mean he has an accomplice in that village. In that case, I think we should ask Judy to go back sixty years to when they were children, and find out where the uncle lived. The surname was Jenkins. She can check with the local council, the property register and anywhere else she can think of. Let's find out where that family are now, and if any of them still live in Pont Daffyd.'

'What do you want me to do?'

'Go back to Pont Daffyd. Take Catren with you, and starting at the crime scene, check out that village. Ask around again, maybe someone will recognise the name Jenkins and know where they live.'

* * *

An hour later, Norman and Morgan were standing in the small clearing where Gareth Jenkins's body had been dumped in the stream.

'What exactly are we looking for?' asked Morgan.

142

'If we knew that, the SOCOs would have found it,' said Norman. He was studying the clear waters of the stream. 'Is it my imagination, or was it flowing much faster when we were here the other day?'

'Yeah,' said Morgan. 'These streams are like that. They can be quite shallow, meandering along at a snail's pace for weeks, then we get a few hours' heavy rain and suddenly they're raging torrents six feet deep, because of the runoff from the higher ground further upstream.'

'Is this a stream, or is it a river?' Norman asked.

'How d'you mean?' asked Morgan.

'Down where the body was found it was quite narrow and shallow. Now, granted this isn't exactly the Thames, it's so much wider and deeper here that I think I'd call it a river.'

'And your point is?'

'If you wanted to make sure a body went right under, you'd pick somewhere with a bit of deep water like this, right?'

'I suppose so,' said Morgan. She pointed to the other side. 'If you snagged it under some of those submerged tree roots over there, as long as it didn't flood, the body could stay hidden for months.'

'Right, but would you throw it in here if you knew how much the level changes when it rains?'

'No, I wouldn't,' said Morgan. 'But then I've lived along-side streams like this all my life. I know what a bit of heavy rain can do to them.'

'Right,' said Norman. 'And that's my point. What if you didn't live in the area? You wouldn't know that the rain might easily cause a flood that could wash the body downstream where it would get caught on the shallows.'

'Are you saying you think we're looking for an outsider?' asked Morgan.

'You disagree?' asked Norman.

'I can see where you're coming from,' said Morgan, 'but if you don't mind me saying, I think there's a flaw in your thinking.'

'Of course I don't mind. Jeez, if I'm talking rubbish, we don't want to be wasting time on it, do we?'

'The thing is, there are plenty of people who've lived here all their lives and have no idea how these streams work.'

'I haven't been here very long, and I know,' said Norman.

'Yeah, but that's because you take an interest in your surroundings, plus the case has brought it to your attention,' said Morgan. 'Trust me, I know people of my age who are hardly aware that there is an environment beyond the screen of their mobile phone.'

'Crap,' muttered Norman glumly. 'I was hoping it might narrow the field a bit, but I guess you're right.'

'If the body had been tied to those roots, it might not have washed away,' said Morgan.

'The SOCOs even brought a diver in,' said Norman. 'They didn't find anything that suggested the body had been tied down, but they did find a couple of big rocks that they think may have been used to weigh it down.'

'Are we assuming Gareth died here, or that he was killed somewhere else and his body was brought here and dumped?' asked Morgan.

Norman shrugged. 'Your guess is as good as mine. Forensics say they found no evidence to suggest he was killed here, but unless they find corroborative evidence somewhere else, they can't rule it out. What's on your mind?'

'Gareth couldn't have weighed much, but even so, it's a long way from the road to carry a body.'

'You couldn't risk doing it in broad daylight,' said Norman, 'and it's so close to the pub you'd have to wait until that closed.'

'So, you'd be looking at the early hours,' said Morgan.

'Which means you'd have to negotiate that first part of the path, where all the loose stones are, in pitch darkness,' said Norman.

'Unless there's another way of getting here that avoids going near the pub,' said Morgan.

Norman looked back towards the path. 'Good thinking. And now we're here, I think we'd better check it out.'

They went back to the path and began to follow it. To the left, they could still catch glimpses of the stream through the spindly trees growing alongside it, then the trees suddenly thickened as they rounded a bend to the right. As the path straightened out again, they could see a small footbridge crossing the stream. The path on the other side led into a thicket of willow trees.

'What do you think?' asked Norman. 'Do we cross the bridge or keep following the path?'

'This path is just taking us further from the village,' said Morgan.

'That's what I was thinking,' said Norman. 'I can't see through those trees, but maybe if we cross the bridge, the path heads back the other way.'

'There's only one way to find out,' said Morgan, and set off across the bridge.

Norman followed her along the path, which narrowed suddenly as it reached the group of trees. The copse wasn't anything like as dense as it had first appeared, but the trees were so close to the path they were obliged to walk in single file. Norman suddenly became aware of an odd sound that gradually grew louder.

'What's that noise?' he asked.

'Come on, Norm. Surely you've lived in Wales long enough to recognise the sound of bleating lambs when you hear them?' said Morgan.

'Where are they? I don't want to find myself knee deep in sheep shit.'

'They're away to our right,' said Morgan. 'And there's a fence between us, so you needn't worry about the droppings.'

'But why are they making all that noise? What's up with them?'

'If they were born early enough, now would be about the time they're taken from their mothers,' said Morgan. 'They cry for a while, but they get over it soon enough.'

'I forgot you're the go-to person for all things farming,' said Norman.

Morgan stopped in her tracks, so suddenly that Norman almost collided with her.

'Now this is interesting,' she said, pointing to the ground.

Norman peered over her shoulder. A well-worn track crossed the path from right to left.

'Well, fancy that,' he said. 'Would I be right in thinking this is how the shepherd gets to and from his fields?'

'Well done, Norm,' said Morgan. 'I'll make a country boy out of you yet.'

'Yeah, good luck with that,' said Norman. 'I reckon it would be a lot easier to carry a body from here, don't you?'

'It must be the best part of four hundred metres from the bridge,' said Morgan. 'And about a hundred and fifty metres from here.'

'I don't know exactly how far that is in old money,' said Norman. 'But I believe you're saying it's less than half as far from here, and I agree. It's also a much more even track. D'you think it comes out in the village?'

'I'd be surprised if it didn't,' said Morgan. 'You're not suggesting we walk it, are you? It's muddy enough here, and the chances are it could get much worse before we reach a road. If I look it up on a map when we get back, we don't need to get any muddier than we already are.'

'I'm all for that,' said Norman. He took one last look around. 'Come on, Catren, there's nothing more to see here. Let's go back and take a walk around the village.'

* * *

'Jeez, has this wind come straight from Siberia?' asked Norman when they reached their car. 'It wasn't like this when we got here, was it?'

'I suppose we were sheltered from it down under the trees,' said Morgan. 'Think yourself lucky you're not a brass monkey.'

'You'd have heard a loud clang by now if I was,' said Norman. He pointed at the pub on the other side of the road. 'In view of the cold, we might as well start there.'

Morgan looked at her watch. 'Isn't it a bit early for a drink?'

'I'm not suggesting we buy a beer,' said Norman. 'Although, now you come to mention it, I suppose we could have an early lunch and ask a couple of questions. I have a feeling in my water that we're going to get lucky, and they'll tell us they have a regular called Jenkins. They might even know where he lives.'

Half an hour later, they were heading back towards their car, Norman beaming happily.

'There, you see, what did I tell you?' he said.

'But they said the guy died over a year ago,' said Morgan.

'Yeah, but at least we know where the house is, and what it's called.'

'They also said his wife died before him and he lived alone,' said Morgan. 'What are you suggesting we do, go to the house and organise a seance?'

'I don't know, but we might as well take a look at the house, now we know where it is.'

As they were just about to cross the road to their car, a small red hatchback zoomed across the humpbacked bridge and passed them, heading down the road. Norman grabbed Morgan and pulled her out of the way.

'Jeez, some people,' he said. 'I mean, who drives that fast across a narrow bridge when people might be crossing the road? For two pins I'd chase them down and give that driver a bollocking . . .'

Morgan wasn't listening. She was staring after the car.

'Are you okay, Catren?'

'I'm sure I recognise that car. I know it's there somewhere in my head, but I can't quite place it.'

'Did you get the registration number?' asked Norman.

'It was going too fast,' said Morgan.

'Well, if you remember who owns it, let me know and I'll get someone from the traffic division to pay them a visit.'

'I wonder what they're doing out here.'

'It's a public highway,' said Norman. 'They don't need our permission to drive through here, they just need to slow down a bit.'

As they were crossing the road, his phone rang. 'Hi, Sarah, what's up?'

'I've just asked Frosty to take Rhiannon to the railway station.'

'Did she tell you anything new?'

'Nothing.'

'Did she tell you where Rhys is?' Norman asked.

'No, but she did admit that he might be in the UK.'

'That's not much help really, is it?' said Norman.

'Ah, but she thinks she knows where he's heading,' Southall said.

'She thinks she knows? Is this more of her obfuscation?'

'Well, I was hoping you could check it out,' Southall said. 'According to her, Rhys inherited a house from his uncle, right there in Pont Daffyd.'

'So he's heading here?'

'That's what she said.'

'You're kidding me!'

'Apparently, now he's finished his contract in the USA, his plan is to renovate the old house so he can bring his wife here to live. The house is called—'

'Bryn Heulog?' said Norman.

'How did you know that?' asked Southall.

'We've just been in the pub asking if they have any regulars called Jenkins. They told us about this old guy called Huw Jenkins who died a while back. As far as they know, he had no family, or at least they'd never seen them. If Rhys has inherited that house—'

'He could have been there all along,' said Southall.

'And we know he has a strong motive,' said Norman. 'I reckon that moves him to the top of our suspect list, don't you?'

'I'll get Judy to find out if he has entered the country,' said Southall. 'You get along to that house and see what you can find.'

'We're already on our way,' said Norman.

Norman ended the call with a happy sigh.

'What's happened?' asked Morgan, starting the car. 'It sounded like the boss knew about the house.'

'According to Rhiannon, Rhys has inherited Huw Jenkins's old house.'

'That's a bit of a coincidence,' said Morgan.

'Isn't it just?' said Norman. 'I said we'd get lucky in that pub, but, jeez, I never expected to get this lucky!'

'Do we need backup?' asked Morgan.

'Good suggestion, but I don't think that'll be necessary,' said Norman. 'We don't even know if the guy will be there, and we won't be too popular if we call the troops out to an empty house. Let's go and see if anyone's at home first, then we can decide.'

'Fair enough,' said Morgan.

'D'you know where we're going?' Norman asked.

'According to what they said in the pub, we head away from the bridge, follow the road from the village for about a mile and look for an old house on the right just after a left-hand bend. *Bryn Heulog* means "Sunny Hill", so that might give us another clue.'

They hadn't gone more than a couple of hundred yards before Morgan slowed down. She was staring at an old house built of stone with leaded windows.

'What's up?' asked Norman.

'There's the car that nearly ran us down,' she said. 'See it? It's sitting there in the driveway.'

'We haven't got time to mess around telling people off about their bad driving, Catren. If this turns out to be a wasted journey and that car's still there when we come back, you can stop and give the driver a piece of your mind. Right now, let's concentrate on our murder suspect.'

* * *

As they rounded the bend they spotted another stone-built house set back about fifty yards from the road among a small group of trees. As they drew closer, it became apparent that the house had suffered years of neglect and was in desperate need of some TLC.

'That must be the place,' said Morgan.

'It is if their directions were spot on,' said Norman.

Morgan pulled over so they could read the faint lettering on a sign by a dilapidated wooden five-bar gate, which sagged heroically across three quarters of the drive, where it appeared to have got stuck.

'Bryn Heulog. There we go.'

'Park in front of the gate,' said Norman. 'It looks as though it would disintegrate if anyone tried to open it.'

'Look up there,' Morgan said. 'That'll be the sunny hill, up behind the house. I bet it's a real sun trap in the summer.'

Norman followed her gaze. 'I see what you mean. It looks a bit overgrown, though. I wouldn't fancy trying to sort out a jungle like that.'

When they got to the gate, Norman stopped and pointed to the ground. 'This gate must be sturdier than I thought. See those drag marks?'

'They look recent,' said Morgan.

Norman looked up at the house. 'Yeah,' he said. 'I'm thinking someone might be home after all.'

'In that case, whoever it is will know we're here,' said Morgan.

'We'll soon find out,' said Norman, marching ahead of her up the drive.

They could clearly see the back end of a silver Jaguar parked behind the house. As there was obviously someone in the house, Norman decided there was no point in messing around. He strode up to the front door and hammered on it with his fist.

'If this is Rhys, he's not trying very hard to hide,' said Morgan.

'Well, if he thinks he's above suspicion, he's got a shock coming,' said Norman.

They waited, hearing the sound of a key turning and bolts being pulled back. The door creaked open to reveal a tanned, athletic-looking man with clear, bright blue eyes. From his grey hair Norman thought he had to be a couple of years older than him, but he could easily have passed for someone ten years younger.

He gave them a winning smile. 'Sorry about that. This door hasn't been opened in years, it's a tad stiff.'

'I'm DS Norman, and this is DC Morgan. We're from the Llangwelli Police,' said Norman, showing the man his warrant card. 'We're looking for Rhys Jenkins.'

'Well, you've found him,' said Jenkins. 'Actually, I've been expecting you.'

'You have?' said Norman.

'My sister, Rhiannon, said you'd be coming.'

Norman suppressed a frown, annoyed that Rhiannon had tipped Rhys off, although it wasn't exactly unexpected.

'I understand you wish to ask me some questions,' said Jenkins.

'Yes, that's right,' said Norman.

'Why don't you come in? It's not the Ritz, or at least not yet, but it's better than standing out there in that cold wind.'

Norman and Morgan stepped into the hall, while Jenkins struggled to close the door, fasten the bolts and lock it again.

'I've been using the back door,' he said. 'At least then I don't have to fight to get in every time.'

'I understand you've recently inherited this house,' said Norman.

'Yes, that's right,' said Jenkins. 'It was a bit of shock when I found out. Apparently, my uncle felt I deserved it, though I can't think why.'

'What about his son?' asked Norman.

'Died in a car crash ten years ago,' said Jenkins, 'along with his wife. Tragic really.'

'Oh, wow! That must have been hard for them,' said Morgan.

'They were devastated,' said Jenkins. 'You don't expect to bury your children, even after they've grown up. I was in the States at the time, so there wasn't much I could do to help.'

'Have you been here long?' asked Norman.

'Just a couple of days,' said Jenkins. 'I flew in at the weekend.'

'Oh,' said Norman. 'I understood your uncle died a while back.'

'That's right. I inherited the house about a year ago,' Jenkins said. 'I was tempted to come over as soon as my contract in the USA finished, but they asked me to stay on for a few months to complete a project. The bonus I got for it is going to pay for the renovation, so I'd have been a fool to turn it down.'

'Yes, I can understand that,' said Norman.

'Look, Sergeant, we both know you didn't come here to ask about my renovation plans, so why don't we cut to the chase?'

'You're right,' said Norman. 'I'm sorry for your loss, but I'm afraid we do need to ask you some questions about your relationship with your brother.'

'Of course, and I do understand why, although I'm not sure you could call it a relationship as such.'

'Yeah, I got the impression you and Gareth weren't exactly best buddies.'

Jenkins offered a rueful smile. 'You might call it an, er, uneasy relationship.'

'Uneasy?' said Norman. 'Didn't he bully you as a kid?'

'He used to take great pleasure in tormenting me when I was a child. Even when he left home to join the army, he'd come back on leave just so he could bully me and make my life a misery.'

'And then he stole your wife and destroyed your marriage. Is that right?'

Jenkins smiled again. 'It wasn't quite like that. They say it takes two to tango, and my first wife wasn't averse to the odd illicit dance, so it would be an exaggeration to say he "stole" her. She was a more than willing partner. Gareth thought I'd be shocked when I caught them together, but—'

'Rhiannon told us you broke his nose,' said Norman.

'Yes, it's true, I did punch him in the face, but it was more a case of revenge for the way he'd bullied me all those years. I'd always wanted an opportunity to hit back, and he'd just presented me with a perfect excuse, so I took it. But you must understand, I had already grown tired of my wife's dalliances by the time it happened. Gareth may have thought he was messing up my life, but in fact he did me a huge favour. Catching them red-handed simply made it so much easier for me to divorce her. It was my escape route.'

'I understand you're a software engineer?' asked Norman.

'Yes, that's right.'

'How did you end up in the USA?'

Jenkins shrugged. 'I was in the right place at the right time. The company I worked for was taken over by a US company and they asked me, as senior engineer, to stay on and oversee the project I had been working on. It meant moving over there, but as I had just left my wife and was at a loose end it was no-brainer, especially when they told me what the salary was going to be.'

'And that was when?' asked Norman.

'More than fifteen years ago now.'

'So, you would agree you're quite handy when it comes to computers and software?' asked Morgan.

'I would hope I'm a little more than "handy",' said Jenkins. 'You don't get to where I was by being anything less than an expert.'

'What exactly did it involve?' asked Norman.

'I was leading a project working on internet security software. Cybercrime is massive. We were trying to find ways of intercepting scams before they could gain momentum.'

'You'd know all about how to set up fake identities and stuff like that then?' Morgan asked.

'Could do it in my sleep,' said Jenkins. 'I assume you're referring to this scam Rhiannon says was perpetrated on Gareth. If so, then, yes, I could easily have set it up. But I didn't. And you'd better hope I'm telling the truth, because if I had, you wouldn't have a chance of tracing it.'

'You seem to be very confident about that,' said Morgan.

'I know my capabilities,' said Jenkins. 'I'm good at what I do. Anyway, why would I need Gareth's money when I've already got more than he ever had?'

'Revenge?' suggested Morgan.

'Revenge for what? My brother did me a massive favour. As far as I'm concerned, the slate was wiped clean the day I caught him in bed with my wife.'

'Can I ask where you were on Friday the sixth of April and over the following weekend?' asked Norman.

'Friday the sixth was the day I finally retired from my job, so I would have been in my office, or at least within the company premises, during the day. I took my wife and our two daughters out to dinner that evening. I spent the rest of the weekend at home with my wife.'

'This is your second wife, right?' Norman said.

'That's correct. I met her in the US.'

'And where's home?'

'It'll be here eventually,' said Jenkins. 'But I meant where we live in the States. We are planning to move to Wales.'

'Is your wife here in Wales now?' Norman asked.

'Unfortunately not,' said Jenkins. 'She's staying in the US until we've sold our house, and then she'll be coming over to join me. She's looking forward to helping renovate the house and can't wait to enjoy her new life in Wales.'

He directed that winning smile at Morgan. 'Look, I understand why you need to ask me these questions. I'd be doing the same in your place, but believe me, going to the States and meeting my wife is the best thing that's ever happened to me. There's no way I'd do anything to spoil that.'

Norman could see Morgan was convinced, but he wasn't so sure.

'Thank you for your time, Mr Jenkins,' he said. 'I think that's all we need to ask you for now, but we may need to speak to you again.'

'Of course,' said Jenkins. 'I intend to be here every day, but I'm staying at a hotel until this place is habitable. But just in case I'm not around, here's my card.' He handed Morgan a business card. 'I don't work there anymore but my mobile number is on the card.'

'Can you write the name of the hotel on the back of the card?' asked Norman.

'Of course.'

* * *

The two of them walked back down the drive.

'Better cross his name off the prime suspect list,' said Morgan as she started the car.

'He's too confident for my liking,' said Norman. 'He even admitted he knows how to set up a fake profile, and then bragged that we wouldn't be able to trace it.'

Morgan turned the car round. 'What he actually said was if he had created one we wouldn't be able to trace it,' she said. 'That's not the same thing. And anyway, if he was in the USA until a couple of days ago, he couldn't have been over here murdering Gareth, could he?'

'We've only got his word for that,' said Norman. 'If that farm track goes anywhere near this house, he goes back to the top of the list.'

'He probably doesn't even know it exists,' said Morgan, heading back into the village. 'Anyway, we'll soon find out.'

'What if he had an accomplice?' asked Norman. 'He stays in the US so he's got a cast iron alibi, while his accomplice does the deed.'

Morgan thought for a few seconds. 'Nah, I can't see it.'

'Really? You think he's kosher?' asked Norman.

'Yes, that's exactly what I think.'

'And you believe all that crap about Gareth doing him a favour by bedding his wife?'

'Why not? I have a friend who just knows her husband is playing away, but she can't prove it. She'd love to catch him at it so she can get concrete proof for a divorce.'

'Jeez, Catren, the fact some good-looking guy smiles at you doesn't mean he's not a murderer.'

'He was rather good-looking, wasn't he?' she said. 'His wife is a lucky woman. I wonder how long she'll be stuck in the States for, because he definitely qualifies for my "I would" folder.'

'Your what?'

Morgan grinned. She just loved it when Norman took the bait.

'He's a good-looking guy, I'm a red-blooded woman. So, yes, why not?'

'Jesus, Catren, he's a murder suspect!'

'Not for much longer.'

'You're unbelievable,' said Norman.

'Why, thanks, Norm, I appreciate the compliment.'

Norman stared at Morgan who kept her eyes resolutely on the road ahead. She was often so candid it was impossible to tell when she was joking. This was one of those times.

'This conversation is over,' he said, turning to face the front again. 'Just take us back to the office so we can bring the boss up to date.'

Smiling to herself, Morgan drove on in silence. She was so pleased with her success at winding up Norman that she forgot to look out for the red car that had annoyed her so much earlier.

* * *

'We think we've found an easier way they could have got Gareth's body to the dump site,' said Norman. 'There's a farm track on the other side of the stream. Catren's just going to check a map to see where in the village it comes out.'

'Oh, well done,' said Southall. 'What about Rhys Jenkins? Was he there?'

'Yeah,' said Norman. 'And his story matched what Rhiannon told you, but then it would, since she tipped him off. He's inherited the house, and he intends to renovate it and then bring his wife over from the USA.'

'I've checked with the Land Registry,' said Southall. 'He does own that house and has done for a year. Have you any idea how long he's been living there?'

'He says he's staying in a hotel for now, and he claims he only arrived in the UK last weekend,' said Norman.

'I'm just going to check with the hotel now,' said Morgan.

'According to him, he was in the US when Gareth was murdered,' added Norman.

'Judy's waiting to hear from immigration exactly when he entered the UK,' said Southall. 'But if it was over the weekend, he can't be our killer.'

'Then he must have an accomplice,' said Norman.

'You seem very sure, Norm.'

'He's just too confident. When we asked him if he could create a fake ID like the one that scammed Gareth, he said he could do it in his sleep. He even went on to boast that if he had done it, we'd never have been able to trace it back to him.'

'He knew about the scam?' asked Southall.

'Rhiannon had tipped him off about that too. I'm beginning to wonder if I'm wrong about her, and that she is involved after all.'

'Except that she was in Warwick when Gareth died,' Southall said.

'Then there must be a third person,' said Norman. 'Someone local.'

Morgan finished her call to the hotel. 'Rhys Jenkins booked into the hotel on Saturday afternoon. He booked his room last Monday, from the US. That ties in with what he told us about spending that weekend at home with his wife.'

'That doesn't mean he's not involved,' said Norman.

Judy Lane called out, 'Rhys Jenkins flew into Heathrow airport at eleven a.m. on Saturday the fourteenth of April. It's his first visit in years.'

'There you are then,' said Southall. 'He can't have murdered his brother.'

Norman set his jaw. 'I still think he's involved.'

'But we have no evidence to prove that, Norm,' said Southall. 'And until we find some, there's nothing we can do.'

'How's your mate doing with that laptop, Frosty?' asked Norman.

'I've not heard anything yet,' said Winter.

'Well, chase him up, will you?' asked Norman. 'I don't like the thought of Rhys Jenkins sitting in his hotel room, laughing at us.'

'And if there's nothing on the laptop?' Southall said.

'Then we've missed something,' conceded Norman.

'And you know what that means.'

Norman sighed. 'Yeah. It means we have to go back to the beginning and start all over again.'

'I've found out where that track comes out in the village,' Morgan said, 'but I'm not sure it's much help. It comes out on the other side of the village, but there are no houses close by.'

'I suppose we couldn't have expected it to lead straight to someone's front door,' said Norman. 'That would have been too much to hope for.'

'Even so,' said Southall, 'we now know it's there, and that someone could easily have used it to get the body to where it was dumped.'

'They'd need the right vehicle,' said Morgan. 'That's a farm track, which means a tractor or a quad bike. Either way, it's so muddy that you'd need four-wheel drive. That might help narrow it down a bit.'

Southall looked at the clock. 'Right, everyone, you're all doing well, but let's call it a day now. We'll head off home, get some rest and clear our minds for a fresh start in the morning.'

CHAPTER TWELVE

Wednesday 18 April

By lunchtime they had gone over the case again, and had come to the conclusion that unless Frosty's mate in the tech department could produce something from the laptop, they had tons of circumstantial evidence, but nothing concrete to point them towards Gareth Jenkins's murderer. That being the case, Southall allocated each of them a specific area to review, and headed for her office.

The afternoon passed in relative quiet. Shortly before five p.m., Norman made his way to Southall's office.

'Can I have a word?' he asked.

'Of course,' she said. 'What's up?'

'I know Gareth died in Pont Daffyd, and the blow to his head caused the heart attack that killed him, but have you forgotten someone was also poisoning him?'

'No, I haven't forgotten, Norm, but we're a small team and there's just so much we can do. I think they're one and the same person, but if we're going to find them, we need to focus on who actually did kill Gareth, rather than on who might have eventually done it if he hadn't been murdered in Pont Daffyd. There seems to have been so much going on in the background that if we can just find out who was behind it all, I'm pretty sure we'll have the killer.'

'You really think it's the same person?' asked Norman.

'What are the chances that two different people were trying to kill the same man at the same time?'

'I see what you mean,' said Norman. 'I guess, statistically, there's virtually no chance.'

'Exactly,' said Southall. 'When we eventually identify a viable suspect and search their house, I'm expecting us to find a supply of warfarin tucked away somewhere.'

'Okay. Fair enough,' said Norman. 'You're the boss.'

* * *

Morgan, who had been allocated the task of reviewing the statements taken from the residents of St David's Place, recalled that most of the neighbours had been out that day. Impatient to get on with her task, she considered going there now. Common sense told her to wait until she'd had time to review the interviews first, so she headed for home. Halfway there, she remembered that she hadn't yet spoken to the people at number fifty-four, who had been away last week. Glad of something to do, she turned round.

Ten minutes later, she was on the front step of number fifty-four. She rang the bell, and, a few seconds later the frosted glass blossomed as a light was switched on inside. A shadowy figure appeared, and the door opened to reveal a short woman with cropped brown hair and a warm smile.

'Mrs Newlands?' asked Morgan.

'Yes?'

Morgan produced her warrant card. 'I'm Detective Constable Catren Morgan from Llangwelli station.'

'Is it about poor Gareth from next door?'

'Yes, that's right.'

'I couldn't believe it when I heard what had happened,' the woman said.

'I wonder if you could spare a minute to answer a few questions.'

Mrs Newlands stepped back and swung the door open. 'Yes, of course. Come on in.'

Morgan stepped inside, and her feet almost sank into the plush carpet. She slipped her shoes off.

'Don't worry about your shoes, I'm sure they're clean enough,' Mrs Newlands said.

'It's okay,' Morgan said. 'I'd hate to spoil your lovely carpet.'

Mrs Newlands smiled. 'I expect you'd like a cup of tea.'

'Well, if you don't mind, that would be lovely,' said Morgan.

'You go and sit yourself down in there, I'll be with you in two minutes.'

Exactly two minutes later, Mrs Newlands appeared carrying a small tray on which two cups were balanced. She offered one to Morgan, and settled in an armchair facing her.

'Now then,' she said. 'How can I help?'

'I was wondering if you could tell me about Gareth, Mrs Newlands,' said Morgan.

'Please, call me Jo.'

'Oh, right, thank you, Jo. Well, we're trying to build a picture of what Gareth was like, and how he passed his time.'

'We've only lived here for just over two years, so I didn't know him that well. Of course, I never got to meet his wife, who died before we moved in. I've heard she was very popular. Gareth, on the other hand, kept himself to himself. But then we can't all be the life and soul of the party, can we? Anyway, I was told Gareth became a changed man after she died, and that I should steer clear of him. But he seemed okay to me. Whenever I saw him he always gave me a smile and a hello.'

'Was he a good neighbour?' Morgan asked.

'Oh yes. He was always polite, and never caused any trouble.' She frowned. 'You seem surprised. Have I said something wrong?'

'Let's just say that not everyone saw Gareth that way,' said Morgan.

'Ah. It sounds as if you've been speaking to Rose Mackie.' When Morgan didn't respond, she said, 'I realise you're not supposed to tell me what other people say, but you don't have to. That woman never has a good word to say about anyone, especially poor Gareth. It was Rose who told me I'd better keep away from him. I can't think what he could have done to make her dislike him so much.'

'She didn't say why you should avoid him?' Morgan asked.

'No, she didn't, but it wouldn't have made any difference. I like to form my own opinion of people,' Jo said.

'You seem to be the only person around here who liked him,' Morgan said.

'I doubt many of them really knew him. As I said, according to them, it was his wife who was the sociable one, while he kept himself to himself. Quiet individuals are often assumed to be unsociable, because people can't be bothered to make the effort to get to know them.'

'What about you? Did you get to know Gareth?'

'He wasn't one for conversation, but I got the impression he was a very sad person. I don't think he ever got over the loss of his wife. I often thought it was only looking after the dog that kept him going. Do you know what happened to her?'

'We found her in the house when we broke in looking for Gareth. One of our detectives is looking after her for the time being,' said Morgan.

'You see, that's so out of character for Gareth,' said Jo. 'He worshipped that dog. I can't believe he would have gone off and left her like that.'

Morgan nodded. 'The only decent thing to eat in the house was dog food.'

'Well, there we are then. That proves just how much he thought of that dog. As for what the neighbours think, it's not for me to say, but I suspect many of them were influenced by his neighbour on the other side.'

'I'm sorry. You mean—'

'Rose Mackie. That woman probably told the entire street to beware of Gareth. I don't understand it. Apparently, her husband used to do odd jobs for him and Alma. You wouldn't do that if you didn't like the person, would you?'

'Did he?' said Morgan. 'I didn't know that. Does he still do odd jobs for him — I mean up to his death?'

'I haven't seen him round there. But now you come to mention it, I don't think I've actually seen him at all.'

'What, never?'

'No, I don't think I have. Mind you if he's at work all day . . .'

'What makes you think Rose has been telling everyone bad stuff about Gareth?' asked Morgan.

'She was quick enough to tell me. Ask my daughter, Maria. She babysits for Rose sometimes. Maria's away on a school trip this week but she can tell you what Rose says about Gareth.'

'Your daughter babysits for Rose? How old is she?' asked Morgan.

'Sixteen.'

'That must be a challenging job. I met Rose's toddler the other day. He seemed a right handful to me.'

'Maria says he's no trouble. Apparently, he sleeps like the proverbial log. She even manages to do her homework while she's round there.'

'Perhaps he wears himself out during the day,' said Morgan. She finished her tea and closed her notebook.

'Well, thank you for your time, Jo. You've been very helpful.'

'Have I? I feel I should know more about Gareth after living here for over two years. Perhaps I should have got to know him better, but I don't think you should force yourself on people.'

'It's not a good idea in my experience,' said Morgan.

'Have you spoken to the couple who lived here before us — Mr and Mrs Hughes? They would have known Gareth when his wife was alive.'

'Do you know where they moved to?' asked Morgan.

'No, I'm sorry, I'm afraid I don't. I do hope you find out what happened to Gareth.'

'I'm sure we will,' said Morgan. 'Thank you for your time. I'll leave you my card in case you think of anything else.'

* * *

Morgan was on her way back to the car when on a whim, she carried on to number fifty, where Rose Mackie lived. Skirting the car parked on the drive, she went to the front door and knocked.

Rose opened the door and stared at her. 'Oh. Detective Morgan. What are you doing here?'

Morgan smiled. 'Sorry to disturb you, Mrs Mackie. I wondered if I might have a word with your husband.'

'My husband?'

'Yes. He wasn't here last week when I called, and as I was passing—'

'He's not here. He's at work, and then he's going out with his mates.'

'Oh, right. Can you tell him I called.' Morgan pulled a business card from her pocket and held it out to her. 'Here's my number. Perhaps you could ask him to call me.'

Reluctantly, Rose took the card. 'Yes. Perhaps I will. Now, if you don't mind, I'm a bit busy.'

Before Morgan could say anything, the door was closed in her face. Thoughtfully, she returned to her car and got in. She started it up, put it in gear, then changed her mind and switched it off again. She got out, walked back to Rose's house and stared at the car on the drive.

After all, why shouldn't there be more than one cherry red hatchback round here? Even so, it's a bit of a coincidence, isn't it?

She made a note of the registration number, got back in her car, and headed for home.

CHAPTER THIRTEEN

The day after her visit to Jo Newlands, Morgan was first to arrive at the office, eager to tell DI Southall all she had learned.

Southall listened, and immediately called the rest of the team to a meeting. 'Catren has something she would like to share with you.'

'Is it relevant to the case?' asked Norman.

'Let's hear what Catren has to say, and then we can decide,' said Southall, stepping aside to give Morgan the floor.

'Just as I was leaving work yesterday, I remembered I had missed out one of Gareth's neighbours, who had been away,' Morgan began. 'The lady in question is called Jo Newlands and she lives at number fifty-four, next door to Gareth's house. In the event, I had quite a long chat with Jo, who painted a totally different picture of Gareth to the one Rose Mackie presented. Rose is the neighbour on the other side of Gareth's house.

'If you recall, Rose told us that Gareth was rude and aggressive. Jo Newlands, on the other hand, called him a sweet old man who wouldn't say boo to a goose. She believes he never got over losing Alma, and that's why he kept himself to himself.'

'It's funny that they saw him so differently,' said Norman. 'But then Rose Mackie's house adjoins Gareth's, doesn't it? Perhaps the walls are a bit thin, and Gareth used to make a lot of noise at all hours.'

'Maybe,' said Morgan. 'But don't forget, Rose has a toddler. Perhaps it wasn't Gareth who was the noisy one.'

'Are you saying you think all the neighbours got it wrong about Gareth except Jo Newlands?' asked Norman. 'Is that likely?'

'She said that whenever she saw him, he always managed a smile, a wave, and a hello,' said Morgan. 'Yes, he kept himself to himself, but she also made the comment that quiet people are often assumed to be unsociable because others don't make the effort to get to know them. I'm wondering how much bearing that might have on the other neighbours' opinion of Gareth.'

'Has she lived there long?' Norman asked.

'Two and a half years,' said Morgan.

'I dunno,' said Norman. 'At least a dozen people say he was a nightmare. Do you want us to dismiss their opinions in favour of someone who was relatively new to the street?'

'She also said Rose Mackie made a point of telling her to steer clear of Gareth. She believes Rose spread the word among the rest of the neighbours, who judged Gareth on what Rose Mackie told them, and not on their own observations. I've met Rose Mackie and I know whose opinion I'd rather believe.'

'I've been thinking about this since Catren told me,' Southall said. 'I'm not sure how much help it is, but it's definitely food for thought. What else did you learn, Catren?'

'Jo reckons Gareth loved the dog, and would never have just gone off and left it. She even said she thinks the dog might have been the only thing keeping him alive.'

'Did she think he was suicidal?' asked Southall.

'She didn't say as much, but I think that's what she meant,' said Morgan.

'But we know he didn't commit suicide,' said Norman.

'Yes, but he was old, lonely and he was probably depressed. Who knows, he might even have had dementia. What if he went to Pont Daffyd because of his state of mind?' said Morgan. 'And when he got there, he was just in the wrong place at the wrong time.'

'I don't think so,' said Norman. 'No one keeps their laptop under a shed in a heavy-duty plastic bag unless they've got something to hide. And there's still Gaynor, and the missing money. No, I think it's all connected, and he went to that village for a reason.'

'Jo Newlands also told me that Rose Mackie's husband used to do odd jobs for Gareth and Alma. She couldn't understand why he would bother if Gareth was really such a pain. So, when I left her house, I went to the Mackies' to speak to the husband, but he wasn't there.'

'Did you ask Rose about him doing these odd jobs?' asked Southall.

'No. I didn't trust her to tell me the truth, and I was hoping to speak to him alone. I'm going to try and find him at work. I also intend to speak to Maria Newlands, that's Jo's daughter, who babysits for Rose Mackie. Apparently, Rose likes to fill her head with poison about Gareth.'

'Sounds like you're developing an obsession with Rose Mackie. I hope it's not going to get in the way of our investigation,' said Norman.

'I think Catren should carry on with this,' said Southall. 'By all accounts, everything was fine up until Alma died, so I'm beginning to wonder if something happened between Gareth and the Mackies after that — or at least, between Gareth and Rose Mackie.'

'That's what I'm thinking,' said Morgan. 'That's why I'd like to speak to Mr Mackie on his own.'

'Okay, everyone. You all know what you have to do today, so let's carry on, shall we?' said Southall.

Norman was turning to go when Morgan held him back. 'Remember that car that nearly ran us down in Pont Daffyd on Tuesday, Norm?'

'You mean that red hatchback?' said Norman. 'Don't tell me you still want to find the driver so you can bawl them out.'

'Guess what car Rose Mackie drives?'

'You're going to tell me it's a red hatchback, right?'

Morgan nodded. 'There was a red hatchback on her drive last week, and it was there again yesterday. It's definitely hers, and now we know the registration number.'

'Yeah, fine, but are you sure it was the one that nearly ran us down? I seem to recall you didn't get the registration number at the time.'

'You know I didn't. It was going too fast.'

'So, the fact that Rose has a similar red car parked in her drive proves nothing really, does it?'

'No, I suppose not.'

'I bet there are any number of small red hatchbacks within a twenty mile radius of Pont Daffyd. Are you sure you're not getting too hung up on Rose Mackie?'

Morgan sighed. 'Perhaps you're right. I'm just so sure that woman's up to something.'

'I'm not saying you're wrong, or that you shouldn't listen to your gut feeling, Catren, but don't let it become an obsession. If she's involved in this, you need to find some evidence to prove it.'

* * *

'Where to?' asked Winter from behind the wheel.

'Mackies,' said Morgan.

'It's number fifty St David's Place, isn't it?'

'No, not Rose Mackie's. Mackies the engineering firm. It's on that trading estate just this side of Carmarthen.'

'Is it a family business?' asked Winter.

'According to their website, Rose's husband's grandfather started it,' said Morgan.

'Wouldn't it have been easier to call at his house, or wait for him to call, if you left him a card?'

'I've missed him twice at home, and I'm not sure I can rely on Rose to give him the message, or the card,' said Morgan.

Winter glanced at her. 'You really don't like her, do you?'

'It's not that I don't like her, it's more that I don't trust her,' said Morgan. 'She's up to something.'

'What about the husband? What if they're in it together?'

'Then he'll tell us the same story as Rose.'

'Yeah, sorry, that was a stupid question,' said Winter, 'though I get the feeling you don't think he will.'

'Jo Newlands has lived in St David's Place for over two years. According to her, she sees Rose Mackie coming and going all the time but she can't recall ever seeing her husband. Don't you think that's strange?'

'I don't know. I know a couple of guys with their own businesses. They often work ridiculously long hours.'

'Says a detective who never knows when his day is going to end, or how early the next one will start,' said Morgan.

'Yeah, okay, but you know what I mean. And it's not as if neighbours socialise like they used to in the old days, is it?'

'Yes, I get that, but we're talking about someone living in the house next door but one over a period of two years, not just a couple of weeks. And even if he does work long hours, what about weekends?' said Morgan. 'You'd see him out in the garden, mowing the lawn or something, wouldn't you?'

'I see what you're saying,' said Winter. 'I'm just not sure I agree. I couldn't tell you what most of my neighbours look like.'

'You live in a poky little bedsit with no garden to go out in,' said Morgan. 'It's not quite the same.'

'Yeah, well, hopefully that's going to change before too much longer.'

'Oh, wow. Really? Are you going to live together?'

'I'd like to.'

'Have you asked her?'

'Not yet. I really believe it's the next step for us, but I don't want her to feel she's under pressure.'

'I think you should ask her,' said Morgan. 'She's a lot tougher than people think.'

'You won't tell her I said anything, will you?'

'Of course I won't. It's not my place, and what sort of friend would that make me?'

They drove on in silence for a few minutes.

'You realise it'll be a bit difficult to hide your relationship once you have the same address,' Morgan said.

'Yeah, I know,' said Winter. 'That's another reason for not rushing it. I haven't figured out how we're going to deal with that.'

* * *

As Morgan had said, Mackies was a small engineering company that occupied a unit on an industrial site a mile or two outside Carmarthen. Winter parked in one of the bays marked 'visitor' and he and Morgan made their way to the entrance. Inside the building, a series of arrows directed them to the reception, where a secretary sat in a partitioned-off area, working at a computer.

As soon as she saw them, she slid the window open and beamed up at them. 'Good morning. How can I help?'

Morgan showed the woman her warrant card. 'We'd like to speak with Ian Mackie.'

'Do you have an appointment?'

'No,' said Morgan. 'We believe Mr Mackie may be able to help us with a case we're working on.'

The secretary didn't seem to know what to do next.

'Perhaps you could ask Mr Mackie if he'd be able to speak to us,' suggested Morgan.

'Oh, yes, of course. He's not in his office but he can't have gone far. He's probably down on the shop floor. If you'd like to take a seat, I'll go and find him. It'll only take a minute or two.'

Two minutes later, the secretary was back at the window. 'Mr Mackie will be with you shortly. Can I get you tea, or coffee?'

'No, we're fine thank you,' said Morgan.

Barely a minute later, a tall, slim, rather good-looking man emerged from a door to the side. He smiled warmly, and offered his hand.

'Ian Mackie. When my secretary said the police wanted to speak to me, I thought it must be about a parking ticket I'm contesting. But that wouldn't need two detectives, would it?'

'Definitely not,' said Morgan, shaking his hand. 'I'm Detective Constable Morgan, and this is DC Winter.'

'Please, come through to my office,' Mackie said. He ushered them in and indicated two chairs in front of his desk. 'Now, how can I help?'

'Is it all right if my colleague takes notes?' asked Morgan.

'No problem. I don't think I've got anything to hide.'

'We're investigating the death of your neighbour, Gareth Jenkins—'

'Gareth? Dead? How?'

The shock on Ian Mackie's face was unmistakable.

'You didn't know?' asked Morgan. 'I'm sorry. I assumed you would, since you live next door to him.'

'I used to,' said Mackie, 'but I haven't lived there for a while now.'

'Oh. Your wife didn't say . . .'

'My wife likes to pretend I still live there. It's three years since we split up, and she still thinks I'm going back. Well, that's never going to happen.'

'Do you mind if I ask why you left?' asked Morgan.

'Oh, you know how it is,' said Mackie. 'People drift apart. I suppose it would be fair to say we wanted different things. But that's all water under the bridge now. What happened to Gareth?'

'He appears to have been attacked,' said Morgan.

'Oh my God, no. Where?'

'In a village called Pont Daffyd. Do you know it?'

'I know of it,' said Mackie, 'but I don't think I've ever actually been there.'

'I understand you did odd jobs for Gareth,' she said.

171

'Yes. I helped him out now and then. It first started years ago when Gareth bought a laptop and then realised he didn't know how it worked. He was struggling to get his email up and running, and Alma asked me if I could help. Neither of them had a clue. Gareth didn't even know you needed a telephone line to get broadband. He seemed to think it was built into the laptop.

'Anyway, I set up an internet connection for him, and showed him the basics. He was particularly keen to know how to use email. Even after I'd set it all up for him, I'm not sure he knew what he was doing half the time. I would have spent more time teaching him, but he said he didn't want to be a nuisance. If you ask me, I think it was more a case of being too embarrassed to ask for help.'

'Did he say why having email was so important to him?' Morgan asked.

'He said something about sending an email to someone every week, and he didn't want to miss it. I assumed he was keen to keep in touch with an old friend or something.'

'Can you remember what make of laptop it was?' asked Winter.

'I think it was an HP, but I couldn't say for sure. It must be ten years ago by now. Is it important?'

'Every little detail helps,' said Winter. 'But you were talking about helping Gareth and Alma.'

'Yes, well, after I'd set up the laptop for them, I realised the poor old things had no one to look out for them. So I kept an eye on them, and did the occasional odd job, like mowing the lawn, and things that needed doing around the house. Nothing major, just putting up the odd shelf, minor repairs, that sort of thing.'

'You must have got to know Gareth quite well then,' Morgan said.

'Gareth wasn't very chatty, to say the least, so the one I really got to know was Alma,' said Mackie. 'She was the talkative one. Gareth was a sweet old guy and seemed happy enough, but he was a real introvert.'

'Did either of them ever mention Pont Daffyd, or anyone who lived there?'

'Not as far as I remember, but as I said, Gareth was quite a private person. He didn't volunteer information easily.'

'We've been told he became a changed man after Alma died,' said Morgan.

'Yes, poor old bloke,' said Mackie. 'Alma was his world. He knew she was ill, and that she had only months to live, but I don't think it ever occurred to him that she would actually die. He seemed to be in total denial right up to the end. So, of course, when she finally did pass away, it knocked him for six. It was a tragic end to a real-life love story.'

'I understand they went travelling before she died,' said Morgan.

'Yes, that's right. I think she must have had a bucket list.'

'We've been told he became aggressive and abusive after Alma died. Is that right?' Morgan asked.

'Aggressive? No. He was certainly very sad, and he became a bit of a lost soul without her around. I suppose he was depressed, which was quite understandable, but he wasn't an aggressive person. Mind you, I stopped going to see him about a year ago. I suppose he could have changed since then, but I find it hard to believe.'

'Why did you stop seeing him? Did you fall out with him?' asked Morgan.

'Good heavens, no. When I first split up with my wife, I was still going to see him every Saturday morning. I'd cut his grass, sit with him over a cup of tea, make sure he had lunch, that sort of thing. But then my wife started to become a problem. She'd block my car in so I couldn't leave, or she'd come round to Gareth's house and doorstep the two of us.'

'That must have been awkward,' said Winter.

'I'll say,' said Mackie. 'I started going at different times to avoid her, but because I work such long hours, I could only go at weekends. Trouble was, being right next door, she always knew when I was there. I'm certain she sat at the window, waiting for me to arrive. Then she started hassling

Gareth even when I wasn't there, and things finally came to a head.'

'Hassling Gareth in what way?' asked Morgan.

'Gareth said she used to stand on his doorstep, ringing the bell and demanding to know what time I was coming, that sort of thing.'

'You should have called us,' said Winter.

'I did think about taking out an injunction against her, but Gareth wouldn't hear of it. He said he didn't want the police involved. Eventually, he said it would be better for all of us if I just stopped going.'

'And you did?' asked Morgan.

Mackie looked away. He seemed close to tears. 'To my shame. I allowed my wife to drive a wedge between me and a harmless, lonely old man. I still saw him now and then but only if I knew Rose wasn't going to be at home. The last time I saw him was about a year ago when I took him to one of those dog rescue places. I thought it would be good for him to have something to care about, and I hoped it would deter my wife if it barked at her. Do you know what happened to the dog? Is it okay?'

'The dog's fine,' said Morgan. 'It's being looked after by one of our detectives.'

'I'm really so sorry,' said Mackie. 'I should never have let her get away with it. Perhaps if I hadn't let Gareth down when he most needed me, he might still be alive.'

'I'm afraid there's no way of knowing that, Mr Mackie,' said Morgan.

He sighed. 'I suppose you're right. If only Rose hadn't been such a cow about everything.'

'If you wouldn't mind, I have a couple more questions,' Morgan said gently.

'Of course,' said Mackie. 'I'll answer as many as you want if it'll help you find out what happened to him.'

Morgan showed him the photograph of 'Gaynor'.

'Did Gareth ever mention this woman? Perhaps when you were helping him with his emails? We believe her name is Gaynor.'

Mackie looked at the photograph and shook his head. 'No, sorry. Who is she?'

'We're not sure,' said Morgan. 'She may have no relevance at all. How would you describe Gareth's financial situation?'

Mackie frowned. 'I didn't know him *that* well. He certainly didn't tell me how much he had in the bank.'

'Of course not,' said Morgan. 'But you must have got an idea. Would you say he was poor? Well-off, or what?'

'Oh, I see what you mean. Well, when I first met Gareth and Alma, they weren't rich, but they seemed pretty comfortable. He did let himself go somewhat after Alma died, but he insisted everything was fine.'

'So, if I told you he was sleeping on a camp bed, had hardly any furniture, no food in the cupboards and no money in the bank, would you be surprised?'

'Surprised! Are you kidding? Jesus, how low had he fallen?'

'What about his health?' asked Morgan.

'He wasn't in the best of health, but he said it was just the usual little aches and pains of old age.'

'He wasn't taking any prescription drugs?'

'Not that I'm aware of. He had a thing about herbal remedies, but he got those over the counter.'

'One more thing,' said Morgan. 'I spoke to the neighbour at number fifty-four, but she's not been there long. She said the couple who lived there before her might have known Gareth better. They were a Mr and Mrs Hughes. Did you know them?'

Mackie looked as if he'd been slapped.

'Er, well, yes.' He licked his lips. 'Of course I knew them, but not well.'

'You wouldn't happen to know where they moved to?' asked Morgan.

'No. Sorry. I have no idea.'

Morgan studied Mackie's face. Was he hiding something? She couldn't be sure.

'Well, thank you for your help, Mr Mackie,' she said, getting to her feet.

'Pleasure,' he said. 'I'm only sorry I didn't stay in touch with poor old Gareth.'

Morgan handed him a business card. 'We'll be in touch if we have any more questions, but if you think of anything else, please call me on that number.'

* * *

'What do you think?' asked Morgan, after they'd been driving for a while.

'I think you're going to suggest it's my turn to buy lunch,' said Winter. 'But I've paid the last three times I've been out with you, so it can't be my turn again.'

'Okay, I'll buy lunch if you're going to be so tight-fisted about it,' said Morgan. 'But that's not what I meant.'

'You're really buying lunch?' said Winter. 'Oh, well, in that case . . . I think Mackie genuinely didn't know Gareth was dead. And he's going to be feeling guilty about not keeping in touch with him for a long, long time.'

'He did seem genuinely shocked when we told him,' said Morgan.

'It's interesting that Gareth wanted to know how to use email,' Winter said.

'That would tie in with that weekly alert thing he set up,' said Morgan.

'Yes, but Gareth managed to find Gaynor, and he seems to have developed a taste for a bit of online porn, so he must have known something about computers,' said Winter.

'Well, he did have ten years to learn about them,' said Morgan.

'If his landline had been cut off, he would have had no internet connection,' said Winter, 'so how was he still sending that weekly email?'

'Yes, I was wondering that,' said Morgan. 'And what about Mackie's reaction when I mentioned the name Hughes?'

'Anyone would think you'd thrown a turd in his face,' said Winter.

'Would you like to hazard a guess as to why?' Morgan said.

'Jo Newlands moved in a couple of years ago, right?'

'Correct,' said Morgan.

'And we know it can take a few months for a house sale to go through.'

'Right again.'

'We'd have to check the timings and what have you, but it's a bit of a coincidence that around the same time Ian Mackie leaves his wife, the Hugheses decide to sell their house and move away. Or am I just being cynical?'

'They say this job makes you cynical,' said Morgan. 'But whether or not that's true, we both seem to be thinking along the same lines.'

'It's intriguing, isn't it?' said Winter. 'Should we have pushed him a bit more about it?'

'Where do you draw the line on privacy?' said Morgan. 'The thing is, if it's not relevant to the case, then we're just being nosy and, anyway, he doesn't have to tell us.'

'Yeah, I suppose there is that,' said Winter. 'And we can always go back for more if it becomes relevant. Mind you, I'd love to find Mr and Mrs Hughes and see what they have to say.'

'My money's on Mr Hughes and Mrs Mackie being the naughty ones,' said Morgan.

'Any particular reason?'

'Mackie seems a decent guy. Not only about Gareth, but he left his wife with the house.'

'Yeah, and a baby,' said Winter.

'Maybe the baby is why they broke up, but he let her stay in the house because of it,' said Morgan.

'I don't think her having the house proves anything,' said Winter. 'I mean, he told us he walked out, but what if he was telling a lie? Perhaps it was the other way around, and Rose booted him out because he was playing away at number fifty-four with Mrs Hughes?'

'It's funny Rose didn't mention any of this when I spoke to her,' said Morgan. 'If anything, she gave me the impression that everything was hunky-dory with her marriage.'

'Yeah, but didn't Mackie just tell us she likes to pretend he's coming back?'

'But it's been three years,' said Morgan. 'She must know by now that that's not going to happen.'

'Perhaps when he first left, Rose was embarrassed to tell anyone, and now it's too late.'

'Embarrassed? I find that hard to believe,' said Morgan. 'Rose doesn't strike me as the sort of person who gives a damn what other people think.'

'What about her harassing Gareth?' said Winter.

'Yes, that was an interesting little nugget of information, wasn't it?' said Morgan.

'D'you think she's capable of it?'

'I certainly wouldn't put it past her,' said Morgan. 'Like I said before, I'm sure that woman is up to something.'

'Does that include murder?'

'I wouldn't rule it out,' said Morgan.

* * *

'Your tech guy, Zack, called while you were out,' Lane told Winter when he returned to the office. 'He asked if you could call him back.'

'Great,' said Winter. 'He must have finished going through the laptop.'

He rushed to his desk, grabbed the phone and sank into his seat.

'Zack? Hello, mate. What have you got for me?'

It was a good ten minutes before Winter put the phone down. He logged onto his PC, printed a copy of the email Zack had just sent him, and headed for Southall's office. The door was open, but Winter knocked anyway.

Southall looked up. 'Frosty. Come on in. What can I do for you?'

'I've just been speaking to Zack from the tech department,' said Winter.

'Wow. That was quick. Perhaps you'd better handle all our tech requests from now on. Did he find anything you didn't?'

'Sort of,' said Winter. 'You know I said the stuff with Gaynor started about three years ago?'

'Yes, you showed me all the emails.'

'Well, the thing is we saw what we were supposed to see, not how things really were.'

'Huh? What does that mean?' asked Southall.

'At first glance it looks as if it all started three years ago, but in reality, all those emails were loaded onto the laptop after Gareth died.'

'I'm not sure I understand what you're saying.'

'The email thread was created on another computer and then loaded onto Gareth's laptop to make it look as if Gaynor and Gareth had been corresponding for years.'

'Can you do that?' asked Southall.

'Zack says you can if you know what you're doing, though most people wouldn't have a clue where to start. And once it's uploaded it's virtually impossible to tell it's not real.'

'Does he know when it was loaded onto the laptop?'

'About a month ago, he says. He's going to send a full report with the exact dates and stuff.'

'Your friend Zack isn't suggesting Gareth did this himself, is he? Didn't your friend say it was done after he died?'

'Zack thinks two people have been using the laptop. One knows what they're doing, and the other is what Zack calls a "fumbler".'

'Gareth being the fumbler,' Southall said. 'So, who is the other user? Could you do it?'

'You mean set up a false email trail like that?' asked Winter. 'I guess I probably could, but I would need someone to give me detailed instructions.'

'Presumably you could find instructions like that on the dark web,' said Southall. 'What about someone like Rhys Jenkins? Could he do it?'

'Computer security is his field, so I'm sure he could,' Winter said.

'We need to let everyone know about this,' said Southall. 'Is there anything else?'

'Zack says the screen saver image of Gaynor was uploaded at the same time as the emails, and in his opinion the image is definitely doctored. The body and the face aren't from the same person. He also said someone had set up internet banking on the laptop some time ago, but he didn't think it was Gareth.'

'Why not?'

'Because it doesn't look as if Gareth ever logged into it.'

'I don't suppose Zack's had a chance to follow the money, has he?' Southall asked.

'Not yet,' said Winter. 'That's his next job.'

'Right, let's tell the others,' said Southall.

* * *

When Winter had finished explaining what Zack had found, Southall said, 'So, it looks as if someone planted Gaynor on Gareth's laptop as a red herring, and we took the bait. We need to find out who that was, and why. What are they trying to divert us from?'

'It has to be Rhys,' said Norman. 'We know he's got the skills, and even if he says he's forgiven Gareth, we've only got his word for it.'

'But he was in the USA,' said Morgan.

'Maybe he has an accomplice over here,' argued Norman.

'Whoever it was, they'd need access to the laptop to add that stuff, wouldn't they?' said Lane. 'Or could it be done remotely?'

'You can do more or less anything remotely these days,' said Winter. 'But the computers at both ends would need to be online. As far as we know, Gareth had no broadband at the house.'

'He must have had access somehow,' said Norman. 'Don't forget, we know for a fact he was sending at least one email every week.'

'Frosty, would your friend Zack be able to find out how Gareth was getting online?' asked Southall.

'Ian Mackie told us he set up Gareth's internet connection when he first got the laptop,' said Morgan. 'He'd know.'

'Talking of Mr Mackie, we can't rule him out,' said Southall. 'He knew Gareth had the laptop and if he was a regular visitor, he might even have a key to the house.'

'But what's his motive?' asked Norman.

'He moved away and stopped going to see Gareth,' said Southall. 'Why did he do that? Did they fall out over something?'

'But he left his wife. Then, when he did go to see Gareth, she caused trouble,' said Winter.

'That's his story,' said Southall. 'But do we know it's true? We need to ask Rose about the marriage break-up and see what she says.'

'I'll go,' said Morgan eagerly.

'In the morning, and Norm will go with you,' said Southall.

'But—'

'Do you have a problem with that, Catren?' asked Southall.

Morgan considered for a moment. 'No, boss, of course not.'

'Good,' said Southall. 'Now, as we're all here, we might as well kick the ball around for a few minutes. If you remember, we didn't find a single piece of paperwork at Gareth's house, not even so much as a bank statement. I think that's very odd. I'm convinced someone removed it all.'

'Yeah, but why?' asked Norman. 'They'd know we can get access to bank statements and phone records, wouldn't they? You see it all the time on TV.'

'Maybe they're not as clever as they think they are,' said Morgan.

'It's funny you should say that,' said Lane. 'As Frosty has been busy, I've been taking another look at Gareth's bank statements. Now we already know there were some large transfers out of Gareth's account, but I noticed something odd in the smaller transactions.

'From the bus pass usage records, we know Gareth used to go to Carmarthen every Monday morning. I thought that was probably to do his weekly shop, and now I've had a chance to have a look at the bank statements, I believe I've confirmed that, because every week, fifty pounds was withdrawn from an ATM at his end of town. The withdrawals were always made between two and three in the morning, either on a Sunday or a Monday.'

'He drew the cash while he was walking his dog?' said Norman.

'That's what I'm thinking,' said Lane. 'It fits perfectly with what we know. But other amounts were also being withdrawn at other times of the day, and from different ATMs. Yet we're told Gareth didn't go out during the day, and that he never went far from home.'

'How much are we talking about?' asked Southall.

'A hundred pounds, sometimes two hundred, once or twice a week,' said Lane.

'Taken out where?'

'Mostly around Carmarthen,' said Lane, 'but sometimes as far as twenty miles away.'

'If it was on a Monday, it could still have been him,' said Morgan.

Lane shook her head. 'These withdrawals are always made towards the end of the week.'

'And this has been going on how long?' asked Southall.

'Over two years,' said Lane. 'The last time was three months before Gareth was murdered.'

'Jeez, no wonder the poor old guy was broke,' said Norman. 'Someone was bleeding him dry.'

'But he must have known,' said Winter. 'I mean, you might miss the odd fifty quid here and there, but surely, if it was happening every week he'd see it on his bank statements.'

'But what if he wasn't getting any bank statements?' asked Southall. 'Zack said someone had set up internet

182

banking on the laptop, but he didn't think Gareth ever used it. I remember when I first set up internet banking, I was given the option to change to paperless statements. What if someone else set up Gareth's internet banking without his knowledge, and what if one reason they did it was to opt for paperless statements?'

'And if they used a fake email address, it would allow them to do it without Gareth knowing, and then steal from his account without him ever receiving a statement to show money was going missing,' said Norman.

'But wouldn't he have checked his balance when he withdrew cash from the ATM?' asked Winter.

'Not necessarily,' said Southall. 'Not everyone does, they don't even bother to get a receipt. And don't forget we're talking about a lonely, depressed and possibly confused old man who we suspect had no idea about internet banking or paperless statements.'

'Now we're beginning to narrow it down,' said Norman. 'It has to be someone who had access to the house, and who Gareth trusted.'

'What about Rhiannon?' said Winter. 'Didn't you say she had a key?'

'Yeah, but she's seventy years old, and she lives in Warwick,' said Norman. 'Are you suggesting she'd come all the way from Warwick to Carmarthen every week just to draw a couple of hundred quid from his bank account? It would probably cost half that to make the journey.'

'Maybe she's in cahoots with the solicitor,' insisted Winter.

'You mean Elwyn Thomas?' said Norman. 'What motive could he possibly have? He's loaded!'

'I think we're looking at Rhys Jenkins, or Ian Mackie,' said Southall. 'But I'm not totally convinced about either of them. Gaynor might not be real, but I think she's key. And I've also got a nagging feeling we're missing something that's right under our noses.'

CHAPTER FOURTEEN

Friday 20 April

Norman and Morgan were about to set off for St David's Place when Norman said, 'I take it you know why Sarah wanted me to come with you.'

Morgan grunted. 'You told her I'm obsessed with Rose Mackie, and she's asked you to keep an eye on me.'

'Is that what you think? Well, I'm afraid you're wrong. I didn't have to tell her, you already did that yourself.'

'I'm perfectly capable of putting aside my personal feelings when I'm on a case,' Morgan retorted. 'I'm not stupid, you know.'

'Yeah, I know that,' said Norman. 'Believe it or not, if you have good reason to suspect Rose Mackie of being up to no good, that's sufficient grounds for us to take note. But Rose isn't stupid either. If the two of you are alone when you question her, it's your word against hers. You should know that. We're on the same side, Catren, but we can't just storm in and accuse her. We need evidence.'

Morgan thought for a moment. 'Yeah, I suppose you're right. I'm sorry.'

Norman smiled. 'There was no need to make an apology, but as it's you, I'll take it as one — for always criticising my taste in music.'

'Oh no you don't. I'm not apologising for that!' said Morgan.

'You just did,' said Norman. 'That being the case, if we can just add catching out Rose to your apology, I'll be having a pretty awesome day.' They pulled up outside number fifty-four, and Norman got out, giving Morgan no time for a retort.

When she opened her front door, it was clear that for her part, Rose definitely wasn't having an awesome day. She glared at the two detectives.

'Mrs Mackie,' said Morgan. 'Good morning. You know me, of course, and this is DS Norman. We have a couple more questions for you.'

'Oh, have you?' said Rose. 'Well, I'm sorry but you've had a wasted journey. I'm just about to go out.'

Norman looked her up and down. 'Barefoot? And in your pyjamas?'

'Look, I have a toddler who is a right handful. I barely have time to put my clothes on.'

'How old is the toddler?' asked Norman.

'He's nearly three.'

'He seems quiet enough now,' said Norman.

'He's asleep.'

'Isn't he a bit young to be left on his own?' Norman said innocently.

Rose almost stamped her foot. 'Of course I wasn't going to leave him on his own.'

'I'm glad to hear it,' said Norman. 'Anyway, now we've established that you're not going out after all, perhaps you'd like to answer our questions.'

Rose sighed wearily. 'Do I have a choice?'

'According to DC Morgan, you said you wanted to help find out who murdered your next-door neighbour,' said Norman. 'Did she get that wrong?'

Rose hesitated. 'Is this going to take long?'

'It'll take a lot longer if you continue to stand here arguing with us,' said Morgan. 'Come on, Rose, let us in. It'll take ten minutes, if that.'

'I suppose I can spare ten minutes. You'd better come in.'

They followed her into the kitchen where she pointed at a table and four chairs. 'Sit down if you want.'

Ignoring the offer, Norman went to the window and looked out. The back garden looked tired and neglected, and the lawn was badly in need of mowing.

'Nice garden,' he said. 'Is that a gate through to Gareth's garden?'

Rose started. 'What?'

'There's a gate in the fence,' said Norman. 'And since Gareth's garden is on that side . . .'

'Oh, that,' said Rose. 'My husband put it there a few years ago. It's been nailed shut for years by now.'

'Was that in the days when you and Ian used to do odd jobs for Alma and Gareth?' asked Morgan.

'Yes, that's right. I'm sure I told you about that last time.'

Morgan nodded. 'Yes, you did. Now Ian's told me what jobs he did for them, what about you? What did you do?'

'You've spoken to Ian?'

'I went to see him yesterday morning at Mackies. He told me he left you about three years ago,' said Morgan.

Rose waved a hand. 'He'll be back, you'll see.'

'Ian says not. He says he's gone for good,' said Morgan.

Rose began to pick at her nails, which were already bitten down to the quick.

'You must have pissed him off big time to cause him to leave you with a newborn baby,' Morgan added.

'I don't know why he left. You'll have to ask him that,' Rose said.

'I did,' said Morgan. 'He says you grew apart.'

'There you are then,' said Rose. 'We grew apart.'

'To be honest, I thought he was being diplomatic when he said that,' said Morgan.

'I don't know what you mean.'

'Oh, I think you know exactly what I mean,' said Morgan. 'Anyway, we can come back to that later. Do you know Pont Daffyd?'

Rose's eyes narrowed. 'Pont who?'

'Pont Daffyd. It's a small village about ten miles from here.'

'Why are you asking me that?'

'It's where Gareth's body was found,' Morgan said.

'I hope you're not suggesting I had anything to do with that. I've never heard of Pont Daffyd, and I certainly haven't been there.'

'Are you sure?' said Morgan. 'Only we saw a car like yours in Pont Daffyd just the other day.'

'Well, it wasn't me.'

'Oh well, if you say so,' said Morgan. 'I must have been mistaken.'

'Yes, you must have,' said Rose.

'I was speaking with Jo Newlands the other day,' said Morgan.

'Who?'

'Jo Newlands. She lives at number fifty-four, the other side of Gareth's house.'

'Oh, her. I hardly know her.'

'She told me you advised her to steer well clear of Gareth,' Morgan said.

'I just warned her what to expect from the miserable old sod. I was being neighbourly.'

'Jo says she found Gareth to be a sweet old boy who wouldn't say boo to a goose.'

'What can I say?' said Rose. 'He might have been nice to her, but he behaved like a shit to me.'

'That's funny. When I asked Ian about Gareth, he agreed with Jo Newlands that he was a lovely, gentle soul. He says Gareth became very sad after Alma died, perhaps even a bit depressed, but he never once saw him lose his temper, or swear at anyone.'

'Yes, well, that's easy for him to say, isn't it? He'd already buggered off by the time the old fart started to become a problem.'

'Is that so?' said Morgan. 'Ian puts it a bit differently. According to him, he used to visit Gareth most weekends, and he was as sweet as ever. Sad and lonely, but never aggressive.'

'Is that why you nailed the gate shut, Rose?' asked Norman.

'The nosy old sod kept coming in through the gate, wandering around my garden with that filthy dog of his, so I asked Ian to nail it shut.'

'Don't you like dogs?' asked Norman.

'I hate bloody dogs,' said Rose. 'Dirty creatures — and they shit everywhere.'

'I find her a sweet little thing,' said Norman.

'Anyway, it wasn't just the dog. The dirty old devil used to come and peer in the windows. I don't know if he was hoping to catch me naked or what, but he scared the life out of me on more than one occasion. It was frightening, being harassed like that. It was like having my own personal stalker living next door.'

'You think he was stalking you?' Norman asked.

'Of course he was. What would you call it?'

'Didn't it occur to you that maybe he was just a sad, lonely old man looking for some company?' asked Norman.

'I'm telling you he was stalking me. I don't know why, but he was.'

'That's funny, because according to Ian, it was the other way round. He says that he used to come and see Gareth after he left you, and whenever he did, you caused so much trouble that eventually he stopped visiting. He hoped you'd stop harassing Gareth if he stayed away.'

'Me? Harassing Gareth?' said Rose. 'I did no such thing!'

'Are you sure about that?' asked Morgan.

'Yes, I bloody well am sure!' Rose shouted. 'How dare you come here making accusations like that.'

There was a brief silence, punctuated by the sound of Rose breathing hard.

'That's quite the temper you have there, Rose,' said Norman. 'I wouldn't like to get on the wrong side of you, I must say.'

'You have to stand up for yourself against perverts like that dirty old man, especially when your husband clears off and leaves you with a baby. You can't let people push you around.'

'I bet you make sure they don't,' said Norman.

'Are we finished now?' asked Rose.

'Just one more question,' said Morgan. 'Jo Newlands suggested that the people who lived in number fifty-four before her would probably have known Gareth better than she did. Their name was Hughes, but she didn't know where they'd moved to. I wondered if perhaps you might know where they are now?'

Rose blenched. 'I didn't know them very well. And I've no idea where they went.'

'It was a bit of a coincidence, wasn't it? Those two deciding to move house at about the time you and Ian split up,' said Morgan.

'What's that supposed to mean?' hissed Rose.

'What, coincidence?' said Morgan. 'It means two apparently unconnected things happening at the same time.'

'I've never thought about it,' said Rose.

'The thing is, Rose,' Morgan said, with a glance at Norman, 'Sergeant Norman here is what you might call an old-school detective. The thing about old-school detectives is that they've been brought up to believe that there's no such thing a coincidence, and that things that are apparently unconnected are nearly always connected in some way. We just need to figure out how.'

Rose glared at Norman. 'Well, I hate to disappoint your *old* detective, but he is completely wrong this time. The fact that the Hugheses moved away just as me and my husband temporarily separated really is a coincidence. Now, if you've no more questions, I have things to do.'

'Okay, Rose, we'll get out of your way,' said Norman, and paused. 'For now.'

* * *

'Rose Mackie would win a gold medal in the Olympic lying final,' said Morgan on their way back to the car.

Norman chuckled. 'Yeah, she is pretty good, isn't she?'

Morgan swung her door open.

'Hang on a minute,' said Norman. 'Before we go, I want to take a look at Gareth's back garden.'

'You do?'

'Humour me,' said Norman. 'There's something I want to check. It will only take a couple of minutes.'

Morgan closed the car door and followed Norman round to the back garden of number fifty-two. 'Are you going to tell me what this is about?'

'Rose just told us the gate between the gardens was put there when Alma was alive, but it had been nailed up. Knowing she has a problem telling fact from fiction, and noticing that her grass hasn't been cut recently, I thought I might check for myself.'

'What does it matter if her grass hasn't been cut?' asked Morgan, trailing after him.

'Well, it looked to me as if the grass had been trampled, as if someone has been walking up to that old gate. Which led me to ask myself why they would do that if the gate didn't open.'

Norman stopped at the gate and pointed at the ground in front of it. 'Right. Here we are. Now tell me what you see.'

Morgan shrugged. 'Grass gone wild, and foot high weeds where there should be a lawn.'

'Yeah, but what about right in front of the gate?'

'Oh, I see what you mean. It's flat, and almost clear of weeds.'

'Right,' said Norman. 'And I would say it got that way through the gate scraping the grass when it was opened.'

Norman pointed back to number fifty-four.

'Now, look at the weeds from here towards the house.'

Morgan followed Norman's pointing finger.

'Oh, now I see what you mean. It's not easy to make out but it's like there was a path there.'

'Right. Only not an old path from three years ago,' said Norman. 'I think we're talking about a path that's been used much more recently, maybe as little as two weeks ago. And unless I'm very much mistaken, it leads from this gate — that Rose says has been nailed shut — straight to the patio outside Gareth's back door.'

'It's not very clear,' said Morgan.

'Yeah, but if it hasn't been used for a week or so, the weeds would have sprung back up, wouldn't they?'

Morgan studied the area Norman had just indicated. 'What about the gate? Does it actually open?'

Norman tried the latch, and smiled as it softly clicked open.

'Well, what do you know?' He opened the gate just enough to make sure it wasn't fixed in place. 'I'm not opening it any wider because I don't want Rose to see what we're doing.'

'That's wide enough to prove it for me,' said Morgan. 'The gate opens, there's definitely a path, and it's been used recently.'

'Right, so now we know her story is full of holes,' said Norman. 'C'mon, let's go.'

'Why don't we arrest her?' asked Morgan, following Norman back to the car.

'Because if we go charging in there now, she'll probably feed us a load more bullshit about how she was only going round there to keep an eye on him. And how are we going to prove any different?'

'You're right,' said Morgan, gloomily. 'She tells so many lies we'd never know what to believe anyway.'

'Exactly,' said Norman, opening the car door. 'We have good reason to believe she's up to something, because we know some of her answers are pure horseshit. For that reason, we don't want to be asking her more questions until we know what the right answers are.'

'We need to build a case first,' said Morgan, sliding into the driver's seat.

'You've got it,' said Norman.

'Okay, so where do we start?' asked Morgan.

'Do you fancy going back via Pont Daffyd?'

'Do you mind telling me why?'

'Remember that old house where you thought you saw a car just like Rose's hatchback? I thought it might be worth a visit. Just to see if they can tell us whose car it was.'

'Ah, you agree it's the same car then?'

'I agree it's possibly the same car,' said Norman. 'It could just as easily belong to whoever owns the house. But, as it won't take more than an extra half hour to drive back that way, and neither of us are in a rush to get back . . .'

'Your wish is my command,' said Morgan. 'Let's find out.'

* * *

It was approaching midday by the time they reached Pont Daffyd. Morgan parked on the road outside the house. There was a dark blue Lexus on the drive, and lights glowed warmly behind the small leaded windows. A sign outside the house read *The Old House*.

'It's not exactly an original name, is it?' Morgan said.

It was an apt description, as Norman pointed out. The Old House was indeed very old, built of stone with a slate roof. 'What more do you want in a house name?'

'A bit of imagination doesn't hurt,' Morgan said.

'Who needs imagination? If I was looking for The Old House, this is exactly the sort of thing I'd expect to find.'

'I suppose I can't argue with that,' said Morgan. 'Though I didn't realise we'd come here to discuss the merits of house names.'

'We haven't. I don't care what the house is called. I just want to ask the owner a couple of questions. At least there's someone at home. That's a good start.'

'Why have they got the lights on?' asked Morgan.

'Those small leaded windows look picturesque all right,' said Norman, 'but they make it as dark as anything inside.'

He stomped off up the drive, leaving Morgan to chase after him.

An oak-beamed porch had been added to the front of the house at some stage in the past. Underneath, the front door appeared to be made of solid oak. Norman was momentarily nonplussed — no one could possibly hear him knock — until he realised that the ancient bellpull wasn't merely decorative.

'Wow! A real bellpull,' he said. 'You don't see many of those these days.'

He tugged at it, and a bell jingled in the depths of the house.

'Hear that?' said Norman. 'It works!'

'It doesn't take much to excite you, does it?' muttered Morgan.

'I think it's an age thing,' said Norman. 'I'm at that stage in life where I take pleasure in the little things.'

Before Morgan could think of a smart answer, they heard a key turn in the lock. A bolt was slid across, and the door creaked open to reveal a tall woman, her age hard to discern in the half-light under the porch. Glossy dark hair fell to her elbows, and she had round, rimless glasses perched on her nose.

'How can I help you?' she asked, giving Norman a dazzling smile. He blushed, acutely aware of Morgan at his side, and that she had a smirk on her face.

'Er, good morning. I'm DS Norman,' He produced his warrant card. 'And this is my colleague, DC Morgan. We're investigating an incident that occurred in the village recently, and wondered if you'd mind answering one or two questions.'

The woman put a hand to her mouth. 'Goodness, how exciting! I've never been questioned by the police before. What have I done?' Her face fell. 'Oh, God. Listen to me, behaving like an overgrown schoolgirl. Of course, you're here about the man who was found dead, aren't you?'

'Could I ask your name, please?' Norman said.

'Millicent Harmsworth. I was so shocked when I heard about that poor man, but I honestly don't see what help I can be.'

'We're not actually here about the murder, Mrs Harmsworth,' said Norman.

She bestowed another disarming smile on him. 'There's no need to be so formal, Sergeant. Please call me Millie.'

'Oh, er, right,' said Norman. 'Well, er, Millie, the thing is, the incident we're interested in happened on Tuesday.'

'What time on Tuesday?'

'Around this time, actually.'

'Ah. We wouldn't have been here. My husband and I were at a business meeting in Cardiff. We didn't get back until quite late.'

'You don't own a red hatchback by any chance, do you?' asked Morgan.

The woman pointed to the saloon on the drive.

'That's mine,' she said. 'My husband drives a Jaguar. Why do you ask?'

'There was a red hatchback parked on your drive last Tuesday,' said Norman.

'A red hatchback? On our drive?'

'Yes, that's right.'

'Did the driver kill that man?'

'I don't think so,' said Norman. 'But we do need to identify the driver.'

'Do you know anyone who drives a red hatchback?' asked Morgan. 'Could they have been visiting, and didn't realise you wouldn't be at home?'

'No, I don't think so. I've one or two friends with small cars, but they're not red. You don't think they were trying to break in, do you?'

'Are you missing anything?' asked Norman.

'Good heavens, no. If anything was missing, I would have called the police.'

'Is your husband here? Maybe he knows someone with—'

'I'm afraid he's away at a conference in Bristol, but I'm sure he doesn't know anyone with a car like that. We have the same friends, you see.'

'And you can't think of any reason why anyone would have been here?' asked Morgan. 'You didn't have anything delivered, like a small parcel?'

'I wouldn't have arranged a delivery knowing I wasn't going to be here. We're both architects and we work from home a lot. I'm sorry I can't be of more help.'

'That's okay, Mrs Harms— er, Millie,' said Norman. 'Thank you for sparing us your time.'

'Do you want to leave me a card or something?'

'I'm sorry?' said Norman.

'A card. In case I think of anything that might be helpful. When I speak to my husband later, I'll ask him. You never know, he might be able to help.'

'Oh, right, I see,' said Norman. He turned to Morgan, who was smirking again. 'Do you have a card for Mrs Harmsworth?'

'Me?'

'Yes, Catren, you. A card for Mrs Harmsworth, please,' said Norman.

'Oh, right, of course. I've got one here somewhere.'

Morgan fished a card from her pocket and handed it over.

Millie Harmsworth looked at the card and beamed at them. 'Excellent. If Martin thinks of anything, I'll let you know.'

As they made their way back down the drive, they heard the door close behind them. Morgan sniggered.

'Don't say a word,' warned Norman.

'Who, me? I don't know what you mean.'

'You know exactly what I mean.'

195

'It's all right, I can understand why you were blushing,' said Morgan.

'I was not blushing.'

'Oh, come on, Norm, you were glowing like a traffic light! And you were even more embarrassed when she made it clear her husband was away. For a minute there I thought I was going to have to take over.'

'You're confusing me with someone else,' said Norman. 'Why should I be interested in where her husband is?'

'Let's be honest here, Norm. She was a very attractive woman, and she obviously took a shine to you.'

'Rubbish! I'm old enough to be her father.'

'Oh, come on, she was fifty if she was a day.'

Back in their car, Morgan leaned back in her seat, ready to enjoy herself.

'What was it she said now? "Please call me Millie." I mean, that's an invitation for a start. And the eyes she was making at you. What was that all about?'

'She was not making eyes at me,' protested Norman. 'Those big round glasses just made it look that way.'

'It's not surprising,' continued Morgan. 'Lots of women fantasise about older men. I know I do.'

'Right, that's it,' said Norman. 'This conversation is over.'

'Are you honestly saying you wouldn't add her to your "I would" list?'

'Listen, Catren, much as it may surprise you, I'm very happy with Faye, in fact I'm happier than I ever have been. Consequently, I don't have, and nor do I need, an "I would" list. Now, can we drive back to Llangwelli without any more of your suggestions about a woman I have no interest in, except perhaps as a potential witness?'

With a happy smile, Morgan started the car. She would never tell him this, but much as she loved to tease Norman, she also adored him. She didn't know much about his past, but whatever had happened to leave him alone at sixty, she was really pleased that he was happy at last, and that he loved Faye so much.

* * *

When they got back to the office, Southall was conferring with Judy Lane, who was looking particularly pleased with herself.

'Have our lottery numbers come up?' asked Morgan.

'Not quite,' said Southall. 'But while you've been out, Judy has managed to locate the Hugheses who used to live at number fifty-four St David's Place.'

'The people who moved from Jo Newlands's house?' said Morgan. 'Have they gone far?'

'Swansea,' said Lane.

'What's that, twenty miles away?' asked Norman. 'Do you want us to go and speak to them?'

'You don't have to go that far,' said Lane. 'I spoke to Rachel Hughes earlier. She's in the area this afternoon, and she'll be happy to speak with us. She'll be here at around two thirty.'

* * *

The first thing Morgan noticed about Rachel Hughes was her huge brown eyes, made even larger by dark shadows that hinted at sleepless nights. Small, blonde and delicate looking, she seemed to be bearing the weight of the whole world on her shoulders. Morgan met her in reception, led her through to the interview room and introduced her to Norman.

'It's very good of you to spare the time like this, Mrs Hughes,' said Norman.

'I often take my lunch break around now, so it's no trouble,' she said. 'Mid-afternoon is a kind of lull before the storm, if you know what I mean. It gets busy later when people pick their kids up from school and even more so when everyone finishes work. When your colleague phoned, she said you wanted to speak to me about Gareth Jenkins.'

'That's right,' said Morgan. 'I take it she told you why.'

'Yes. I had no idea anything had even happened to Gareth. Poor thing. He was such a nice old man.'

'You got on well with him?' asked Morgan.

'It's funny, isn't it? You think you know someone, but when you stop to think about it, you realise you didn't really know them at all, if that makes sense. He was nice enough, but it was his wife, Alma, that I knew best. She was lovely. It was very sad when she died.'

'Do you remember how Gareth reacted to her death? Did he change at all?' Morgan asked.

'He was very sad. Getting more than a word or two out of him had been difficult before, but after Alma died, it was almost as if he'd lost the ability to speak. He sort of turned in on himself and shut the world out, if you know what I mean.'

'Was he ever any trouble?' Morgan asked.

'Trouble? Gareth? Good heavens, no. If he saw you, he'd say hello and maybe ask how you were, but otherwise you would hardly have known he was there.'

'So, as far as you're concerned, he was a good neighbour and you got on with him?' asked Morgan.

'I'd say so, yes. And I felt desperately sorry for him. After Alma died, I used to worry that he wasn't eating enough, so I made the odd thing for him, you know, like a stew or a cake. Even now I've moved, I still cook him the odd cake if I'm going to be coming out this way.'

'That's good of you,' said Norman. 'How did he feel about that?'

'He was always grateful, but try as I might, I never managed to get more than a thank you out of him, let alone a conversation. It was like squeezing blood out of a stone, you know?'

'When was the last time you did that?' asked Norman.

'I've been very busy recently, so I can't say exactly. At a guess, I'd say it was probably about a month ago, but I can look in my diary if you like.'

'How did Gareth seem on that occasion?' asked Morgan.

'I don't think I saw him that last time. I always brought the cake in a tin, so if he didn't answer the door, I could leave it on the doorstep.'

'That would explain the empty cake tin we found in his kitchen,' said Morgan.

'What about your husband?' asked Norman.

Rachel looked surprised. 'My husband?'

'Did he get on with Gareth?'

'Oh, I see what you mean. I'm not sure what he'd say about that, if I'm honest.'

'Sorry, I don't quite get that. You're not sure what he would say?' asked Norman.

'We're separated. We have been for nearly three years now.'

'Oh, I'm sorry to hear that,' said Norman.

'I'm not,' said Rachel. 'I was glad to be shot of him. Bastard.'

'Bit of a shit, was he?' asked Morgan conspiratorially. 'Let me guess — playing away from home?'

'Next door but bloody one isn't playing very far,' said Rachel bitterly.

'Are we talking about Rose Mackie?' asked Morgan.

Rachel nodded. 'I thought she was my best friend, but what best friend has your husband's baby? Best friend, my arse!'

'Oh, wow. That must have hurt,' said Morgan. 'Is that why you moved?'

'I was too embarrassed to stay there once I found out. I felt such a fool,' Rachel said.

'How did you find out?'

'Daniel works from home. Someone told me they'd seen him sneaking round to see Rose while I was out at work. Ian Mackie works long hours, so he was out of the way, too. We were both taken for a pair of fools. When I confronted Daniel about it he said it hadn't meant anything, whatever *that* means. It was actually him who suggested we sell the house, move away and start again.'

'It didn't work out?' asked Morgan.

'I would probably have forgiven him eventually, but when Rose announced she was having Daniel's baby, it was a step too far. I kicked him out after that little bombshell landed.'

'Are you going to divorce him?'

'If I do that, I'll have to give him half the house. There again, unless I get right away from here and make a fresh start, I'll probably never get over it.'

'Where's Daniel living?' asked Norman.

'I don't know, and I don't care,' said Rachel. She looked at her watch. 'I'm sorry, but I'm going to have to get back to work.'

'That's okay,' said Norman. 'I think we've finished for now.'

'Let me show you out,' said Morgan.

'I hope I haven't bored you with my problems,' said Rachel when they got to the door.

'That's okay,' said Morgan. 'We all need to vent now and then.'

'Did I answer your questions all right?'

'Yes, thank you,' said Morgan. 'You've been very helpful.'

* * *

She got back to find Norman waiting for her. 'So, you were right about Ian Mackie,' he said.

'What about him?' asked Morgan.

'He told you him and Rose had "grown apart," but you said you thought he was being diplomatic.'

'I guess he didn't want to admit she'd made a fool of him.'

'Yeah, I suppose so,' said Norman. 'Anyway, it's definitely another one we can add to Rose Mackie's list of fibs.'

'What about Rachel?' asked Morgan. 'Did she seem credible to you?'

'We saw the cake tin, so we know that much is true,' said Norman.

Morgan regarded him shrewdly. 'But?'

200

'Maybe we should have pushed her more on her husband's whereabouts.'

'You think she knows where he is?'

Norman shrugged. 'I'm wondering how she is going to send divorce papers to him if she doesn't know his address.'

'Don't forget you can do anything online these days,' said Morgan.

'Yeah, but even so, I'm sure she'd still need his address.'

'Perhaps she doesn't intend to divorce him,' said Morgan. 'I mean, she's not obliged to, is she? She said she doesn't want to give him half the house. Maybe she means it.'

Norman shrugged. 'Maybe I'm behind the times, but wouldn't Daniel have some sort of say in it? Bastard or not, he might insist they divorce. He'd probably get half the house in that case, whether she wants him to have it or not.'

'Maybe Rachel hasn't realised that yet,' said Morgan. 'Changing the subject slightly, if Daniel's the father of Rose's baby, do you think he's still seeing her?'

'Yeah, that little bit of news opens up a whole new can of worms, doesn't it?' said Norman. 'And I wonder how Ian Mackie feels about it? Perhaps he was being diplomatic to hide his real feelings.'

'It's getting complicated, isn't it?' asked Morgan.

'More so every day,' said Norman.

CHAPTER FIFTEEN

'So, it seems that Gareth was very different from the way he was initially portrayed,' said Southall. 'Far from being the isolated, crabby old man Rose Mackie described, he was in fact a sweet old thing for whom Ian Mackie did odd jobs and Rachel Hughes made cakes.'

'And now we know that the gate between the gardens was never actually closed off, it appears Rose Mackie may have been visiting him. Or do we believe her version, and Gareth was in fact stalking her?'

'I'm sorry, but I can't believe a thing Rose says,' said Morgan. 'Especially after Norm proved the gate does work, and has been used fairly recently.'

'Now we know people did visit Gareth, it opens up a new possibility,' said Southall. 'What if one of these visitors saw he was struggling to cope, and took it upon themselves to help him? Perhaps that someone informed him that banks no longer send statements.'

'That would be the same someone who was simultaneously emptying his bank account, right?' said Winter.

'Unless there's more than one person involved,' said Southall.

'My money's on Rose,' said Morgan.

'But we can't ignore Ian Mackie, Rachel Hughes, Daniel Hughes, along with some other visitor we're not yet aware of,' said Southall. 'And let's not forget Rhys Jenkins. As Norm said, what if he had an accomplice? It could even be one of the neighbours, or ex-neighbours. Is there a link between any of them and Rhys?'

'I think we learned something else from Rachel Hughes, even though she never actually mentioned a name,' said Norman.

'Go on, Norm,' said Southall.

'We know Rose Mackie and Daniel Hughes were having an affair, right? Rachel said she found out about it when someone told her they had seen Daniel sneaking round to see Rose when he was supposed to be at home working. I think we all know who that someone is.'

'It could have been anyone,' said Winter.

'Yeah,' said Norman, 'it could have been, but most of the people who live around there are out at work during the day. I think it's more likely to be someone who was around. And who do we know who was nearly always at home?'

'You mean Gareth?' asked Southall.

'Yeah, why not?' said Norman. 'He lived next door to both of them. He could easily have noticed what was going on; he might even have been spying on them.'

'But Gareth himself was heartbroken, wasn't he?' asked Morgan. 'It's a bit rich to dob another guy in for breaking their partner's heart.'

'Don't forget, Ian and Rachel used to look out for him,' said Norman. 'He could have been fond of both of them and didn't like the idea of Rose and Daniel cheating on such nice people. Or maybe he just didn't like Rose and Daniel. Jeez, does it really matter why he did it? The fact remains he did. And if I'm right, it gives Rose and Daniel a powerful motive for murdering him.'

'But we don't even know if they're still in contact,' said Southall. 'Of course, if we knew where Daniel Hughes lived . . .'

'Yeah, I'm sorry,' said Norman. 'I should have pushed Rachel about it, though to be fair, we didn't even know they were living apart until she told us.'

'Who's to say it isn't Daniel *and* Rose?' said Morgan. 'It could be either of them, they both have a motive.'

'I don't think we should rule out Ian or Rachel,' chipped in Winter. 'They were two happy couples until the affair came to light. Now Ian and Rachel have lost all that, and they might blame Gareth for taking it away from them.'

'I'm not disagreeing with any of these theories,' said Southall, 'but it concerns me that we still don't know why Gareth went to Pont Daffyd.'

Morgan's mobile phone started to ring. She headed for the kitchen to answer it, while the others sipped patiently at their tea. A few minutes later, she emerged from the kitchen with a broad grin on her face.

'That was Millie Harmsworth,' she said. 'It seems she had a chat with her husband about that red hatchback, and he thinks he knows why it was on their drive. It turns out they have a chalet at the bottom of their garden. They were going to rent it out as an Airbnb, but then a friend told them of someone who urgently needed a place to stay. Anyway, it turns out the lodger has a girlfriend who often visits him and, according to Martin Harmsworth, she drives a red hatchback.'

'So?' said Norman. 'That doesn't really help us, does it? How come you look so pleased with yourself?'

Morgan's smile grew even wider. 'What if I told you the lodger is called Daniel Hughes? That help, does it?'

'You mean the hatchback is Rose Mackie's, and she was visiting Daniel Hughes?'

'Yep,' said Morgan.

Norman grinned at Southall. 'Well, there you go. Didn't you say there was something right under our noses?'

'And what have I been telling you?' said Morgan. 'I knew it was her car.'

'Jeez, he was probably right there when we were talking to Millie Harmsworth,' said Norman. 'If only we'd known . . .'

'Yes, except we didn't,' said Southall. 'And anyway, we don't know for sure that it's even the same Daniel Hughes.'

'It's too much of a coincidence, Sarah,' said Norman. 'It must be him.'

'I can see how it looks, and I'm sure you're probably right,' said Southall. 'But we need to make sure of our facts before we jump to any conclusions. Who said they don't believe in coincidences, eh?'

'What if Rose or Daniel enticed Gareth into going to Pont Daffyd?' asked Morgan.

'And how did they do that?' asked Norman. 'From what we know of Gareth, it would need to be one hell of an incentive to get him out of his house and on to a bus, unless he was going shopping. And that only happened on Mondays.'

'Hold on. Didn't I just say we shouldn't jump to conclusions?' said Southall. 'Let's start by establishing that it is Daniel Hughes.'

'I've just thought of something else,' said Winter. 'Our theory is that someone was staying in Gareth's house because they were looking for his laptop, but they didn't find it because Gareth had hidden it under the shed, right?'

'I think we're all agreed on that, Frosty,' said Norman.

'Are we assuming it was this person who planted Gaynor and the other stuff on it?' asked Winter.

'That's a fair assumption,' said Southall. 'What's your point?'

'Well, Gareth wouldn't have hidden the laptop from someone who was helping him with it, so why couldn't they find it after he died?'

'I see what you mean,' said Southall. 'You think there were two people.'

'I think it's got to be a possibility,' said Winter.

'But if it was two people working together, they'd both know where the laptop was,' said Morgan. 'Unless, of course, they weren't working together!'

'Two different people looking for Gareth's laptop at the same time? I think that might be just too much of a coincidence,' said Southall.

'There is another possibility,' said Norman. 'We're told Gareth had no clue about how to use computers, but what if he managed to figure out that someone was messing with the laptop? Perhaps that's when he decided to hide it under the shed.'

'And that's why they couldn't figure out where it was,' said Morgan.

'Right,' said Norman. 'I mean, who keeps a laptop outside?'

'That works for me,' said Morgan.

'This is all very clever,' said Southall, 'but it still doesn't explain why Gareth went to Pont Daffyd.'

'I still think Gareth's brother, Rhys, is involved,' said Norman. 'What if Gareth went looking for the house Rhys had inherited? Maybe he thought he would find him there.'

'Yes, but why?' asked Southall.

'Maybe he wanted to ask for his help,' suggested Winter. 'If he'd figured out someone was messing with the laptop, maybe he thought Rhys could help him sort it out.'

'Now that's an interesting take on things,' said Southall.

'Yeah, except we know Gareth and Rhys hadn't spoken in years,' said Norman. 'Wouldn't he be more likely to turn to Ian Mackie, since he'd helped him in the past?'

'What if Rhys and Rhiannon are keeping the truth from us?' said Morgan. 'Don't forget Rhys said that as far as he was concerned, the slate had been wiped clean. Maybe he'd been in touch with Gareth all the time.'

'I can't see it,' said Norman. 'We found no evidence on the laptop to suggest such a thing.'

'Or, as I said earlier, what if Daniel or Rose enticed him?' said Morgan.

'Why would he want to see Daniel?' asked Southall.

'I think I might know the answer to that,' Judy said, looking up from her screen. 'Daniel Hughes is a software engineer.'

'So is Rhys,' said Norman.

'But we know Rhys was in the USA at the time,' said Lane, 'whereas Daniel Hughes is a freelance games designer and mostly works from home. Maybe Gareth was going to Daniel for help with the laptop.'

'I have a problem with this line of thinking,' said Norman. 'If Gareth was going to Pont Daffyd to ask for help with his laptop, why did he hide it under the shed? Wouldn't he have taken it with him?'

'Good point,' said Winter. 'Even the cleverest expert can't fix a laptop if he hasn't got access to it.'

'So, what are we thinking?' asked Norman. 'Because I'm now wondering if perhaps Gareth wasn't on that bus because he was looking for help, but because he'd worked out who was messing with his laptop and draining his bank account.'

'Are we seriously suggesting Gareth went to see Daniel Hughes to have it out with him?' asked Southall. 'Is that something a man as sick as Gareth was would be likely to do?'

'I get what you're saying,' said Norman, 'but don't forget Ian Mackie said Rose had been tormenting Gareth for three years. Imagine that was you, and then on top of that you found out Daniel had been messing with your laptop and emptying your bank account. Don't you think that would be enough to tip you over the edge?'

Southall thought for a moment. 'You're now saying you think Rose and Daniel are in it together? What about Rhys? I thought he was your number one suspect.'

'I'm not ruling Rhys out,' said Norman, 'but it makes sense that Rose and Daniel are both involved, doesn't it? Especially if Gareth was the one who revealed their affair.'

'I think we can all agree on that,' said Southall. 'However, right now it's just conjecture. We're going to need a lot more evidence if we're going to ask for a warrant to search their properties.'

'As it's the weekend, we're unlikely to get one before Monday, anyway,' said Norman.

'Don't worry about that, Norm. If we can gather enough evidence today, I can get a search warrant signed off tomorrow,' said Southall.

'You plan to start early on Monday?' asked Norman.

'That's exactly what I'm planning,' said Southall. 'Then we can be knocking on their doors with search teams at six a.m. They'll love that. However, as I said, if we're going to go ahead with it we need more evidence, and we need it today.'

'That's what we're here for,' said Norman.

'Right then, Norm. As you and Catren already know where this house is, I'd like you two to head over to Pont Daffyd. Speak with this Daniel Hughes, and confirm he's the one we're looking for.'

'It'll be a pleasure,' said Norman.

'Frosty, I'd like you to come with me,' said Southall. 'We'll call in on Ian Mackie to see if he confirms what Rachel Hughes said about the affair. We also need to speak to Jo Newlands's daughter, Maria. I'd have liked to speak to her before Rose Mackie, but she's away on a school trip, so we're going to have to wait till she comes back.'

'I'll contact Jo Newlands and see if Maria's back,' said Lane. 'If not, she must have a mobile phone. I'll ask for her number, then you can speak to her straight away.'

'Good thinking, Judy,' said Southall. 'It's worth a try. Let's all meet back here later so I know we've got what we need. As it's Saturday, we can have a working lunch, my treat.'

* * *

Half an hour later, Morgan and Norman were in Pont Daffyd and pulling up outside the Old House.

Morgan switched off the engine and turned to Norman with a mischievous smile. 'If you want to check in with your friend Millie, I can stay here for a couple of minutes so you can speak with her in private.'

'That remark is beyond contempt,' said Norman, 'and not worth a response.'

'Ooh. Have I said too much?' she asked.

'Listen, Catren. I put up with your messing about because it seems to make you happy, it's rarely offensive, and it's often quite funny, but if you really want to start moving up the ranks, you need to understand that there's a time and a place for it. As we're about to come face to face with a man who could be Gareth Jenkins's murderer, I don't think this is it, do you?'

'No, I suppose not,' Morgan said in a small voice.

'It's not as if we haven't spoken about this before, is it?'

'I was only trying to lighten the atmosphere.'

'There'll be plenty of time for that afterwards,' he said.

'Yes, of course, you're right,' said Morgan. 'I'm sorry.'

'Right. To answer your original question, what's going to happen now is that we forget what just happened and concentrate on the job we came here to do. That means you are going to walk up to the house, ring the bell and inform the householder that we're on the premises but there's no need for her to be alarmed. Then you're going to tell her we're looking for the lodger and could she please point the way to the cabin.'

'Chalet,' said Morgan. 'They call it a chalet.'

'Believe it or not, I don't give a toss what the correct terminology is. All I want to know is how to get to it. When you've found that out, I'll join you and we'll go and speak to Daniel Hughes. Is that clear?'

'Yes, perfectly,' said Morgan.

Norman sat in the car and watched Morgan walk to the house and tug at the bell pull. When he saw the front door open, he got out and loitered at the bottom of the drive until he saw Morgan step away from the front door. Millie Harmsworth spotted him immediately, and waved enthusiastically, so that he was obliged to wave back. Then she disappeared inside, and he was able to breathe a sigh of relief.

'Okay then, which way?' he asked Morgan.

She led him towards a gate at the side of the house. 'Through this gate and follow the path down to the end of the garden.'

'Is he here? I don't see a car,' Norman said.

'He doesn't park on the drive. There's parking for the chalet at the bottom of the garden, apparently,' said Morgan. 'You get to it from a lane that joins the road.'

When they got to the gate, Norman stopped and let out a gasp.

'Jeez! Look at the size of this garden. And that lawn! It must take all day to mow.'

'I expect they can afford a sit-on mower,' said Morgan.

'You'd certainly need one,' said Norman.

The path led them around the edge of the lawn and behind a group of huge rhododendron bushes.

'Are you sure this is right?' asked Norman. 'I don't see any chalet.'

'She said the chalet is hidden by the bushes,' Morgan said.

They followed the path beneath the overhanging branches of the rhododendrons. The effect was not dissimilar to the 'tunnel' where Gareth's body had been found.

'This seems eerily familiar,' said Norman.

'Perhaps it's a sign,' said Morgan.

'I'm not sure I believe in that stuff, but I hope you're right.'

After about fifty yards the rhododendrons began to thin out and the chalet finally came into view. It was the size of a small bungalow and was built like an Alpine chalet. A white picket fence completed the effect.

'Ah! Isn't it cute?' said Morgan. 'It's just how I imagine the gingerbread house in the middle of the forest. You know, like in the fairy-tale.'

'It does look pretty quaint,' said Norman. 'But somehow I don't think it's made of gingerbread. That building is made out of wood, so I'd say that makes it a log cabin.'

'A pedant might argue it was made out of planks, not logs,' said Morgan.

Norman turned a withering gaze on her.

'Not that I would,' added Morgan hastily. 'I think pedantry is highly overrated.'

'I'm glad to hear it,' said Norman. 'Now, come on, let's go and see if Hansel's at home.'

'Who?' asked Morgan.

'Hansel. As in Hansel and Gretel. Weren't they the ones in the gingerbread house? Or have I got my fairy tales mixed up?'

Morgan rolled her eyes. 'And you say I'm the one who goes off on a tangent.'

'It's hardly a tangent if you've already raised the subject,' said Norman. 'Besides, compared with you I'm a complete beginner.'

They made their way along the side of the chalet, Norman peering in through the windows as they went.

'I can't see anyone in there,' he said. 'I hope we haven't trekked all the way down here for nothing.'

'Someone must be at home,' said Morgan, rounding the front of the chalet. 'Look, there's a car.' She pointed to a mud-spattered, dark green Range Rover Discovery parked on the far side of the building.

'Look at how muddy it is,' she observed. 'D'you think he's been driving down any farm tracks recently?'

'I like your thinking, but it's been nearly two weeks since Gareth's body was dumped,' said Norman. 'Anyone with half a brain would have washed the mud off their car the very next day. Anyway, look at this lane. You couldn't possibly drive up and down here without getting mud on your car.'

Norman led the way to the front door. There was no bell, so he thumped hard on it. He waited a few seconds and then raised his fist to knock again, but dropped it on hearing movement inside.

When the door finally opened Norman found himself looking straight at a man's chest. Apparently, their talk of fairy tales had been spot on, and this was a giant. Daniel Hughes was at least six feet six inches tall, possibly more.

He obviously worked out too, as could be seen from his broad shoulders and the muscles rippling under his tight-fitting T-shirt. He had what Norman often heard described as a ruggedly handsome face, with piercing blue eyes and brown shoulder-length hair tied back in a ponytail. He wasn't smiling.

'Daniel Hughes?' asked Norman.

'Who wants to know?'

Norman showed his warrant card. 'I'm DS Norman, and this is DC Morgan. We're from Llangwelli station.'

Hughes managed a grudging half smile. 'Police? What can I do for you?'

'We're investigating the death of Gareth Jenkins. His body was found here in Pont Daffyd just over a week ago.'

'Oh, yeah. I heard a body had been found. I mean, I was sorry to hear about it, but what's it got to do with me?'

'You knew Gareth, didn't you?'

'Did I?'

'We understand you used to live in St David's Place, Llangwelli.'

'That's right, I did,' said Hughes. 'Oh, wait a minute. Of course! He was the old guy who lived at number fifty-two, wasn't he?'

'That's him,' said Norman.

'I still don't see how I can help. I moved from there almost three years ago.'

'We're trying to build a picture of what Gareth was like. As a former neighbour, you may be able to fill in one or two blanks for us, or perhaps confirm the odd fact.'

Hughes seemed about to refuse, and then relented. 'Why don't you come in? It's a bit on the small side, but if you don't mind—'

'Small is fine with us,' said Norman.

'Sorry to be so suspicious, but you can't be too careful, you know?' Hughes said, and stepped back for them to enter.

'Do you need to be careful?' asked Norman.

'Out here in the middle of nowhere having people turn up unexpectedly on your doorstep isn't exactly a regular occurrence,' Hughes said.

'I see what you mean,' said Norman.

Hughes ducked through the doorway to a room on the left. A small television screen was affixed to one wall, with two armchairs facing it on either side of a small open fireplace.

'Do you like being out here in the middle of nowhere, or are you hiding?' asked Norman.

'Hiding? No. I came here because I needed somewhere to stay, and at the time this was all I could find. And then when I got here, I found I enjoyed the solitude, so I stayed.'

'Was that after your wife kicked you out?' asked Morgan.

Hughes grimaced. 'That's not quite how it was.'

'Rachel told us she kicked you out because she found out Rose Mackie was having your baby.'

'Look, I admit I had an affair with Rose, but that's all,' said Hughes. 'Rose says the baby's mine, but I've seen no proof. Anyway, I told Rachel it wasn't mine and she accepted that. She even thought we could get over it if we moved house. Sadly, it didn't work out, so, as it was my affair that had caused the problem, I thought it only right that I be the one to move out.'

'How very noble,' said Morgan.

'Now wait a minute,' said Hughes. 'You're out of order judging me.'

'You're right, we are out of order,' said Norman. 'But can I ask how the affair came to light?'

Hughes shrugged. 'I don't know. I suppose Rachel must have got suspicious.'

'You don't think someone told her about it?'

'I have no idea. And anyway, what's the failure of my marriage got to do with some old guy dying?'

'Come on, Daniel, show a bit of respect,' said Norman. 'He wasn't just "some old guy", he was someone you knew. And he didn't just die. He was murdered, and then his body was dumped in a stream.'

'You're right,' said Hughes. 'No one deserves to die that way and, yes, I do owe him more respect than that.'

'Did you know him well?' asked Norman.

'Hardly at all if I'm honest. We used to say hello but that was about it. I'm not a great one for socialising, that's why it suits me out here, where people can't find me.'

'So you are hiding,' Norman said. 'Are people looking for you?'

'Only Rachel.'

'You're hiding from her? Why?'

'Because she wants us to get back together and try again. I've told her it won't work, but she keeps on and on at me. If she knew I was here, I'd never get any peace. She writes to me all the time, you know.'

'Email, or letters?'

'Both,' said Hughes. 'I managed to stop the emails, but I still get two or three letters a week.'

'How do her letters get to you if she doesn't know where you live?' asked Norman.

'When I left Rachel, I had all my mail redirected to a PO box in Carmarthen. The postman doesn't deliver out here, so I've kept it on. I collect my mail whenever I go into town.'

'What about Rose Mackie?' asked Norman. 'Do you still see her?'

'No, I don't,' said Hughes. 'Rose was a mistake, and not one I intend to repeat.'

'Is she looking for you?'

'Why would she be looking for me?'

'Well, if you're the father of her baby . . .'

'I just told you, I am not that baby's father.'

'Why would Rose tell Rachel and Ian Mackie that the baby is yours if it isn't?' asked Norman.

'I don't know. Maybe she wanted to cause trouble. She's like that.'

'So, you haven't seen her recently, and she hasn't been here. Is that right?' asked Norman.

'Why would she come here?'

'You just said she likes to cause trouble. I'm just asking if she's been here causing trouble?'

'Of course not. She has no idea where I live.'

'What do you do for a living, Daniel?' asked Norman.

'I'm a freelance computer games designer.'

'Wow. Impressive,' said Norman. 'I guess you need to be pretty handy with software coding and what have you to do that.'

'I'm pretty good at it,' said Hughes proudly.

'Do you work from home?'

'There are two bedrooms here, so I use one as an office. That's where I was when you knocked.'

'You have broadband out here then?' asked Norman.

'5G,' said Hughes. 'There's an antenna not far from here so the signal's pretty reliable, and fast.'

'Can I ask where you were on Friday the sixth of April between midday and midnight?' asked Norman.

Hughes looked taken aback. 'I'm not a suspect, am I? I thought you just wanted to know more about Gareth.'

'It's just routine,' said Norman. 'No one else has refused to tell us.'

'I'm not refusing,' said Hughes. 'It's just that I thought you guys worked by — well, you know, detection, not by making lucky guesses. Does this mean you have no idea who did it?'

'We're asking everyone we speak to,' said Norman. 'If you could just give us an answer . . .'

'I would have been here, working,' said Hughes.

'What about the evening?'

'I lead a pretty boring life, I'm afraid, so that would be sport, a film on TV, and maybe a beer or two.'

'Can anyone verify that?' asked Morgan.

'As I said, I like my solitude,' said Hughes. 'It was the whole point of my coming out here. Now, if there's nothing else, I have work to do.'

* * *

True to her word, Southall had supplied sandwiches and cakes, and by the time Norman and Morgan arrived, Winter had just come in with a tray of coffees.

'Right, said Southall. 'Before we start, Judy's had a busy morning, and she has some information I'd like you all to hear.'

'Well, a few days ago I started contacting everyone involved in the removal business — moves furniture, buys furniture and does house clearances — hoping someone might remember taking the movables from Gareth's house. I was beginning to think I was wasting my time, but then this morning a guy called David Marsden got back to me. He does house clearances and says he was asked to clear the furniture from Gareth's house just over a year ago.'

'But why would Gareth ask him to do that?' asked Morgan.

'That's the thing. It wasn't Gareth who asked him. It was a woman who said she was Gareth's daughter. She told David Marsden that her father had gone into a nursing home and that she wanted all the furniture removed so she could clean the house and put it up for sale.'

'Did he see the woman?' asked Norman.

'Oh yes. She was there at the house when he did the clearance.'

'Did he describe her?'

'Vaguely.'

'Is it Rose Mackie?'

'I couldn't tell from his description. It was too vague,' said Lane.

'You say it's too vague, but does he think he would recognise her from a photo?' asked Norman.

'I'm setting up a virtual ID parade,' said Lane. 'He's coming in on Monday morning before he starts work.'

'Oh, wow! That's brilliant, Judy,' said Norman. 'If he does pick her out on Monday, she's gonna have a hell of a lot of explaining to do.'

'There's more,' said Southall. 'Go on, Judy, tell them the rest.'

'I also managed to get Maria Newlands's mobile phone number from her mother. Maria babysits for Rose, and according to her, Rose never has a good word to say about most of her neighbours — with two exceptions. The two people she doesn't run down are Gareth and Maria's mother, Jo, although Maria thinks that's because she doesn't want to lose her babysitter.'

'She doesn't slag off Gareth?' asked Morgan. 'That doesn't make sense. She told me she hated the guy.'

'According to Maria, Rose thinks Gareth needs looking after.'

'Does she know where Rose goes when she asks her to babysit?'

'She admits that she's never been particularly interested in where Rose is going. She knows Rose has a friend called Kylie who she sometimes goes out with, but other than that, she hasn't a clue.'

'Has she ever seen Rose go round to Gareth's house?'

'She says Rose doesn't always get dressed up to go out, and she doesn't always take the car, but she doesn't know where she's off to on those nights. She knows about Rose's affair with Daniel Hughes. She added that, in her words, "as Rose is a bit of a slapper, maybe she's seeing someone else's husband", but that's just speculation.'

'So, Rose could have been round at Gareth's?' asked Norman.

'I know what you're getting at, Norm, but we can't say one way or the other,' said Southall.

'Did you ask her about the night Gareth died?' asked Norman. 'Did Rose ask Maria to babysit then?'

'Rose wanted her to, but Maria said she couldn't because she was going on the school trip.'

'How did Rose react to that?' asked Norman.

'Maria said she was disappointed.'

'Yeah, I bet she was,' said Norman. 'Did she find someone else?'

'Maria doesn't know.'

'Pity,' said Norman.

'Okay,' said Southall. 'At this point we can't prove Rose was out of the house that night, but even so, we've got more than enough to bring her in for questioning.

'While Judy was on the phone to Maria Newlands, Frosty and I managed to track down Ian Mackie. He repeated his previous assertion that Rose didn't care about Gareth, or about Alma. According to Ian, she despised both of them and hated him doing odd jobs for them.'

'Even if Rose did tell Maria Newlands that Gareth needed looking after, I think I'd believe Ian Mackie on that one,' said Norman.

'Rose herself told us how much she disliked Gareth, so I don't think that's in question,' said Southall. 'Ian Mackie also confirmed that it was Gareth who told him about the affair between Rose and Daniel Hughes. Apparently, Gareth saw Daniel sneaking around to the Mackies' house so often that in the end, he felt he ought to tell Ian. He believes it was also Gareth who told Rachel Hughes.'

'Does Ian know who the baby's father is?' asked Norman.

'He says Rose insisted the baby was his, so he took a paternity test that proved it wasn't.'

'That doesn't necessarily mean Daniel Hughes is the father,' said Norman.

'Of course it doesn't, though it's unlikely to be anyone else. Only a DNA test will prove who the father really is. Anyway, I don't think we need to worry about that. In my view, it's not relevant to our murder case.'

'I must admit I'm struggling to see what difference it makes,' said Norman.

'Now it's your turn,' said Southall. 'I take it you found Daniel Hughes?'

'Oh, yeah,' said Norman. 'He's our man all right, and he fits the bill in so many ways I was almost tempted to bring him in there and then.'

'I'm glad you didn't,' said Southall. 'I haven't got the search warrant yet! What did you learn?'

'For a start, he has no alibi. He admits he's good with coding and computers in general. He's also got a Land Rover Disco, which would cope easily with that muddy track we found the other day. And he wouldn't have had any trouble carrying Gareth's body to the dump site. He must be at least six foot six, and he has muscles everywhere.'

'What about his relationship with Rose?' asked Southall.

'He says there is no relationship, and that Rose has no idea where he lives. According to Daniel, no one knows he's living out there except the Harmsworths.'

'You didn't mention Rose's car having been seen at the house?' Southall asked.

'I thought we'd save that for Monday,' said Norman. 'There was one thing he said that seemed to be at odds with what we've been told. I'm not sure it matters, but he says Rachel is desperate to get back with him, which is the exact opposite of what she led us to believe.'

'I wonder which one of them is telling lies,' said Frosty.

'I'd be more interested in why,' said Lane.

While they were talking, Morgan had been busy at her computer.

'Here's something else that points to Daniel Hughes,' she announced. 'Looking at this ordnance survey map, if you follow the lane that leads up to the chalet where Hughes lives, and then keep on going past the chalet, it meets up with another track. Guess where that one goes?'

'The field where the lambs were?' asked Norman.

'You got it in one, Norm. Daniel Hughes can actually drive from his chalet out to the dump site, and the chances of anyone seeing him are pretty slim.'

'Right,' said Southall. 'That's more than enough grounds to put in for a search warrant!'

CHAPTER SIXTEEN

Monday 23 April

At 05.58, Norman, along with Morgan, a transit van carrying four scene-of-crime officers and two uniformed police constables in a patrol car pulled up outside the chalet at the Old House.

Within fifteen minutes, Daniel Hughes had been roused from sleep, arrested, read his rights, and was now on his way to Llangwelli, in the custody of the two uniformed officers.

Norman walked across to the SOCO van and knocked on the driver's window. It slid slowly down to reveal a bleary-eyed technician who, despite all his best efforts, was unable to stifle a yawn of epic proportions.

Norman took a hasty step back. 'You want to be careful doing that. You could easily end up swallowing someone.'

'Sorry about that, Norm,' said the man. 'Late night.'

'Yeah, well, you'd better wake up. The chalet is all yours and I need you guys to carry out a thorough search. I'm off to Llangwelli, but Catren will be sticking around for a while to give you a hand. Make sure you get all his computer equipment.' He pointed to the Land Rover Discovery. 'We need that car taken apart as well.'

'It's too mucky to do that out here,' said the SOCO. 'I'll get it picked up and taken back to the workshop.'

Not long after Norman had left, one of the technicians called out to Morgan.

'Catren, you'd better come and have a look at this.'

Morgan followed the voice into the lounge, and found one of the technicians staring at the fireplace.

'Is that what I think it is?' she asked, peering over her shoulder.

'It's not complete and it's a bit charred, but it certainly looks like it,' the technician said.

'Can you fish it out and hold it up so I can take a photograph before you bag it?' said Morgan, feeling in her pocket for her mobile phone.

The technician reached for the object and held it up.

Morgan took three photos. 'Fantastic! I'll send these on to the DI.'

A second technician appeared in the doorway. 'Catren, when you've finished there, come and have a look in this cupboard.'

* * *

At the precise moment Norman and Morgan drew to a halt at the chalet, Southall arrived at Rose Mackie's house. She, too, was followed by a SOCO van and a patrol car containing a pair of uniformed officers. The residents being all still in bed, their cars lined the street and it was difficult to find a space to park. Two minutes later, Winter turned into the drive of number fifty-two, jumped from his car and joined Southall outside the house.

'Why didn't I think of parking there?' asked Southall.

Winter smiled apologetically. 'Well, I thought the owner wouldn't object, especially as he's dead. I can move my car if you want to park there.'

'No, leave it there,' said Southall. 'I'll be going back to the station once we've got Rose, but you'll be here for a while. Where's Social Services?'

As she spoke, a pink Mini turned cautiously into the street.

'This is her,' said Winter. 'Karen, from Social Services.'

The Mini crawled towards them and came to a halt in the middle of the road. The window slid down to reveal the bleary-eyed, stressed-looking face of a young woman whose hair bore testament to the fact that she'd only just got out of bed. She gazed helplessly at Winter.

'Tell her she can't park there, Frosty,' said Southall. 'She'll have to find a space further down.'

Winter went across and bent down to the car window. After a brief confabulation, the Mini crept further down the street, eventually pulling into a space a good fifty yards away.

'Is she okay?' asked Southall when Winter rejoined her. 'She looks terrified.'

'She's never been on an early-morning police raid before,' said Winter. 'I told her there won't be gunfire or anything like that, but I'm not sure I convinced her. She's a bit scared.'

The young woman, now looking rather more business-like, came up to join them. Her hair had been tied back, and she now wore a pair of round gold-rimmed spectacles.

Winter introduced Southall, who held out her hand, smiling reassuringly.

'Karen, from Social Services,' said the young woman, glancing nervously at the police vehicles.

'Don't look so worried, Karen,' said Southall. 'We're not going into a war zone. I can pretty well guarantee plenty of verbal abuse, but I'm not expecting any violence. Having said that, we don't want to be putting you in any danger, so why don't you wait out here until we call you. With any luck, she'll let us in without too much fuss. When we do get inside, I'd like you to keep the boy in his bedroom until we've taken his mother away.'

'Yes, of course,' said Karen. 'How old is the child?'

'About three, we believe. His name's Billy.'

'And it's his mum you're arresting?' Karen asked.

'Yes, that's right,' said Southall.

'Can I ask why?'

'She's a suspect in a case we're investigating.'

Karen's eyes widened in alarm. 'Oh my God. Really? What . . . what sort of case?'

'You don't need to know that,' said Southall. 'We just need you to look after little Billy while we search the house and take his mother in for questioning.'

'Yes, of course.'

The two uniformed officers now approached.

Southall patted her pocket for the search warrant that she knew perfectly well was there. 'Right. Are we all ready?'

'Ready,' said Winter.

The two officers nodded. 'Ready.'

'Got the big door key?' she asked.

One of them held up the door enforcer he was carrying under his arm. 'Just say the word, ma'am.'

Southall smiled at his eagerness. 'Let's try knocking first, shall we?' She marched up to the front door and pounded on it.

Winter bent down and shouted through the letterbox, 'Police! Open up.'

A light came on in an upstairs window, the curtain swished back and an angry-looking Rose Mackie leaned out.

'You've got to be kidding. Do you know what time it is?'

'As a matter of fact we do,' called up Southall. 'Now come down and open the door.'

'Come back at a sensible time, and I might be willing to open it for you. Meanwhile, you can bugger off and let me get back to sleep.'

'If you refuse to let us in, we'll just have to break your door down,' said Southall.

'Now you're having a laugh,' said Rose.

Southall turned to the PC with the enforcer. 'Show her.'

The PC held it up for inspection.

'Does that look like a laugh?' she asked.

'What do you want anyway?' asked Rose.

'To take you in for questioning, that's what,' Southall said.

'What about?'

'Come on, Rose, the whole street can hear us,' Southall called.

'I don't give a shit who hears, I'm still not coming down.'

'What about Billy?' asked Southall. 'What effect do you think all this is having on him?'

'If he's upset it's your bloody fault, not mine,' yelled Rose. 'Why don't you all piss off and come back at a more reasonable hour?'

'I'm afraid that's not going to happen, Rose.'

Rose stared down at Southall for a few moments, and then drew the curtains again.

'Is she coming down or blockading the place?' asked Winter.

The frosted glass pane in the door suddenly blossomed with light.

'Here we go,' said Southall.

The door was flung open to reveal Rose, resplendent in a pair of Paddington Bear pyjamas.

Southall showed her the search warrant.

'What's that?' asked Rose.

'It's a warrant to sea—' Before Southall could finish speaking, Rose snatched it from her hand, screwed it up and threw it down on the doorstep.

'Look at that,' Rose said, folding her arms. 'Litter, on my doorstep.'

'Do you really want to turn this into a battle, Rose?' asked Southall. 'There are four of us here, so I doubt you'll come out the winner.'

'I'd like to know what the hell you are arresting me for,' Rose said. 'Surely you don't think I killed the old fool next door?'

'Did you?' asked Southall.

'Of course I didn't. And if that's why you're here, you're making one hell of a big mistake.'

'You don't say,' Southall responded. 'I wonder how many times I've heard that before.'

'I mean it,' said Rose. 'You've got it all wrong.'

'Maybe we have,' said Southall, 'but the fact remains you're going to be arrested and taken to Llangwelli station. I've brought someone from Social Services to look after Billy, but she can't do that unless you cooperate. If you don't, Billy will just have to come to the station with us. Do you really want that?'

'Billy's going to be stressed enough when he wakes up and finds you lot here,' said Rose.

'If that's the case, how's he going to feel when the search team starts going through your house? I'm surprised he's not awake and crying already.'

'Search team? You can't do that!'

'Yes, I can, Rose. The sheet of paper I handed you — the one you just screwed up and threw on the ground — was a search warrant.'

'What do you think you're going to find?'

'I have my suspicions,' said Southall.

'Well, you're wasting your time.'

'It's actually you who is wasting our time right now,' said Southall. 'So, before my patience runs out completely, I'm going to start counting. If you haven't allowed the social worker to go in and see to Billy by the time I get to ten, the search team is coming in regardless.'

Rose's capitulation was sudden and unexpected.

'Oh, go on then,' she said. 'But make sure you look after him properly.'

'At last,' said Southall.

Winter called to Karen, who scuttled up the stairs in search of Billy.

'Now then, Rose, you've got five minutes to put some clothes on before we set off,' said Southall.

'What's wrong with what I'm wearing?'

'Pyjamas?' said Southall. 'Come on, Rose. You don't want to go in pyjamas, do you? Suppose you end up waiting in a cell?'

'In a cell? You can't do that.'

Southall smiled grimly. 'You think?'

'Okay,' said Rose. 'I'll have to go upstairs to get my clothes though.'

'Fine,' said Southall. 'I'll come with you.'

* * *

Ten minutes later, Rose was on her way to Llangwelli in the back of the patrol car, Southall following in hers. Winter had remained at the house with the search team, who were now working their way methodically through the kitchen.

Winter had just slipped on a pair of latex gloves ready to start poking around in the lounge, when he heard Karen calling him from the top of the stairs.

'Karen? Did you call?'

'I think you'd better come up here a minute,' she said.

Winter ran up the stairs and into Billy's bedroom. Karen was standing by the child's bed looking worried.

Billy appeared to be sound asleep, though he looked a bit pale.

'What's up?' Winter asked.

'I can't wake him,' Karen said. 'I think he's been drugged.' She held up a small bottle and shook it so it rattled. 'I found this on the dresser.'

Winter turned pale himself. 'Oh, Jesus! He's not going to die, is he?'

'I hope not,' said Karen, her mobile in her hand. 'I'm just about to call an ambulance.'

'Yeah, of course,' said Winter.

Karen, surprisingly calm given her previous demeanour, made the call. When she'd finished, Winter asked what was in the bottle.

'It's called Zopiclone,' she said.

'What's it for?'

'It's a prescription-only sleeping pill for adults. It's usu-ally only given for short-term use because it's quite powerful and it can become addictive.'

226

'Bloody hell,' muttered Winter. 'You think Billy's mum's been using it to keep him quiet?'

'I can't say for sure but I'm afraid it looks that way,' Karen said.

'Will he be addicted?' asked Winter.

'I hope not, poor kid, but I guess that will depend on how much he's been given, and how often.'

CHAPTER SEVENTEEN

'Have you finished your tea?' Southall said.

'Yeah,' Norman said, lifting his empty mug. 'I think they've had long enough to think about what they're going to tell us, don't you? Who do you want to start with?'

'Suppose we start with Rose,' Southall said.

'Is Frosty okay now?' asked Norman. 'It must have been one hell of a shock. It's always worse when it's a kid, isn't it?'

'He's spoken to the social worker who is over at the hospital. She says Billy's going to be okay,' said Southall. 'I feel guilty about it now. I should have made sure Billy was okay before I left.'

'Come on, Sarah, give yourself a break. You had no reason to think the kid was in any danger. If anyone should be feeling guilty, it's Rose Mackie.'

Southall sighed. 'I suppose you're right, but—'

'It is what it is, Sarah, and dwelling on it won't change that,' said Norman. 'Frosty, for one, certainly won't be blaming you.'

'Yes, but as senior investigating officer, the buck stops with me,' said Southall.

'What buck?' said Norman. 'Didn't you just say Billy's going to be okay?'

'Yes, but—'

'And would you have done anything different if you had gone up to check?'

'Well, no, but—'

'So why are you beating yourself up about it?' said Norman. 'Frosty did exactly what you would have done, so why not be proud of your young DC, and stop blaming yourself for something that didn't happen.'

'Of course I'm proud of Frosty—'

'There we are then,' said Norman. 'End of story.'

Southall stared open-mouthed at Norman.

'What?' he said. 'You keep telling me I'm like a father figure around here, right? Well, the way I see it, part of that role involves maintaining morale among the younger members of my team, even if one of those younger people outranks me. Of course, if you're not happy with that . . .'

Southall grinned. 'Does that mean I have to call you "Dad"?'

'I don't think that will be necessary,' Norman said, returning the smile. 'I feel old enough as it is.'

'Come on, Dad — sorry, Norman,' said Southall. 'Let's go and catch us a murderer.'

* * *

Five minutes later, Southall and Norman were seated in an interview room, facing Rose Mackie and a duty solicitor across a table. Southall flipped open the folder in front of her, looked up at Rose and smiled.

'Right then, Rose,' she said. 'Is it okay for me to call you Rose?'

'Call me what you like,' said Rose. 'You haven't told me why I'm here yet.'

'Now you know that's not true,' said Southall. 'I distinctly remember reading you your rights and informing you of your arrest in connection with the murder of Gareth Jenkins.'

'Well, I don't remember it,' said Rose.

'Perhaps you weren't listening,' said Southall. 'Whatever, you were cautioned before witnesses, so you can't claim not to have been told.'

'Why would I want to kill the miserable old fool anyway?' asked Rose.

'Sorry, Rose, that's not how it works. It's me who asks the questions, while you provide the answers.'

Rose said nothing.

'Now then,' said Southall. 'Tell me about your relationship with Gareth Jenkins.'

'I didn't have a relationship with him.'

'Are you sure about that?'

'All right, so I used to help out before Alma passed away, but I stopped after she died, because he became aggressive and abusive towards me. I've told you all this before.'

'According to your husband, you never "helped out", even when Alma was alive,' said Norman.

'He's lying,' said Rose.

Southall raised her eyebrows. 'You describe Gareth's behaviour as "abusive and aggressive". What do you mean by that?'

'It's clear enough, isn't it?' said Rose. 'He was a miserable old sod.'

Southall frowned. 'Now that's what I'm having trouble understanding. You see, it's not just your husband who disagrees with you, all your neighbours thought Gareth was a lovely old fellow. Granted, he kept himself to himself but no one who knew him has a bad word to say about him, except you.'

'I can't help that,' said Rose. 'I can only tell you what he was like towards me.'

'Why would he be like that towards you in particular?' asked Norman.

'I don't know,' said Rose. 'I never did anything to him.'

'Is that right?' said Norman.

'We'll come back to that in a minute,' said Southall. 'Why do you drug your son?'

'What?' Rose turned to her solicitor, who merely shrugged. She glared at Southall. 'What's my son got to do with anything? I thought you wanted to talk about the old guy.'

'Then you don't deny you drug Billy.'

'Of course I bloody deny it.'

'So, the Zopiclone we found is yours, is it?'

Rose's foot began to tap on the floor. 'I have trouble sleeping.'

'That's fair enough,' said Southall, 'I'm not the best of sleepers myself, but why do you keep the tablets in Billy's room?'

'I don't.'

'Well, that's where we found them,' said Southall.

'That's where you say you found them,' said Rose.

'Are you accusing us of planting evidence?' Southall said.

'It wouldn't surprise me,' said Rose.

'Really?' said Southall. 'What if I told you we couldn't wake Billy this morning? Would that surprise you?'

The foot tapped faster. Rose's eyes darted between Southall and Norman.

'That's your fault,' she said. 'He's not used to being woken that early.'

'He wasn't asleep, Rose, he was unconscious. We had to call an ambulance.'

For the first time Rose looked genuinely alarmed. 'If you've hurt my Billy—'

'He's being examined in hospital as we speak,' said Southall. 'Not because we hurt him, but because he has been drugged.'

'Why would I drug him? He's my son.'

'Well, here's the thing,' said Southall. 'Some of the neighbours have reported seeing lights on in Gareth's house after he was murdered. He was even seen walking his dog in the early hours. Now, since we don't believe in ghosts, that means someone was inside the house.'

'Well, it can't have been me. I have a toddler, and I wouldn't leave him on his own for anything. What if he woke up and I wasn't there?'

'Yeah, that's what we thought at first,' said Norman. 'But then this morning we realised that you regularly drug your little boy. If he'd been given a sleeping pill as strong as Zopiclone, he wouldn't have woken up while you were round at Gareth's house, would he?'

'This is rubbish. I've never been inside that house.'

'You're sure about that, are you?' asked Southall.

'Yes, I am. What would I want to go in there for?'

'Maybe you were looking for something,' said Norman.

'It's a shithole,' Rose said. 'It's so bad even squatters wouldn't want to live there.'

'How do you know that if you've never been inside?' asked Southall.

'I've heard,' said Rose.

'Really? Who told you?'

'I can't remember.'

'That's convenient,' said Norman.

'You know what it's like because you've been in there,' said Southall.

'Rubbish. You can see what it's like through the windows.'

'As you know, we took your fingerprints when we brought you in. We'll compare them with the ones we found in Gareth's house. Are we going to find a match for your prints, Rose?'

'If you do, it's from years ago, when Alma was alive,' Rose said.

'Alma died five years ago, didn't she?' said Southall.

'If you say so,' said Rose.

'So, you're saying you've not been inside the house in the last five years?'

'That's right.'

'And yet you know the house is in a state and that most of the furniture is gone.'

'Like I said, someone told me,' said Rose.

'Do you know a man called David Marsden?' asked Norman.

'I don't think so,' said Rose.

'He knows you though,' said Norman.

'Fame at last, eh?' said Rose. 'Who is he anyway?'

'He buys and sells furniture.'

Rose's foot suddenly stopped tapping.

'In that case I probably bought some furniture from him,' she said. 'As far as I know, buying furniture isn't a crime, is it?'

'No, you didn't buy furniture from him, Rose,' said Norman. 'He says he bought furniture from you.'

Rose shook her head. 'I think I'd remember if I had done that.'

'David Marsden says a woman sold Gareth's furniture to him,' said Norman. 'And I'm betting he'll pick you out when he comes in for the identity parade later.'

'How can he pick me out? I haven't been in any identity parade,' said Rose.

'That's one of the great things about computers,' said Norman. 'We can do them virtually these days. Instead of having to find people who look alike, we use photographs. It's so much easier.'

Rose looked at her solicitor. 'They can't do that, can they?'

'I'm afraid they can,' he said.

'David Marsden says you arranged for him to take the furniture from the house of a Gareth Jenkins. Apparently, you told him Jenkins was your father, who was going into a nursing home. The thing is, Gareth didn't have a daughter, so it had to be someone with access to the house.'

'Well, he's lying,' said Rose. 'It wasn't me.'

'Another one,' said Southall. 'All these people lying about you. Why do you think they're doing that, Rose?'

'I don't know, but they are.'

Southall fell silent, paging slowly through the file. Rose resumed tapping her foot.

This went on for several minutes, until Southall suddenly said, 'Why did you want a babysitter on the night of Friday the sixth of April?'

'When?' asked Rose.

'Two weeks ago last Friday,' said Norman. 'You asked Jo Newlands's daughter but she couldn't do it because she was going away.'

'I remember now. There was a concert I wanted to go to; a friend of mine had tickets.'

'Good concert was it?' asked Norman.

'I wouldn't know,' said Rose. 'Since I couldn't get a babysitter, I wasn't able to go.'

'You were at home that night?' asked Norman. 'Can anyone prove it?'

'There's only me and Billy,' said Rose. 'And he can't tell you, can he?'

'What's the name of your friend who had the tickets?' asked Norman.

'Kylie Swann,' said Rose.

'I'll need her address. We'll be paying her a visit so we can check your story,' said Norman.

'You do that,' said Rose. 'Ask her, she'll confirm it.'

Just then a knock on the door was heard.

Norman went to see who it was, and was handed a sheet of paper, which he set down on the table in front of Southall. She glanced at it and her eyes widened.

'Rose, do you take warfarin?'

'No, I don't.'

'Then why do you have them in your house?'

Rose shrugged. 'I didn't know I had. I've got a box full of stuff of my dad's that I've never got around to sorting out. They must have been in there.'

'Your father's?' said Southall.

'Yes,' said Rose. 'He used to take warfarin. What's the big deal?'

'It's a big deal because someone had been poisoning Gareth with warfarin for a considerable length of time before he was struck and killed.'

Rose pushed herself up from her chair. Her solicitor took hold of her arm and pulled her down again.

'Now wait a minute,' she said. 'You can't pin that on me. It's true I didn't like the old bugger, but I didn't poison him. I didn't even know I had any warfarin!'

'Do you know where Daniel Hughes lives?' asked Southall.

'Who?'

'Daniel Hughes,' said Southall. 'He was Gareth's neighbour on the other side — number fifty-four. You can't say you've forgotten Billy's father.'

'Yes, of course I know Daniel, but I haven't seen him since they moved away,' said Rose.

'You're not still in a relationship with him then?' asked Southall.

'No, I am not,' said Rose. 'The bastard won't even admit to being Billy's dad.'

'But you know where he lives,' said Southall.

'No. Last I heard they'd moved to Llanelli, but I don't know where.'

'How do you and Daniel communicate?'

Rose frowned. 'We don't.'

'And you have no idea where he lives,' Southall said.

'I just said so, didn't I?'

'What would you say if I said your car had been seen parked on the drive of the Old House in Pont Daffyd?' asked Southall.

'I'd say someone was mistaken,' Rose said, averting her gaze.

'According to what you say, an awful lot of people seem to be telling lies about you. Why do you think that is, Rose? What's going on?'

'I don't know,' said Rose. 'I just mind my own business and get on quietly with my life.'

'Is that right now?' said Southall. 'Shall I tell you what I think?'

'As if I had a choice,' said Rose.

'I think Gareth Jenkins was very fond of your husband, Ian. He was fond of Rachel Hughes too, because they were kind to him and looked out for him. I think Gareth worked out that you and Daniel were having an affair, and he didn't like the pair of you cheating on his friends, so he told Ian and Rachel about it. How am I doing so far?'

'I have no idea what you're talking about,' said Rose.

235

'When your partners heard of the affair, it destroyed both of your marriages,' continued Southall. 'Because of that, you and Daniel decided to make Gareth's life a misery. You persecuted him, sold all his furniture, stole all his money, and began slowly poisoning him. Only he figured out who had been stealing his money and threatened to tell us about it. That's when you panicked, wasn't it? You realised the warfarin wasn't killing him fast enough, so you enticed him to Pont Daffyd where you murdered him and then dumped his body.'

Rose stared open-mouthed at Southall.

'Nothing to say?' asked Southall. 'That must be a first.'

Still Rose said nothing.

'We're going to call a halt for now,' said Southall. 'You'll be put in a cell while we check a few things. It'll give you time to consider just how much trouble you're in, and what you're going to do next. And before we reconvene, I suggest you have a chat with your solicitor.'

* * *

'You do remember that we didn't find many unidentified fingerprints at Gareth's house?' asked Norman on their way back to the office.

'Of course I do,' said Southall. 'They cleaned up pretty thoroughly, but Rose can't know that for sure.'

'If it did worry her, she certainly hid it well,' said Norman.

Southall received a message on her phone. She scrolled through it and handed the phone to Norman.

'Take a look at these photos.'

'Jeez! Is that what I think it is?'

'They fished it out of the fireplace,' said Southall. 'And they found the other one in a cupboard in the hallway.'

'Wow,' said Norman. 'That was a bit careless, considering all the trouble he went to in creating Gaynor and laying that false email trail for us to follow.'

'It just goes to show he's not as clever as he thinks,' said Southall.

'Maybe something interrupted him while he was doing it,' said Norman.

'Whatever,' said Southall. 'I'm looking forward to hearing his explanation.'

'I'm ready when you are,' said Norman.

'C'mon then,' said Southall. 'Let's go.'

* * *

Five minutes later they were back in the same interview room, this time facing Daniel Hughes and a different solicitor.

'Tell me about your relationship with Gareth Jenkins,' said Norman.

'I already told you, I barely knew the guy.'

'But you lived right next door to him,' said Norman.

'Living next door to someone doesn't necessarily make you best mates,' said Hughes.

'So, you didn't help him like Ian Mackie and Rachel?'

'Rachel?'

Norman raised an eyebrow. 'Erm, your wife?'

'Yes, I know who she is,' said Hughes testily. 'I just don't understand the question.'

'Ian Mackie used to do odd jobs for Gareth, like cutting his grass, that sort of thing. Rachel says she used to bake him a cake now and then, or make him the odd casserole. I'm just wondering what you might have done for him. You're good with computers and stuff. Maybe you helped him with his laptop.'

'I didn't do anything for him,' Hughes said.

'Didn't you like him?'

Hughes shrugged. 'Not particularly. He was forty years older, we had nothing in common.'

'What about Rose Mackie?' asked Norman.

'What about her?'

'I understand you had an affair.'

'If you've spoken to Ian and Rachel you already know that. You don't need me to confirm it.'

'How did Ian and Rachel find out about the affair?' Norman asked.

'I would imagine someone told them. Anyway, what's an affair that ended three years ago got to do with it? I thought I was arrested in connection with a murder.'

'That's right,' said Norman. 'You're here to help us with our enquiries. Rose is here for the same reason.'

Hughes blinked, obviously startled.

'Come on, Daniel,' Norman said. 'That surprised you. Don't try and make out it didn't.'

'Frankly, I'm surprised by this whole thing,' said Hughes. 'I have no idea why I'm here. As I said, I hardly knew the old guy, and I left St David's Place three years ago.'

'Tell us about Rose's baby,' said Norman.

'I'm sorry?'

'Rose Mackie's baby, Billy. She claims you're the father.'

'She can claim what she likes. There were other guys, it could just as easily have been one of them.'

'Which means you don't know for sure that you're not Billy's father?' asked Norman.

'He's not mine,' insisted Hughes.

'Are you still in a relationship with Rose?'

'No.'

'Are you sure about that?' asked Norman. 'Only her car was seen on the drive just days ago.'

'What drive?'

'The drive of the Old House,' said Norman.

'How do you know it was her car?'

'It was a red hatchback.'

Hughes smiled. 'Are you saying that in the whole of Wales, Rose is the only person who drives a red hatchback? Even if it was her, it had nothing to do with me. Maybe she was visiting Millie.'

'Why would she visit Millie?' asked Norman.

'I don't know, do I? Anyway, if she knew where I lived she would have come down the lane and parked by the chalet, not the front drive.'

'We parked out on the road when we went to see you,' said Norman.

'Yes, but you didn't know any different, did you? If Rose was the frequent visitor you seem to be suggesting, she'd know where to park, wouldn't she?' said Hughes triumphantly.

'You think?' said Norman. 'We came down that lane of yours this morning. Now I know how muddy it is, I'd park on the drive and walk across the garden, rather than risk getting stuck. Rose has got a small hatchback, so I'm sure she thought the same.'

'Anyway, it's irrelevant,' said Hughes, 'since Rose has never been to my chalet.'

Norman smiled. 'Okay, Daniel. Whatever you say.'

'Tell us about Gaynor,' said Southall.

'Who?'

'Gaynor. Her photo is the screen saver on Gareth Jenkins's laptop. We were led to believe Gaynor was emailing Gareth for years, but it turns out it was a false trail someone created, and Gaynor a fake persona.'

'I have no idea what you're talking about,' said Hughes.

'Oh, I think you know exactly what I'm talking about,' said Southall. 'It was a clever idea, but we're not quite as dim as you thought we were.'

'I've never set eyes on his laptop. I didn't even know he had one. And why would I do something like that anyway?'

'Well, you see, someone was taking money from Gareth's bank account, supposedly Gaynor asking him for money. The sums transferred correspond to the requests in Gaynor's messages. We haven't yet traced where that money really went, but we will, you can be sure of that.'

Hughes frowned. 'And you're saying I did this? I'd like to see your proof.'

'There's more,' said Southall. 'We believe the same person was also using Gareth's debit card to take cash from his bank account.'

'All very fascinating, I'm sure,' said Hughes, 'but I don't see—'

Southall pushed a photograph across the table. 'Apologies for the quality. Of course, we'll use the real thing when we present it as evidence.'

Hughes looked down at the photo, and then back up at Southall.

'Am I supposed to know what this is?'

'I thought you might, as it was found in your fireplace,' Southall said.

'I don't ever light a fire,' Hughes said.

'Maybe not to keep warm,' said Southall. 'But it's a handy place to burn pieces of evidence, isn't it?'

'What evidence?'

Southall tapped the photograph. 'That photograph shows a charred debit card. It was found in your fireplace.'

'Yes, I can see that. My bank sent me a new one. They tell you to destroy the old one, so I did.'

Southall smiled. 'Take a closer look. Go on, don't be shy. There's still a bit of the name that hasn't been burnt. The initial is a "G" and the surname starts "J E N". We can probably do better when we get it back to the lab, but is that close enough for now?'

Hughes shifted uncomfortably in his seat. 'Look, I swear that's not the card I destroyed. It was my old one. The bank sent me a replacement. Have a look in my wallet. Check with my bank.'

'Oh, we will,' said Norman. 'You can count on it.'

Hughes turned to his solicitor. 'You're the lawyer. Do something. You can't just sit there and let them fit me up like this.'

The solicitor shrugged. 'I can't stop them asking you questions.'

'But this is all bollocks,' said Hughes desperately. 'I didn't do it!'

'There's something else we found at your house,' said Southall.

'You can't have,' said Hughes.

'I haven't told you what it is yet.'

'It doesn't matter what it is. There is no evidence in that chalet that links me to Gareth Jenkins.'

Southall slid a second photograph across the table.

'What's this?' asked Hughes.

'You tell me,' said Southall.

'I can't tell you. I don't know what it is or where you found it.'

'It was hidden in the cupboard in the hall, behind your vacuum cleaner.'

'No way,' said Hughes. 'I never use that cupboard. As my former wife will tell you, I have an aversion to housework.'

'How did it get there then, Daniel?'

'I don't know. Anyway, you still haven't told me what it is.'

'It's a shoe box containing about two thousand pounds in ten- and twenty-pound notes, all new,' said Southall.

Hughes gaped at her. 'It's what?'

'Two thousand pounds in cash,' said Southall. 'We're assuming it's part of the money that was being stolen from Gareth's bank account.'

'And you think I did that?'

'It's in your cupboard.'

'How am I supposed to have stolen it?'

'We know it was being withdrawn from ATMs around Carmarthen, using Gareth's debit card,' said Southall. 'And we've just shown you the card, which we found in your fireplace.'

'This is like a nightmare,' said Hughes. 'I thought my world had gone to shit when Rachel found out about the affair, but this . . .'

'Come on, Daniel,' said Norman. 'You can see the evidence we've got. You might as well come clean. It'll be better for you in the end.'

'Come clean about what?'

'You want some help? Okay, I'll tell you what we think happened, and then you tell me if I'm right. See, we think it was Gareth who told Ian and Rachel about your affair. I can imagine the trouble that must have caused. I bet you and Rose were well pissed off, right?'

'No comment,' said Hughes.

'Oh, so that's the way you're playing it now, is it?'

'No comment.'

'As I was saying, you and Rose were pretty unhappy with old Gareth, so you embarked on a campaign to make his life a misery. You stole all his money, and when that ran out, you enticed him over to Pont Daffyd and murdered him. Am I right?'

'No comment.'

'Okay, Daniel,' said Southall. 'Now you have an idea of the size of the hole you're in, we'll take a break so you can consult with your solicitor. That okay with you?'

'No comment,' said Hughes.

* * *

'Which one's going to break first, do you think?' asked Norman as they headed back to the office.

'I actually thought Rose would have cracked by now,' said Southall, 'but apparently she's a tougher cookie than I thought.'

'She might not be quite so tough when she hears what we found at Hughes's chalet,' said Norman.

'We'll let her stew for a while before we tell her,' said Southall. 'In fact, why don't we wait until Frosty and Catren get back? Then we can hit Rose with everything we've got.'

'Good idea,' said Norman. 'Because my stomach's telling me I need to eat.'

As soon as they arrived at the office, Southall went straight over to Lane's desk. 'Has your removals man been in yet? We could do with some firm evidence against Rose.'

'Not yet. Sorry. On the plus side, I had an interesting call from a lady called Donna Walker who lives opposite the Old House. She'd been away so she missed all the recent excitement in the village, but she's good friends with Millie

Harmsworth, who told her about Daniel Hughes and the mysterious red hatchback we were trying to identify.'

'That's it? She called to let you know she's heard all the gossip?' asked Norman.

'Wait a bit, Norm. She called because she has one of those doorbells with a security camera built in.'

'And what? She's had a break-in?' asked Norman.

Lane sighed. 'Her doorbell camera happens to take in the Harmsworths' drive, just at the end by the road. After Millie told her about the red hatchback, she thought she might look back at the footage, just in case.'

'Jeez, she doesn't have footage of the red hatchback, does she?'

'Yes, she has, and since she was so keen to help, I asked her if she could download any footage she has from the beginning of April to now, and email it to me.'

'Have you watched it?' asked Southall.

'There's twenty-two clips to go through, but I've made a start. The first five were useless, but you'll want to see the one I've just been watching. Do you want to see it now?'

With Southall and Norman watching over her shoulder, Lane played the first film clip.

'The definition isn't great,' said Southall.

'I seem to recall that both houses are set back from the road,' said Norman. 'It must be quite a distance between the two front doors. See, you can't even see the Old House, just the top end of the drive and the road between them.'

As they watched, a red hatchback came into view and turned in through the gates of the Old House.

'What date was this taken?' asked Norman.

'Tuesday the seventeenth of April at two p.m.,' said Lane.

'That's the day me and Catren went out to Pont Daffyd,' said Norman. 'I remember Catren slowing down to look at the car, because the driver had almost run us down.'

On the screen, the car moved slowly further up the drive until it was out of shot.

'Bugger,' said Southall. 'We're not going to see the driver getting out.'

Lane fast-forwarded the film until the car reappeared. This time it was reversing. A man appeared and started running after it. The car swung out onto the road and stopped, and the man bent down and spoke into the driver's side window.

'That's Daniel Hughes,' said Southall.

The driver could be seen looking up at Hughes.

'Hallo, Rose,' said Norman. 'Never been to Pont Daffyd, have you?'

Daniel and Rose were clearly arguing. After a few minutes, Rose roared away, leaving Daniel staring after her.

'What a pity there's no sound,' said Southall. 'I'd love to know what that was about.'

'Yeah, he doesn't look happy, does he?' said Norman. 'But it proves they've both been lying — again.'

Lane swung her chair round to face them. 'I'm assuming most of the videos won't show anything, but I'm happy to keep trawling through them just in case.'

'I think you'd better,' said Southall, 'but we're going to take a short break for lunch, and I think you should, too. Have you heard from Frosty and Catren?'

'I spoke to Frosty half an hour ago. He said they were just about winding up, so he won't be long. Catren should be back at about the same time.'

'Perfect,' said Southall. 'When they get back, tell them to have some lunch, and then I'd like Catren to check with Rose's friend Kylie about the concert they were supposed to be going to on the night Gareth died. And ask Frosty to find the doctor who was treating Rose's father. We want to know if he was prescribed warfarin, because Rose claims that's where she got it from. And see if you can chase up the removals man.'

CHAPTER EIGHTEEN

'Okay, Rose, you've had time to think, perhaps you'll be a bit more honest with us,' said Southall. 'I'll ask you again: did you poison Gareth Jenkins with warfarin?'

'I swear I didn't poison anyone. I already told you I didn't even know the tablets were there.' Rose sat back and folded her arms. Clearly she had no intention of helping them out.

'Okay, let's try another one,' said Southall. 'Did you persecute Gareth Jenkins?'

Rose glanced at her solicitor, who gave a slight nod. 'Look, I admit I gave the old guy a hard time, but I wouldn't call it persecution. I only went round when I knew Ian was there.'

'Why?' Southall asked.

'I was angry with him for spending time with Gareth when he wouldn't even speak to me. It wasn't fair. He even took my name off the joint bank account. I had a baby and no money. What was I supposed to do? The only time I could get to him was when he was next door.'

'And were you still persecuting Gareth after Ian stopped going round?' asked Southall.

'Of course not. Like I said, I was only interested in Ian and what he owed me. After he agreed to give me an allowance, there was no need to keep chasing after him.'

'When did you start receiving this allowance?' asked Norman.

Rose considered. 'Eighteen months, two years ago. Something like that. I can't remember the exact date.'

'We'll be checking your bank account,' said Norman.

'Fine.'

'Ian says you caused so much hassle he stopped coming, because it was upsetting Gareth.'

'Only on Saturday mornings,' said Rose. 'He still went round at other times.'

'What about that gate between the gardens? Use that, did you?' said Norman.

'What?'

'You said it was nailed shut, but it opened easily enough when I tried it. I think you used that gate so no one would see you going to Gareth's.'

'Why would I do that?' Rose said.

'So you could search the house and feed the dog.'

'What would I be searching the house for? And I certainly didn't feed the dog. I already told you, I hate dogs.'

'So why is the grass trampled? There's a distinct path from your back door, through the gate to Gareth's.'

'Path? I haven't seen any path.'

'You can even see it from your kitchen window,' Norman said.

'I don't have time to look after Billy and do the garden, and Ian won't help me,' Rose said. 'The garden's a mess, so I don't go out there. And as far as I know, that gate doesn't open. It hasn't been opened since Ian nailed it shut, trying to stop me going round there.'

'Trying to stop you?' Norman said. 'So you continued to go round.'

'He forgot I could still go round the front, didn't he?' Rose said.

'When was this?' asked Southall.

'Around two years ago,' said Rose. 'Before Ian started giving me an allowance.'

'And that's when you stopped using the gate? Two years ago?' asked Norman.

'I just said so, didn't I? Anyway, how could I use it if it was nailed up?'

'Are you still in a relationship with Daniel Hughes?' asked Southall.

Rose looked startled at this abrupt change of tack. 'What?'

'Daniel and you. Are you still in a relationship?'

'No, we are not. I already told you that.'

'Do you know where Daniel lives?' Southall asked.

'No.'

'Have you ever been to Pont Daffyd?'

'How many times do I have to tell you? No!' said Rose.

Southall took a photograph from her folder and slid it across the table.

'This is a still taken from a video we watched earlier on today,' she said. 'Is that you driving the car in this photo, Rose?'

Rose swallowed, hard.

'The game's up, Rose,' said Norman. 'Everyone can see it's you, and we can all see that the man is Daniel Hughes. It's also perfectly clear that you're outside the Old House in Pont Daffyd. There's no point you denying it.'

'D'you want to tell us what the argument was about?' asked Southall.

'He was angry because I called him a murderer,' Rose said after a moment's hesitation.

'Or was it about the money?' asked Norman.

'What's that supposed to mean?' asked Rose.

'We found Gareth's debit card and a load of cash in a cupboard at Daniel's chalet,' Norman said.

'I can't tell you anything about that. I haven't been inside that old man's house, and I would never have taken his money. Whatever else I might be, I am not a thief.'

'Are you telling me you don't know anything about Gareth's money going missing?' Norman said.

'That's exactly what I'm telling you,' Rose said.

'What about Gaynor?'

'Who?'

'The screen saver on Gareth's laptop. The fake persona sending him emails,' Norman said.

Rose shrugged. 'I didn't even know he had a laptop.'

'Ian set it up for him when he first got it,' said Norman.

'Oh, yes. I remember now,' said Rose. 'I remember because when Ian set it up, he logged him into our broadband without asking me. But that was years ago. How would I know he still had it?'

'Oh, come on, Rose,' said Norman. 'You were in his house every night after he died, trying to find the damned thing!'

'How many times do I have to tell you, I haven't been in his house.'

'Okay,' said Southall. 'Let's go back to why you continued to persecute Gareth even when Ian wasn't there.'

'Can you imagine what it's like finding yourself all alone with a hyperactive kid, living in a place where everyone knows your husband has left you because you had an affair? They look down on me like I'm nothing more than a lump of shit, and it's all because of that nosey old bastard. If he hadn't told Ian and Rachel, none of this would have happened.'

'Oh, so now it's all Gareth's fault, is it?' asked Norman.

'If he'd only kept his mouth shut—'

'You and Daniel wouldn't have murdered him. Am I right?'

'I didn't murder anyone,' said Rose. 'I didn't even know he was dead until you lot came round asking questions about him.'

'Do you seriously expect us to believe that?' asked Norman. 'Maybe you need to take another look at this photo. We've got you on video in Pont Daffyd, with Daniel.'

'All right. I admit I did go to see Daniel, but look at the date stamp on that photo. It was after you told me the old bloke was dead.' Rose sat back, smiling.

Norman couldn't argue with that. 'Okay. But I still want to know why you went to see Daniel.'

'I saw him in St David's Place. When you guys told me the old bloke was dead, I thought Daniel might have murdered him,' Rose said.

'When was this?' Norman asked.

'Over the weekend.'

'Which weekend?'

'The weekend of the murder.'

'Did he tell you what he was doing there?' Norman asked.

'I asked him if he'd killed Gareth, and he told me I'd got it wrong, and that it wasn't him.'

'Could he have been looking for Gareth's laptop?' Norman asked.

'I told you I didn't even know there was a laptop.'

'Daniel's pretty good with computers, isn't he?' Norman said.

'I should think he'd have to be since it's his job,' said Rose.

'Do you think he created Gaynor?'

'What is all this stuff about bloody Gaynor?' Rose said. 'I know nothing about any Gaynor, and I don't know anything about the old bloke's laptop.'

'The trouble is,' said Norman, 'I can't quite see how you were happy to persecute the poor old guy, yet you wouldn't dream of taking his money.'

'You know what?' said Rose. 'I really don't give a shit what you can or cannot see. I'm not proud of what I did, but I stopped once I got what I wanted out of Ian. I didn't try to poison anyone, or kill anyone, and I've answered all your questions. Now, if you don't mind, I'm very tired, and I'd like a rest.'

Southall regarded Rose, who did indeed look exhausted.

'Okay,' she said, 'we'll take another break.'

* * *

Back in the office, Southall asked Lane how she was getting on with the videos from the security camera.

'I've been working my way back from the most recent one, but so far, nothing's come up. I'm just about to watch Friday the sixth.'

In Southall's opinion, she should have started from the sixth and worked forwards, but now wasn't the time to bring it up. She turned to Winter.

'Have you spoken to Rose's father's GP?'

'Yes, I have,' said Winter. 'He confirms that her dad had been prescribed warfarin, and had been taking it for a while before his death.'

'Where exactly did you find the tablets?' Southall asked.

'In a box of stuff that was sitting in the garage,' Winter said.

'What else was in this box?'

'Just odds and sods really, not the sort of stuff I'd have expected someone like Rose to have.'

'Her father died last year,' said Southall. 'Could it have been his effects?'

'That would make sense,' said Winter. 'The box was covered in dust, like it hadn't been moved or opened in a long time.'

'And you're quite sure the tablets were inside this box?' asked Southall.

'Yes. We've got it on video. The doctor also said the number of tablets left in the bottle was more or less what he would expect if the patient was taking the tablets as prescribed.'

'Crap!' said Norman. 'That means Rose could be telling the truth about them.'

'I don't think we'd ever have been able to prove that she was giving them to Gareth anyway,' said Southall.

'If you want some more bad news, I've spoken to Rose's friend, Kylie,' said Morgan. 'She confirms she bought two tickets for the concert, one for her and one for Rose. She said she was a bit annoyed when Rose said she couldn't make it, but she has kids of her own, so she understands babysitters aren't always there when you need them. She managed to find someone to buy the spare ticket, so there was no harm done in the end.'

'That doesn't prove Rose wasn't out with Daniel murdering a defenceless old man,' said Norman.

'No, that's true,' agreed Southall. 'But it does show that not everything she's said is a lie, and at this stage we've nothing to prove she was inside Gareth's house, or in Pont Daffyd on the night he died. We can't even disprove what she told us about visiting Daniel Hughes.'

'I can't believe she's not in it up to her neck,' said Norman.

'I'm not saying you're wrong, Norm, but we're going to have trouble charging Rose with the evidence we've got at the moment.'

Norman was about to respond when Judy Lane let out a gasp.

'You're going to want to see this.' she said.

The whole team crowded around to watch. The footage started with a view of the empty drive of the Old House. A car whizzed by, heading into the village, followed by another going in the opposite direction. The time displayed was 15.07 when the small, hunched figure of a man shuffled into view.

'I'm sure this is Gareth,' whispered Lane. 'He's very small, and you can't see his face, but the clothes match what he was wearing on the bus.'

'Jeez,' said Norman. 'Look how slowly he's walking. He really wasn't a well man, was he?'

'It looks as if he's walked all the way from the village,' said Morgan.

'He's practically tottering,' said Winter. 'Poor old devil looks exhausted.'

As they watched, the man stopped to read the sign at the end of the drive, and began to make his painful way up the drive.

'Jeez, I can hardly bear to watch the poor old guy,' said Norman.

'He must have had a really powerful reason for putting himself through that,' said Lane as the figure disappeared from view.

'He's going to have it out with Daniel Hughes,' said Southall.

'Gotta be,' said Norman. 'He must have figured it all out and wanted to put a stop to it. It's not looking good for Daniel, is it? A charred debit card, a stash of cash, and now this.'

'I can't wait to hear what he has to say,' said Southall.

As the others returned to their desks, Lane fast-forwarded the video. She was just reaching for her mug of tea when a vehicle turned off the road and headed up the drive. It happened so quickly Lane wasn't even sure she'd seen it, so she ran it backwards and watched it again.

'I've got a car entering the drive,' she announced. 'Forty-five minutes after Gareth arrived.'

Again the team assembled behind her chair.

'Is it Rose Mackie?' asked Norman.

Lane set the video running at half speed. A grey saloon car appeared, from the direction of the village.

'That's not a red hatchback,' said Morgan.

'No shit, Sherlock,' said Norman. 'Maybe Rose borrowed a car and came this way to avoid the mud.'

'Anyone recognise the make?' asked Southall.

'VW Passat?' guessed Winter.

The car came to a stop at the sign outside the gate. The driver read the house name and turned onto the drive. Lane stopped the video.

'It's not Millie Harmsworth's car,' said Morgan. 'She has a blue Lexus.'

'And she said her husband drives a Range Rover,' said Norman.

'Jaguar,' corrected Morgan.

'Either way, it's not him,' said Norman.

'I might be wrong about it being a VW,' said Winter, 'but that's definitely not a Jag.'

Lane zoomed in on the vehicle. 'The definition isn't great, but Frosty's right, it's a VW. You can just about make out the badge.'

'We need to know who owns that car,' said Southall. 'Can you get the registration number?'

'It's a bit blurry,' said Lane, 'but Frosty's so clever I'm sure he can get it so it's readable.'

'Right,' said Southall. 'Frosty, I want you to find out who owns that car. Judy, I want a still of Gareth walking up the drive, and one of that car. Then I want you and Catren to watch the rest of that video. Norm, I think it's time we had another chat with Daniel Hughes.'

* * *

Norman settled in his seat alongside Southall. On the other side of the table sat Daniel Hughes, looking haggard. Being questioned and kept in a cell does that to people, Norman thought, however muscular they might be. Especially if they have a guilty conscience.

'Okay, Daniel,' he said. 'Can you tell us what you were doing on the afternoon of Friday the sixth of April?'

'I would have been at home, working. It's what I do most days,' Hughes said.

'And you work alone, right?' said Norman.

'I do.'

'So, no one can verify that you were, in fact, there.'

'Why would I need someone to verify it?' Hughes asked.

Ignoring the question, Norman said, 'Did you have any visitors?'

'I just said I was alone, didn't I?'

Norman slid the shot of Gareth Jenkins shuffling up the drive of the Old House across the table.

'What about this guy?'

'What about him?' asked Hughes.

'Do you know who he is?'

Hughes studied the photo. 'It's not exactly high definition, is it? Apart from that, how can I tell from this angle? If I could see a face it might help, but from the back of their head? I mean, come on. They call it facial recognition for

253

a reason. You can't identify someone by the back of their head.'

'It's Gareth Jenkins,' said Norman. 'Why do you think he was walking up the drive?'

'I have no idea,' said Hughes.

'Are you saying he didn't come to see you that afternoon?'

'At the chalet? Of course not.'

'You're sure about that, are you?' Norman said.

'He did not come to my chalet.'

'We think he did,' said Norman. 'We think Gareth had worked out that it was you and Rose who'd been bleeding his bank account dry and messing with his laptop.'

Hughes shook his head. 'I've already told you I don't know anything about that.'

'And Gareth was right, wasn't he? That's why you had his debit card and all that cash.'

'I also told you I've never seen that card or that money before.'

'How did it get there then, Daniel?'

'I don't know. Anyway, if I'm as clever and devious as you seem to think, would I be likely to leave evidence lying around where you could find it?'

Norman smiled. 'You say you like it out there because you don't get any visitors. And if you don't get visitors, what are we to think? That it got there by magic?'

'No comment.'

'I must say you did a great job of covering your tracks at Gareth's house,' Norman said. 'But maybe you got a bit complacent when it came to your own place.'

'I don't know what you're talking about. I've never been in his house.'

'Yeah, you could be right. It was more likely to have been Rose who cleaned up the house, as she lives right next door. So she's going to be pretty pissed off when we tell her you messed up at your end.'

'I don't know why you persist with this idea that I'm in some sort of conspiracy with Rose. I told you, I don't see

Rose. I haven't seen or heard from her since I moved away from St David's Place.'

'But that's not quite true, is it?' said Southall.

Hughes, obviously struggling to remain impassive, said nothing.

'Rose told us she came to see you on Tuesday the seventeenth,' said Southall. 'And we know that's true because DS Norman and another detective were in Pont Daffyd that day, and they saw her car on the drive. We also have video footage of her pulling up outside the house. It clearly shows you at the car door arguing with her before she drives off.'

Hughes's face crumpled. 'All right. Yes, Rose did come to see me that day.'

'What did she want?'

'She said you lot had been round asking questions. She said the old guy was dead and that she thought I was the killer.'

'Why would she think that?' asked Southall.

Hughes sighed. 'When the shit hit the fan after he spilled the beans about the affair, I told her I'd like to strangle the old sod. But it was just angry words, I had no intention of actually killing the wanker.'

'Maybe not at first,' said Norman. 'First you decided to steal all his money. But I suppose when the money ran out, you had no reason not to finish him off.'

'I keep telling you, I don't know anything about the money,' Hughes said.

'Let's go back to the afternoon of Friday the sixth,' said Southall. 'We've established that Gareth Jenkins came to your chalet—'

'He did not come to my chalet,' insisted Hughes.

'The Harmsworths weren't at home, and we know Gareth didn't come back down the drive,' said Southall. 'If he didn't go to your chalet, where else would he have gone?'

'I don't know.'

Just then there was a knock on the door. Norman went to see who it was, and found Winter, who handed him a sheet of paper. Norman glanced at it. When he saw the name written on it, his mouth fell open. 'Seriously?'

'Yeah, it surprised us too,' said Winter.

'You'd better do some background che—'

'We're already on it,' said Winter.

'Good work,' said Norman.

Back in the interview room, he handed the page to Southall, who raised her eyebrows.

'There's no mistake,' he said.

Southall took a second image, also from the video, and slid it across the table.

'Perhaps the driver of this car can tell us,' she said.

Hughes looked as if he'd been struck by a hammer.

'Ah, so you know whose car this is,' said Southall.

Hughes said nothing.

'Why did Rachel come to see you that afternoon, Daniel?'

'She wanted us to get back together.'

'Is that so? According to Rachel, it was you who wanted to get back together.'

'You've gotta be joking,' said Hughes. 'Rachel's not the "forgive and forget" type, she's much too vindictive. If I moved back in, I'd have her forever on my back, sniping away about Rose. I know I made a mistake, I don't need Rachel reminding me of it fifty times a day.'

Norman leaned forward slightly. 'Rachel's vindictive, is she? Exactly how vindictive?'

'Oh, she comes across as all meek and mild, ready to help anyone, but trust me, get on the wrong side of that woman and she won't forgive you — ever.'

'How long was she at the chalet for?' asked Southall.

'Twenty minutes.'

'And where was Gareth Jenkins?'

'I already told you I didn't know he was there.'

'Do you think Rachel saw him?'

Hughes shrugged. 'I have no idea. She didn't say she had.'

'How did Rachel react when she found out about the affair?' asked Norman.

'How do you think?' said Hughes. 'She went ballistic. She even tried to stab me with a kitchen knife at one point.'

'Is that why you came out here to hide?' asked Norman.

'Stupidly, I thought she'd never find me. I nearly shat myself when I opened the door and found her standing there.'

'How did she feel about Gareth?' Norman asked.

'How do you mean?'

'Wasn't it him who told her about the affair?'

'Oh, I see. Well, she wasn't exactly pleased with him.'

'I think maybe we should call a halt for now,' said Southall.

* * *

Both brooding over the news about Rachel, Southall and Norman walked back to the office in silence.

As soon as they appeared, Lane called out, 'Forensics phoned. I'm afraid Rose's fingerprints don't match any of those found in the house.'

'Bugger,' said Southall. 'I was afraid of that.'

'Does that mean you believe Rose really did go to see Daniel to ask if he murdered Gareth?' asked Norman.

'You just heard Daniel confirm her story.'

'Yeah, but if they're in it together . . .'

'I understand what you mean, but how would we ever prove it?' said Southall. 'And now Forensics say we have no evidence she was ever in Gareth's house. All we have is the warfarin tablets, and now I'm inclined to believe she's telling the truth about those.'

'Crap!' said Norman. 'Is it just me, or does anyone else think we've been played?'

'It's beginning to look that way,' said Southall.

'If it's not Daniel and Rose, what about Daniel and Rachel?' Norman said. 'Surely you don't think she turned up when Gareth did just by chance?'

'Why would Rachel want to murder Gareth?'

'You just heard what Daniel said. She's vindictive. What if she had it in for Gareth because he told her about the affair and caused the break-up of their marriage?'

257

'But she says she doesn't want Daniel back,' Southall said.

'Yeah, but what if she's lying? Daniel says the exact opposite, doesn't he?' said Norman. 'What if those cakes she used to bake for Gareth were laced with warfarin?'

'Judy,' Southall said, 'what do we know about Rachel Hughes?'

Lane rifled through the papers littering her desk. 'Ah. Here we are. I found her CV.' She began to read it out.

'What did you say her occupation was?' asked Southall.

Lane read it out again, light slowly dawning. 'Oh. It's been there in the file all the time, but she wasn't a suspect so it never got picked up.'

'Well, it's been picked up now,' said Southall. 'I want her found and brought in.'

'It's getting pretty crowded down there,' said Norman. 'We'll need more cells if we're going to bring anyone else in.'

'Let Rose go,' said Southall.

'Seriously?' asked Norman.

'We've got no grounds for holding her, have we? And anyway, she'll have her hands full explaining to Social Services why she's been feeding drugs to her son; she won't have time to do a runner.'

* * *

Norman returned some twenty minutes later. 'Rose sends her regards.'

'A bit annoyed, is she?'

'Incandescent more like,' said Norman.

'She'll get over it,' said Southall. 'If she hadn't lied so much in the first place, she might never have fallen under suspicion.'

'Yeah, I did tell her that, but she was so busy complaining she didn't hear.' Norman looked around the office. 'Where is everyone?'

'Judy's in my office making a phone call,' said Southall. 'Catren and Frosty are on their way to Rachel's to invite her in for a chat. She's only down the road, so they won't be long.'

* * *

Half an hour later, Southall and Norman were back in the interview room seated opposite Rachel Hughes. Norman gave the overworked duty solicitor a nod of commiseration.

'Can I ask why I'm here?' asked Rachel.

'We have a few things we'd like your help clearing up,' said Southall.

'What things?'

'You told us you still brought Gareth Jenkins a cake whenever you were in the area, even after you moved away from St David's Place.'

'That's right,' said Rachel. 'I did.'

'Why didn't you take him one last week?' asked Southall.

'I'm sorry?'

'You were in the area all last week, so why didn't you take round a cake for him?'

'Why would I bake a cake for a dead man?'

'The thing is, Rachel, you clearly stated that you didn't know anything about what happened to Gareth until we told you on Friday morning. So, I'll ask you again: why didn't you bake a cake for him last week?'

Rachel waved a hand airily. 'Oh, that was a generalisation. I didn't mean I took him one every single time.'

'Oh, I see,' said Southall. 'So, it wasn't because you already knew that Gareth was dead?'

'Of course not. As you said yourself, I couldn't have known he was dead then. I only heard when your detective told me.'

'What do you do for a living, Rachel?' asked Norman.

'I'm a pharmacist. I do locum work for a chain of pharmacies.'

'Did you say "pharmacist"?' asked Norman.

'Yes, that's right.'

'Don't you mean pharmacy assistant?' said Norman. 'As far as we can tell, you're not fully qualified. According to the hospital in Swansea where you were doing a placement as part of your degree course, you left under a cloud after some drugs went missing.'

Rachel's eyes flashed. 'I resent that accusation. It was never proved conclusively.'

'Why'd you drop out then?' asked Norman.

'Why do you think?' said Rachel. 'I couldn't stay there with everyone thinking I was a thief.'

'The hospital say they had good reason to suspect you, but since your marriage had just gone pear-shaped, they gave you the benefit of the doubt and refrained from blacklisting you.'

'That doesn't stop tongues wagging though, does it?' said Rachel bitterly.

'Upset you, does it, when tongues start wagging about you?' asked Norman.

'Doesn't it upset everyone?'

'I hear you have a mean streak,' said Norman. 'You like to hit back at anyone who gets on the wrong side of you. Daniel says you even tried to stab him.'

Rachel sniffed. 'You can't believe everything Daniel says.'

'Yeah, maybe,' said Norman. 'But perhaps you might want to poison a person who crosses you. That would stop their tongue wagging, wouldn't it?'

'Poison? What are you talking about?'

'The hospital never found the missing warfarin tablets,' said Southall. 'But we have a pretty good idea what happened to them. We think you took them so you could poison Gareth Jenkins and stop him talking.'

'Huh? That is just ridiculous,' said Rachel.

'Is it?' said Norman. 'You could easily have crushed a few tablets and added them to a cake mix.'

'I don't have any warfarin tablets.'

'We'll see if that's true when we search your house,' said Southall.

'Anyway, I thought you said Gareth died from a blow to the head,' said Rachel.

'No, we told you nothing of the sort,' said Southall. 'All we said was he died in suspicious circumstances.'

'It sounds to me like you knew Gareth was dead before we told you,' said Norman.

'Of course I didn't!'

'Where does Daniel live?' asked Southall.

'Who?'

'Daniel. Your husband.'

'I told you before, I don't know where he lives.'

Southall sighed. 'The more you lie to us, Rachel, the worse it gets for you.'

'I'm not lying.'

Southall took a photograph from her file and slid it across the table.

'This is your car,' said Southall. 'And don't deny it. We know it's yours, and Daniel has confirmed you were there.'

Rachel's eyes glinted. 'Bloody Daniel.'

'Why were you there?' asked Southall.

'Daniel had been begging me to go back to him. I went to tell him to stop bothering me, that it was over between us.'

'Are you sure about that?' asked Norman. 'According to Daniel, it was the other way round, and you were pestering him. He says he moved out to the middle of nowhere so you couldn't find him. He was horrified when he saw you on his doorstep — he said, and I quote, "I nearly shat myself".'

Southall slid another photograph across the table.

'The person in this photograph is Gareth Jenkins. The date shown on both photos is Friday the sixth of April. According to the time stamp, Gareth arrived not long before you. We have another photograph that shows you driving away, but there is no record of Gareth leaving. We believe you and Daniel enticed him there that afternoon with the sole purpose of murdering him.'

At Southall's words the colour drained from Rachel's face. 'No, no, no, you've got it all wrong. Why would I kill him? He was a nice old man.'

'He was, wasn't he? Until he revealed that Rose and your husband were having an affair,' said Norman. 'Those wagging tongues again. You tried hounding him, you tried poisoning him, but none of that worked, so you decided you needed a quicker way to silence him.'

'It wasn't me,' Rachel said. 'It was Daniel. The old man attacked him, Daniel pushed him away and he fell and banged his head.'

'Where did this . . . attack happen?' asked Norman.

'Outside Daniel's shack.'

'Come on, Rachel,' said Norman. 'Gareth weighed next to nothing. He barely had the strength to walk his dog. How could he possibly attack a guy the size of Daniel?'

'He had a walking stick—'

'He could have had a shotgun,' said Norman. 'It would have made no difference. He didn't have the strength to even lift a gun.'

'I'm telling you—'

'What? Tell me anything you like, I still won't believe you,' said Norman.

'All right. I think we need to take a break,' said Southall. 'And, Rachel, you need to understand just how much trouble you're in.'

* * *

The cell was cramped enough with just a single occupant, but with Southall and Norman in there too, there was barely enough room to move.

'Okay, Daniel,' said Southall. 'I hear you want to speak with us.'

Hughes cast his eyes around the cell. 'I can't do this anymore. I want to tell you what really happened that day.'

'Is it going to be the truth, or have you just had time to think of a good story?'

'It's the truth, I swear it,' said Hughes.

'Okay,' said Southall. 'We're listening.'

'I was working at home that Friday afternoon when I heard someone hammering on the front door. As I said before, it was Rachel, and my first thought was that she'd come to have another fight — or to try and stab me again. I expected her to start yelling at me, but she just stood there shaking, like she was in shock.

'This was something new. The look on her face — it made me truly worried for her. I mean, after all's said and done, she is still my wife. Anyway, I brought her into the chalet, sat her down and tried to find out what had happened to her.

'She told me she'd parked on the drive and started walking towards the path that leads to my chalet when he suddenly appeared from round the side of the house and demanded to know where he could find me.'

'When you say he—'

'The old guy, Gareth Jenkins,' said Hughes.

'You told us Gareth wasn't there. You're changing your story, are you?' said Norman.

'I said he didn't come to my chalet, and he didn't. I'm guessing he didn't know about the chalet, so he was going to ask for me at the main house, except there was no one there.'

'How did he know you were even in Pont Daffyd?' asked Southall.

'I don't know.'

'Didn't you ask him?'

'Well, that's the thing. I never actually saw him that day. At least, not alive.'

'What does that mean?' asked Norman.

'Rachel told me Gareth started shouting in her face, so she pushed him away. He fell back and hit his head. That's when she ran to my chalet. By the time I got to him, it was too late, he was already dead.'

'So, there you were with a dead body,' said Norman.

'Yeah, exactly.'

'If it was an accident, why didn't you call the police?' Norman asked.

'Because Rachel wouldn't let me. She said if I didn't help her hide the body, she would say she saw me attack Gareth and murder him.'

'So, it was you who dumped the body?' said Norman.

Hughes hung his head. 'I'm not proud of that.'

'I should hope not,' said Norman. 'I suppose you used the track from your chalet that leads down to the river. And of course, you have a car that can cope with the mud.'

'I know it was wrong, but I knew Rachel meant what she said about—'

'But why would she accuse you?' asked Norman.

'I told you, Rachel is vindictive,' said Hughes.

'But I thought she wanted to get back together with you,' Norman said.

'Well, that's what she said. She'd been going on about it for months,' said Hughes.

'You think she set you up?' asked Southall.

'I don't see how the old guy could have known I was in Pont Daffyd unless someone told him.'

'Did Rachel know where you dumped the body?'

'She said it was better if I didn't tell her.'

'So, it wasn't you and Rose working together, but you and Rachel?' asked Norman.

'No!' said Hughes. 'I wasn't working with either of them.'

'You set up the money scam on your own?'

'I swear I have never set eyes on that money before, or that debit card.'

Norman locked eyes with Hughes, who returned his stare without blinking.

'Where was Rachel when you went to check on Gareth?' asked Norman. 'Did she come with you?'

'No. She was in too much shock to be of any help, so I left her in the chalet.'

'You will have to make a formal statement,' said Southall. 'Are you willing to do that?'

'Yes, I'll do it whenever you want.'

* * *

Relieved to be out of the cell, Southall and Norman made their way along the corridor towards the stairs.

'Do you believe him?' asked Southall.

Norman considered this for a moment. 'It's difficult to believe anything anyone says in this case, but it'll be interesting to hear Rachel's take on Daniel's version of events.'

'Since we're here, why not ask her?' Southall said.

'D'you mind if I slip out for a while?' said Norman. 'There's a couple of things I need to do.'

'Sure,' said Southall. 'Three's a crowd in these cells anyway.'

CHAPTER NINETEEN

Two hours later, Norman was back. 'Rachel says Daniel is lying to save his own neck, and if what he said was true, she would have called the police,' Southall told him.

'I take it you explained why that would have been risky,' said Norman.

'Yes, I told her that even if his death was accidental, there would have been an autopsy which would have shown that he was being poisoned.'

'What did she say to that?'

'She still swears blind it wasn't her, but that's sounding less convincing now the SOCOs have found warfarin tablets in her kitchen.'

'Did she say who she was working with?' asked Norman.

'Huh! Fat chance. According to our Rachel, she knows nothing about anything.'

'So, what do you think? Which one is the liar — Daniel or Rachel? Or is it both of them?'

'I'll tell you one thing, Forensics didn't find any of Daniel's fingerprints on the money we found, nor on the debit card. Mind you, they didn't find anyone else's prints either.'

'Seriously?' said Norman. 'Jeez, I can't believe anyone could have handled all that cash with leaving at least one print somewhere on it.'

'Maybe he didn't handle it at all,' said Southall.

'You think Rachel set him up?'

'If she was in the chalet on her own while Daniel was dealing with the body, she would have had plenty of time. But that creates another problem. If Daniel wasn't working with her, who was?'

'I might be able to offer a suggestion there,' said Norman.

'Is that right?' said Southall. 'Would this have anything to do with where you've been for the last two hours?'

'I had to hook up with my builder.'

'Your builder? In the middle of a murder—'

'I needed his advice,' said Norman, 'and you'll see why in a minute.'

'Okay. Fire away.'

'Rose Mackie insisted the gate between the gardens had been nailed shut, right? She said Ian had done it months ago, yet when I tried it, it opened fine. There was even a faint path from Rose's back door to Gareth's, so it seemed obvious that Rose was lying about the gate. But Rose hates dogs. Would she really have been going over to that house every night, feeding the dog and walking it in the early hours? I don't think so.'

'But we know she was drugging the boy,' said Southall.

'True,' said Norman. 'But then I got to thinking. We seem to have got most things wrong about Rose, so what if we got that wrong too? What if she really does drug him because it's the only way she can get any peace? Don't get me wrong, I know it's not right, but we've all heard stories of mothers, especially single ones, who are at the end of their tether with having to deal with a hyperactive kid. And you can't deny that Rose does look frazzled.'

'Okay, so what's your theory?' asked Southall.

'When I tested the gate, I didn't look closely at it, I just wanted to see if it opened, and I didn't want Rose to see me doing it. Just now I got my builder to have a close look at it. He says the gate had been nailed shut, but at some stage someone levered the nails out.'

'Can he say when?'

'Not with any certainty but he's sure it's been done fairly recently. He pointed out marks on the gate where a claw hammer or something similar pressed against it. You can even see that some of the nails snapped off in the process, and they're not rusty. One thing he did say is that you'd have to be standing on Gareth's side of the gate to remove the nails.'

'Go on.'

'Okay, so, if we assume Rose is telling the truth and she hasn't been using the gate to get to Gareth's house, and we know the nails were removed from Gareth's side, I think it also makes sense to assume that someone has been coming through the gate from Gareth's house and going to Rose's back door, trampling a path through the grass in the process.'

'To make us think it was Rose going over to Gareth's house,' said Southall.

'Exactly,' said Norman.

'Wait a minute,' said Southall. 'Are you saying you think Gareth really was stalking Rose?'

'No way. I don't believe that any more than you do. But I do believe someone was trying to throw us off the scent and make it look as if Rose was harassing Gareth. And if that person also knew Gareth's dog, they would have been able to come and go without the dog raising the alarm. What's more, if they were a dog lover they wouldn't want it to suffer, right?'

'Didn't Ian Mackie say he took Gareth to the dog pound so he could pick a dog?'

'That's exactly what he said,' said Norman.

'But did he know the dog?' asked Southall. 'He said he stopped going to Gareth's just after that.'

'That's what he told us,' said Norman, 'but if you remember, Rose said she thought he was still coming over, just not at the weekends.'

'This is all very well,' said Southall, 'but where's the connection between Ian Mackie and Rachel Hughes?'

'I dunno,' said Norman. 'Maybe there isn't one.'

'I'm not following,' said Southall.

'Just bear with me,' said Norman. 'Early on in the case, wasn't it you who said we might be looking for two people who were each unaware of what the other one was doing?'

'Yes, I think I did say that,' said Southall.

'Right,' said Norman. 'So, what if those two people are Rachel — who was trying to poison Gareth — and Ian Mackie, who just wanted to ruin him.'

'Why can't they have been working together?'

'Maybe I've got it wrong, and they are,' said Norman. 'But we haven't yet found a single thing to suggest that, have we?'

'But if Ian Mackie was syphoning off the cash, and they weren't working together, how did Rachel come to have the debit card and cash to frame Daniel?'

Norman's face fell. 'Shit! How stupid am I? Of course — that is the link.'

'I think it's time Mr Mackie was brought in to answer some more questions, don't you?' said Southall.

'Hmm? Oh yeah, for sure,' said Norman absently.

'Are you okay, Norm?' asked Southall.

'That was such an obvious link, and I hadn't seen it,' he said. 'It's not the first time that's happened recently either. I'm just wondering if age is starting to catch up with me and I'm losing my touch.'

'Losing your touch? How can you say that when you've just worked out what's been going on with the gate?'

'Anyone could have worked that out.'

'But anyone didn't, did they? You did, all on your own. No one gets it right every time, we all know that. And going out on a limb with some wild theory is what you do.'

'I suppose so,' said Norman, still sounding unconvinced.

'Come on,' said Southall. 'Let's get hold of Ian Mackie.'

Just then there was a tap on the door. 'Before you two go anywhere, you might want to take look at this,' Judy Lane said. 'It's Rachel Hughes's mobile phone records.'

* * *

As they pulled into the car park at Mackie's Engineering, Ian Mackie was on his way out. Norman pulled up behind his car, blocking his exit. Southall jumped out and strode towards him. Mackie stopped, an expression of alarm on his face.

'Detective,' he said, forcing a smile. 'Sorry, but I'm just going out.'

'Oh no you're not,' said Southall.

Mackie frowned. 'I'm sorry?'

'You should have picked a cleverer partner in crime,' said Southall.

'I don't understand . . .'

'Then let me explain,' said Southall. 'You're a smart guy, right? I mean you'd have to be to set up Gareth Jenkins's laptop the way you did, but you chose the wrong partner. Rachel isn't quite in the same league as you.'

'Rachel? Rachel who? I've no idea what you're talking about.'

Norman walked across to them, fiddling with his phone. Almost immediately Mackie's phone sounded from his pocket. He went to reach for it, but changed his mind.

'Aren't you going to answer that?' asked Norman.

'It can wait,' said Mackie.

Norman held up his own mobile phone. 'I got your number from Rachel Hughes's call list. Now do you remember who Rachel is?'

'Lots of people have my number,' said Mackie.

'Yeah, I bet they do,' said Norman. 'But there's only one who sends you texts about Gareth Jenkins.'

'Christ.'

'Rachel left a nice trail of breadcrumbs for us to follow. There are still a few things we're not clear about, but I'm sure you can help us with those.'

'Why did you take all his money?' asked Norman. 'It's not as if you need it.'

'To punish him, of course,' said Mackie.

'He trusted you,' said Norman.

'Yes, but then he ruined everything — for both of us.'

'He was looking out for you,' said Norman. 'He didn't like seeing Rose and Daniel make fools of you. He did what he thought was right.'

'Yes, I know,' said Mackie. 'But I was perfectly happy before. Sometimes it's best not to know — ignorance is bliss and all that.'

'He didn't deserve to die for it,' said Southall.

'He wasn't supposed to die,' said Mackie. 'That wasn't my plan at all.'

'But Rachel was poisoning him,' said Norman.

'That was her doing, not mine. I told her to stop when I found out.'

'Well, I've got news for you,' said Southall. 'According to the post-mortem, she was still slipping warfarin into his food when he died.'

Mackie's shoulders slumped. 'I admit I took his money, but I had nothing to do with his murder. I wasn't even there.'

'But you knew he was dead, right?' asked Norman.

Mackie looked up, surprised.

'You were in his house after he died,' said Norman. 'What were you doing there, looking for his laptop?'

'Where had he hidden it?' Mackie said.

'I'm not telling you that,' said Norman. 'It was a clever move — switching lights on after dark and walking the dog in the early hours. It certainly made people think Gareth was still alive.'

'It's a strange thing, I didn't feel guilty about Gareth but I couldn't leave the dog to starve. That just wouldn't have been right.'

'What was Gareth doing at Daniel Hughes's house that afternoon?' asked Southall.

'He thought it was Daniel who had taken his money.'

'Why did he think that?' she said.

'He finally worked out that he was broke, and he asked me how it could have happened. I think I may have mentioned that someone like Daniel Hughes would know how to get access to his laptop.'

'You think you *may* have mentioned it?' said Southall.

'All right, I did mention it, but I never for one moment thought he would track Daniel down and go over there!'

'Whose idea was it to frame Daniel?' asked Southall.

'He was an obvious suspect — and I owed him one.'

'And Rachel agreed?'

'I told her the police were closing in and that if she planted the money at his house, we'd be in the clear. She's dumb enough to do whatever I tell her.'

'Well, Rachel's not quite as dumb as you think,' said Southall. 'She did try to stick to her side of the bargain, but she couldn't do anything about Daniel crumbling first. And just in case it did go pear-shaped, she left a trail of text messages that led us straight to you.'

His mouth working, Mackie stared at Southall.

'You're under arrest, Ian Mackie,' said Southall. 'Read him his rights, Norm.'

THE END

THE JOFFE BOOKS STORY

We began in 2014 when Jasper agreed to publish his mum's much-rejected romance novel and it became a bestseller.

Since then we've grown into the largest independent publisher in the UK. We're extremely proud to publish some of the very best writers in the world, including Joy Ellis, Faith Martin, Caro Ramsay, Helen Forrester, Simon Brett and Robert Goddard. Everyone at Joffe Books loves reading and we never forget that it all begins with the magic of an author telling a story.

We are proud to publish talented first-time authors, as well as established writers whose books we love introducing to a new generation of readers.

We won Trade Publisher of the Year at the Independent Publishing Awards in 2023. We have been shortlisted for Independent Publisher of the Year at the British Book Awards for the last four years, and were shortlisted for the Diversity and Inclusivity Award at the 2022 Independent Publishing Awards. In 2023 we were shortlisted for Publisher of the Year at the RNA Industry Awards.

We built this company with your help, and we love to hear from you, so please email us about absolutely anything bookish at feedback@joffebooks.com

If you want to receive free books every Friday and hear about all our new releases, join our mailing list: www.joffebooks.com/contact

And when you tell your friends about us, just remember: it's pronounced Joffe as in coffee or toffee!